A HOMELESS
MAN'S BURDEN

She was only nine

Wesley Murphey

Lost Creek Books
La Pine, Oregon

A HOMELESS MAN'S BURDEN: She Was Only Nine
by Wesley Murphey

Published by Lost Creek Books, La Pine, Oregon
lostcreekbooks.com

A Homeless Man's Burden is a work of fiction, though the idea for the book came from a real crime. Names, characters, businesses, organizations, places, events, and incidents either are the product of the author's imagination or are used fictitiously, except that the names Lt. Calley and pioneer family Bristow are, or were, actual historical people. No other names used in this novel are those of any real persons that the author knows or has ever heard of.

Cover Design- Howard Rooks Graphic Design, Pleasant Hill, Oregon
Cover photo subjects: Dale and Sarah Moffitt, Cody Murphey, all 2010.

ISBN 978-0-9641320-8-5
Library of Congress LCCN 2010911680

Printed in the United States of America
Printed by Sheridan Books

Printing 10 9 8 7 6 5 4 3 2 1

1

Under the Bridge

The middle-aged fur trapper pulled hard on his oars to bring his green, wooden drift boat out of the McKenzie River's strong current and into the backwater a quarter mile from the International Paper Plant in Springfield, Oregon. He rowed mechanically past his first two sets, noting both conibear traps were missing—a good indication they held dead beavers underwater at the end of their cables. His heart wasn't into the trapping today, however, because his head told him he was about to find a situation he hoped to never face.

The trapper slept little the past two nights worrying about the old man in his sleeping bag home under the bridge. He knew he should have checked the old man on his last run, two days ago, when he didn't stir while the trapper worked a couple sets near him. Since then, the trapper had considered driving to the bridge to see if he was okay, but as always was bogged down in his garage, skinning and handling too many animals. He couldn't take time out for a humanitarian mission.

The old man isn't my responsibility anyway, he told himself—no more than the dozens of other homeless people strewn along the banks of all three of the local rivers he trapped. Fact was if there was anything he disliked about trapping the rivers, it was the homeless being there.

Society viewed them as the dregs of humanity, shifty, dishonest, alcoholics and drug addicts, prostitutes, ex-cons, and the mentally ill. People who didn't have enough going for them to live like normal people. He liked to think he viewed the homeless with more compassion— "but for the grace of God, there go I." But since he'd had several traps come up missing not far from their jury-rigged camps, *even he* didn't trust them.

Some of the trapper's favorite places to trap over the years were now littered with pieces of broken boards, tin, plywood, rotting particle-board, mildewed blankets, clothes, and sleeping bags, beer cans and broken wine bottles, all kinds of drug paraphernalia, and other garbage that had washed downstream from the make-shift camps during high-water conditions that caught the homeless unprepared. Like they really could prepare.

As he eased the boat into the twenty-foot-wide canal that flowed under the Interstate 105 bridge, his heart sped up; his mouth grew dry.

One of the things he had loved most about trapping, in the thirty-five years since his dad got him started in his late-teens, was the anticipation he felt as he approached each set as if it was a present to be unwrapped on Christmas day. But *now* he was filled with dread.

"Please God," he prayed silently, as he forced his biceps and triceps to work the oars, "let him be okay."

Only sixty more feet. He turned his head to look over his shoulder, through the willows and alders, at the area up underneath the edge of the bridge. "Let him be sitting up, watching me, like he was the first time I saw him." He had hated him being there then, that is, until he saw he was an old man. The old guys never caused problems. They always left his traps alone.

The trapper had talked to the old man for twenty minutes that day, as he put his traps in the water near the bridge. The old man had been curious, but friendly.

Finally, the boat glided free of the willows. Then the trapper saw it—the dingy, brown sleeping bag—still there, still half-full with the old man's body. "God, let him be alive," he prayed. He started to call the old man's name, then realized he didn't even know it.

As he pulled up alongside the rocks and dropped anchor, he said, "Hey, are you okay?"

No answer.

Maybe he's just sleeping. Please just be sleeping.

The trapper climbed out of his boat, wearing his hip waders, and clumsily climbed up the rock piling to the dirt shelf fifteen feet above him, where the man lay motionless with all but the top of his head concealed inside the bag.

When he reached the shelf, he shook the bag gently, and said, "Sir. Sir, are you okay?"

To his surprise, the man groaned, and said hoarsely, "What? What do you want?" He rubbed his eyes, trying to focus as he looked up at the trapper.

The trapper pulled the sleeping bag down enough to get a good look at the old man's face, which now shown in the light of the mid-afternoon sun. The rest of the bag was shaded by the bridge.

"Are you okay, sir? You don't look so good."

"I had a heart attack three days ago. I haven't had any food since then, and I ran out of water yesterday morning."

The man's face was ashen; his lips were dry and cracked. The trapper looked around and found a couple milk jugs that he guessed the old man kept his water in. They were empty. He quickly descended to his boat, retrieved the water jug and brought it back up to the shelf. He carefully poured water from his jug into one of the old man's milk jugs, without contacting the opening. If the old man had AIDS, or some other communicable disease, the trapper sure didn't want him drinking directly from his own jug.

"Here, let me help you." The trapper held the old man's head up and poured water into his mouth from the milk jug.

The old man took several swallows, as traffic rumbled past above them, then said, "I never thought water could taste so good."

"You're going to be alright now... What is your name?"

"Sam," he said quietly. "Ease my head back down. I'm in bad shape."

"My name is Shane. Shane Coleman. I'm going to get you some help. I don't have a cell phone or I'd call 911." He looked around for something to place under the man's head to get it off the ground. There was nothing. He quickly took off his life-jacket and placed it beneath the man's head. "I'll go up on the highway and flag down some help."

"No. You can't do that."

"But you need medical help."

"I'm just an old man who doesn't matter. I just want to be left alone to die. It's my time."

"You're wrong Sam. It's not your time, and you do matter."

"You don't know anything about me."

"Give me a chance to help you. You're right. I don't know anything about you. But I want to. My dad died two years ago at the age of eighty-five. He died alone at home without calling any of us for help. He could have been saved. I'm not letting you die."

"It's not your choice, son."

"I'm not going to leave you to die. And definitely not alone."

"It's my time. You can't change the hand of God." He coughed a couple times, then said, "There's something I want to tell you before I die. It's the reason I'm under this bridge. It's the reason so much of my life has been so difficult. God has judged me."

The trapper tried to guess how old the man might be as he looked at his face which was partially covered by a long, thin, gray beard. When he'd talked to him on the earlier run it was at a distance. In his present condition he undoubtedly looked older than he was. The trapper figured him to be in his mid-to-late seventies.

"How old are you anyway?"

"I'm sixty-six."

"That's way too young to die."

"I've lived fifty years longer than I had a right to already."

"What do you mean?"

"Could you give me another drink of water?"

The trapper tipped the jug up against the man's lips, while once again holding his head up.

"That's some good water. Where'd you get it?"

"Up river, a mile below Bellinger Landing where I put in this morning. There's a spring that runs in off a rock cliff on the north side of the river. I always get fresh water there when I run this stretch. It's better than the city water I have at home."

"You're not kidding."

"Now what is it you want to tell me, Sam?"

"I'll get to it soon enough, son. What'd you say your last name was?"

"Coleman."

"You aren't related to the Coleman's out in the Dexter-Lost Creek area are you?"

"Not anymore. None of my family lives out there anymore. But my dad was the mail carrier for twenty-five years in the Dexter and Lost Creek area."

"Buck Coleman? You're Buck Coleman's boy?"

"Yes," he answered, getting excited. "You knew my dad?"

"Of course I knew your dad. I grew up out there. He was our mailman."

"I used to ride along on my dad's route from time to time. Where did you live?"

"None of that matters right now. I have to get this thing I've carried for the last fifty years off my chest first. God is giving me this opportunity by you coming along to free my soul of its burden. That's what I have to do."

"What kind of burden could you have carried around for so long? If you're sixty-six now, that means you've been carrying it since you were sixteen."

"That's right. And I've paid a terrible price for it all these years."

"Something happened to you when you were sixteen? Or you did something?"

"Nothing happened to me, and I didn't do anything. It's what I knew and didn't tell."

"You've got my attention."

"It was mid-August 1960. It happened in one of the Dexter-area bean fields." He coughed and didn't speak for several seconds.

The trapper's stomach tightened; he suddenly felt nauseous. The date and the location were still etched in his mind after all these years. He had heard the story he was sure he was about to hear many times from when he was old enough to remember, around 1962. The story about this man.

He wanted to run down the bank and get in the drift boat. Get out of there. He forced himself to take long, deep, calming breaths. He was a man now—a strong, two-hundred-ten pound, six-foot one-inch, middle-aged man. There was nothing to fear. He was God's tool, a priest so to speak—like the Catholic priests of his childhood to whom he hated to confess his own sins—brought here by God to allow this beast to relieve himself of his life-long spiritual burden.

But the old man said he didn't do anything back then. That he just didn't tell what he knew. *He wasn't the killer.* Maybe he was and this was the closest he would come to admitting it.

"My buddies and I had picked in that bean field every summer from the time we were about ten."

Most people would have asked which bean field. But the trapper not only knew which one, he had worked in that very field— Duncan's—himself from age eight through fifteen, 1965 to 1972. *This story* had always kept him, his siblings, and their friends from wandering off alone while working or playing there, or anywhere else for that matter. This story had been used by countless parents back in the sixties to keep their kids from venturing off on their own. This very story had reportedly caused a few mothers to have nervous breakdowns when their kids *did* wander off and were gone too long. In fact, the trapper's own mom came close to breaking down a couple times herself because of it.

"One of my friends stayed home sick one day from picking. At least he said he was sick," the old man said, speaking slowly, haltingly. "He had just got his driver's license a couple months before. I often rode to the bean field from Lost Creek with him in his dad's '52 Chevy pickup. That day he didn't come to work, a terrible thing happened. A nine-year-old girl named Ellen Brock, that picked beans in the field with her aunt and two siblings, came up missing sometime after lunch. After an hour or so of other bean pickers searching for her, the police were brought in. Over the next several days dozens of law enforcement officers and local volunteers searched all over for her, but came up empty. Dogs were never used because the police thought that with so many people's scent around, the dogs wouldn't do any good.

"Two weeks after her disappearance, a man who picked in the field found her under some blackberry bushes, partly in the water, in one of the sloughs that ran through the edge of the bean farmer's place. Her half-naked body was pretty badly decomposed already, what was left of it. Some animals and birds had eaten away a lot of the flesh. The police determined she had been there in the blackberries all along—back underneath a rotten old maple stump and covered with moss—but only recently, she had been drug out where she was visible, undoubtedly by a neighbor's dog or some wild animal.

"The man who found her was immediately suspected, but said he only found her because he had seen some buzzards fly in there at a distance and that got him curious.

"For weeks the police questioned everyone who picked in the bean field and hundreds of local people to try to solve the case. They even questioned me and my friends. When her body was found, there was speculation that a wild animal had killed her, which would have been a comfort to many people. But the authorities ruled that out when they found her neck had been broken and her skull crushed, plus her shirt was never found—*Except by me.*"

2

The Shirt

"**You** found her shirt? Where?"

"The second week of September, I was messing around up in my best friend's hay loft one afternoon when he wasn't home. I uncovered a small, pink shirt that was a perfect match for the one in the photo of the little girl which the police had initially shown everyone. The photo was black and white of course, but the shirt had a big heart on the front with the words, 'Daddy's Angel,' on it. There was dried blood on it. It was the same shirt the parents reported the girl as wearing the day she came up missing.

"When I found the shirt, I visualized her wearing it, playing and laughing at the head of her aunt's bean row near the filled and partially filled bean sacks. I cried.

The trapper asked, "What did you do when you found the shirt? Did you confront your friend? What was his name anyway?"

"I wasn't sure what to do? My friend was a lot bigger than me. I was pretty skinny. I knew he could beat the tar out of me, and if he killed a little girl, who knew what he might do to me," the old man said, without giving the friend's name.

9

"Maybe he didn't actually do it. Maybe she left that shirt there some other day, and he really didn't do it," offered the trapper, partly trying to rid the old man of his guilt, and partly attempting to relieve himself of the burden that he already felt so heavy upon his own shoulders.

"If you'll be patient, I'll give you more details." He coughed a few times. "Could you help me get another drink?"

After the old man took a few swallows of water, the trapper eased his tired head back down on the life jacket, then offered to get him a sandwich from the boat. He declined.

The old man went on, "The girl had never been in that barn or at my friend's place. She lived miles away."

"Where did your friend live?" the trapper asked.

"Up Lost Creek."

"Where up Lost Creek?"

"I'll get to that in due time. A few minutes after I found the girl's shirt, I stuffed it down the back of my jeans and immediately went home to our barn. I hid it in a false wall to keep it safe until I decided what to do. I ate hardly any of my supper that evening, and then tossed and turned all night long, hardly getting any sleep."

"I day-dreamed in school all the next day and avoided my friend. He had no idea that I had found the evidence. I finally decided I had to tell someone, but then I worried they wouldn't believe my story about where I found the shirt. In fact, they might think I was actually the one who killed the girl. Then I knew I was in a worse predicament than before." He coughed several more times, then closed his eyes and breathed labored breaths.

"Are you okay?" the trapper asked after half a minute. "I need to go get help."

The old man immediately opened his eyes, and said, "Do you want to hear the rest of my story or not?"

"Okay," the trapper conceded, "I'll stay here for now. How about some more water?"

"Yes, more water."

A few minutes later, after the old man had drunk some water and rested a bit, he went on. "I finally made up my mind I had to go to my friend and tell him I knew he was involved in the girl's disappearance and death."

"Did you go?"

"Yes. The next day after school, I went to his house. We went out to the back pasture away from the barn, and I told him I was sure he knew something about what happened to her. I wanted to give him the chance to confess to me. He couldn't look me in the eyes. He just kept looking off to my side. I knew I was right."

"What did he say?"

"He denied it. He insisted he had stayed home sick that day. He said we'd been friends since third grade, and he would never have done what I accused him of. He said he couldn't believe I would accuse him of such a thing. And then he threatened to hurt me bad if my suspicions didn't end right there. The whole time we talked, he never looked me in the eyes. I knew he knew I knew. But he made me swear to never bring it up again to him or anyone else."

"Did you tell him you found the shirt?"

"No. I knew no matter what happened, there had to be a good explanation for it. He would never have hurt her deliberately. At least I wanted to believe that."

"What did you do with the shirt?"

"I got up around midnight that night and snuck back over to his barn. I put the shirt back where I found it and covered it up with hay. Many times in the next few days I considered telling someone so they could go find the shirt, but I could never bring myself to do it. And I worried that my fingerprints would be on it. I was screwed no matter what I did."

"Did you ever go back later to see if your friend did anything with the shirt?"

"Yes, a couple weeks later. The shirt was gone, and that was that."

"Is your friend still living in the area? What's his name?"

"His name doesn't matter. After all these years none of it matters. Everyone has moved on years ago."

"You haven't. You said so yourself, how it always ate at you."

"It didn't *always* eat at me. I stuffed the whole thing away a long time ago."

"But you said not telling what you knew screwed up your life."

"That's right. I can look back now and know that God judged me for not telling what I knew. And with his judgment came some very hard times for me."

"But what about Ellen's family? And don't you think the killer should have to pay for what he did?"

"It was fifty years ago. I didn't tell you about it to stir up trouble, or to bring back bad memories for anyone. I only told you so I could get it off my chest before I die. No one besides that man knows I knew anything. I never told anyone else."

"So now you're just going to die without giving me the guy's name?"

Suddenly the old man groaned loudly and clutched his chest.

"Sam. I've got to go for help."

The old man grabbed the trapper's arm and said, "No. Stay here with me. Don't leave me alone."

At that, all his strength left him, he released the trapper's arm, and lay still. The trapper felt for a carotid pulse but found none. The old man was dead. Within a few minutes his face grew cold and clammy.

The trapper was torn up inside with all kinds of thoughts and emotions. He had known the old man for less than a week, and only talked to him for a total of an hour or so. The trapper felt a deep grief come over him. He wasn't sure if it was because this old man dying made him realize what dying must have been like for his own dad. Or maybe it was because he had learned about the old man's connection to his dad. There was so much he had wanted to ask the old man.

He sat next to the old man's body for twenty minutes, not sure what to do, or even how to feel. He shed some tears as he contemplated going up on the highway to wave down help. But what good would that do?

Someone had to deal with the old man's body. He couldn't just leave it lay there. On the other hand, the trapper was reluctant to tell the authorities that he was trapping this stretch of river. He was perfectly legal; it wasn't that. Rather it was that he always tried to maintain a low profile on his trap lines.

The light was beginning to fade now. He knew he didn't want to go through the Hayden Rapids downriver in the dark to get to his take out just below Hayden Bridge. He finally decided he had no choice. He had to let the authorities know that the old man was there, dead.

He lifted the old man's head, removed the life jacket from beneath it, and gently laid his head down on the ground. He put the life jacket on, climbed down the rock piling, got back in his drift boat, and floated downriver. He quickly tended to his remaining traps and barely got through the rapids before dark. After he reached the landing, he hastily loaded his boat on the trailer, then drove to his house in Springfield off Jasper Road.

As usual, his wife came out to greet him as he was backing the boat in. She was a perfect match for him, a real outdoor woman. Though she didn't get into the trapping herself, she was always interested in what he caught. At least she did a good job of acting interested.

When he got out of the truck and hugged her, he held on tighter and longer than normal. She sensed it, and asked, "Honey, are you okay?"

"Yes, I'm okay… Well actually I'm not okay, exactly."

"What's wrong?"

"An old man died on my line today?"

"What?"

"You know all those homeless people living on the rivers?"

"One of them died?" she said. "How did you know that? You always try to stay away from them."

"You say that like they're a cancer or something."

"Boy, you are sensitive tonight. I didn't mean it like that. I just meant that you never like them to see your sets, and you try to work around them. I've watched that myself when I've run your line with you."

"I'm sorry, sweetie. You're right, I *am* overly sensitive tonight."

"So what happened?"

"There was this old guy down near International Paper living in his sleeping bag under the 105 bridge. He was in bad shape when I got near him today. Then while we were talking, he had a heart attack and died."

His wife, Marlene, grabbed him tight to her and said, "I'm so sorry, honey. That probably brought back some pain about your dad, didn't it?"

He wanted to say, you don't know the half of it. But instead said, "Yes, partly, but partly just because he was an old man who died out there living all by himself without a home or anything."

"When you talked to him before he..., well did he say if he had any family or anything?"

"I wasn't clear on that," Shane said. "He died before I really got much information. I didn't even get his last name." He hadn't decided how much, if any, of what he'd learned from the old man he would share with Marlene, or anyone else for that matter. Or even what he would do about it. Maybe he would let the old man's secret die with him.

"Did you stop anywhere on the way home and report it?"

"No. I'm a little reluctant to do that."

"But you have to. You can't just leave him out there to rot."

"I'm not going to *just leave him out there to rot*," he said, getting defensive.

"I didn't mean to say it like that," she said. "So why wouldn't you call it in?"

"I just don't want to draw anymore attention to my trapping than necessary. You know how I am about that. I know I need to report it. I'm just not sure how to do it without the possibility of raising questions. You can imagine the stir it could make."

"Well the longer you put it off, the more questions will be raised when you do report it."

"I know that."

"This is one of those times when you have to forget about what it means to your trapping and do the right thing. Call it in. Tell them all you know about him."

That's not happening, he thought, at least not yet, and maybe not at all.

Shane and Marlene had been married for twenty-six years, had three grown kids, and were still madly in love. He met her while going to Lane Community College after completing his four-year Navy tour. Her small five-foot four-inch beautiful figure, big blue eyes, black hair, infectious smile and laugh, and easy-going nature, could easily fool the casual observer into thinking she was a push-over. But she definitely was not.

Shane had always been a man's man, an independent leader. But both he and Marlene knew she could get him to do almost anything she wanted by approaching him tactfully, using her feminine charms, unlike the tactics several of her friends who had been married and divorced multiple times tried to use on their men. The ones who bought into the women's lib philosophy of, "I am woman, hear me roar…" He was a lucky man. And because he was sensitive and attentive to her needs and input, she was a lucky woman.

"You're right, sweetie, let's go in."

"911, what is your emergency?"

"I don't have an emergency, but I couldn't get anyone on the non-emergency lines." Shane said.

"If you don't have an emergency, then you need to call one of the law enforcement offices during business hours."

"It's not something that should wait until then."

"Okay, sir, what is the problem?"

"There's a dead man on the McKenzie River."

"Did he drown?"

"No, ma'am, he didn't drown. He died of a heart attack."

"Where is the man, and how do you know about it? Is he related to you?"

"He's under the I-105 bridge near International Paper, the one over the canal that feeds one of the mill ponds."

"Are you Shane Coleman at 45382 Jasper Road?"

"Yes. The man isn't related to me. He was a homeless guy living under that bridge. I met him while running my traps on the river there."

"Do you have his name?"

"Sam. He said his name was Sam. I didn't get his last name, and I'm not totally sure Sam is his real name either."

"Was there any identification on him?"

He wanted to say, *what are you a rookie dispatcher? If the old man had ID, I'd know his name now wouldn't I?* But he bit his lip and said, "I didn't look for ID."

"I've got a couple officers en route to the bridge and one on the way to your place. Were you with him when he died?"

"Yes. He died about 3:45 this afternoon."

"Why are you calling just now?"

You're lucky I called you at all, lady. If it wasn't for my wife, I might not have. "Because I didn't have a cell phone with me, so I called when I got home."

"Is the man white?"

"Yes."

"Do you know his age?"

"He told me he was sixty-six."

"I'll fill the officers in on what you've told me. I'm sure they'll have more questions for you. I'll let you go now, but please stay near your phone in case we need further directions to find him."

Great, just when I have a boat full of fur to unload and wipe down.

From under the bridge ten minutes later—

"We've got a deceased white male with no identification, no wallet, nothing," said one of the Springfield Police officers on his radio to the officer at the Coleman place. "Nothing new there. *They* never make our job easy, do they?"

"No, they don't."

"Dispatch, we need the county coroner to come pick him up. Nothing here looks suspicious. He just looks like another old, homeless man who is finally out of his misery."

The police officer at the Coleman's asked Shane several more questions. Then Shane said, "When you find out his whole name, would you let me know it. It only seems right that the last guy to talk to him should know his name."

"I understand. That won't be a problem, assuming *we can* figure out who he is. Some of these guys just get put under with a John Doe, such and such a number, label. That's about all we can do if they aren't reported missing—which they rarely are—and no one claims them, or they have no criminal record and therefore no fingerprints on file. Most the time homeless people have been in trouble with the law at some point, and have been fingerprinted. But who knows with *this one*."

"What about dental records?"

"Those are great when a person is much younger and a veteran; then we can check the military data base. There's also a nation-wide criminal database for all criminals who have had dental x-rays taken while in custody. Of course the only time we would need those would be when the criminal's finger tips are missing or mutilated. Other than that, we don't have access to dental records kept in local dental offices, unless we have a person's name. It's a catch twenty-two."

"Will there be a news release in the local papers?"

"Yes. It will be a one-inch notice buried deep inside the paper somewhere simply stating that an old, homeless man, who went by 'Sam,' died under a bridge in Springfield. It will include a one sentence appeal for anyone who might be missing a homeless relative to contact the local police. No fanfare or accolades."

"You sound kind of cold," Coleman said. "No offense intended."

"As a police officer, you can't help but get a little thick-skinned when you deal with the transient population as much as we do. We get so many calls about this tramp or that one, male or female, being a nuisance somewhere. It might be at a local business, or in a local neighborhood, maybe hanging out around a park or school with their booze, or strung out on dope, sleeping on someone's property, or getting into their garbage. You name it. *Those people* do it.

"It's so sad that an old man like this can just die out there in the elements all alone and un-known, and nobody cares," Marlene Coleman said.

"All that while professional ball players hold out, or refuse to sign, unless they get their five or ten million yearly contract, so they can have another mediocre season hitting for a two-forty average and belting a whopping twelve homers," Shane Coleman added. "America: the land of opportunity, the land with the infinite gulf between the haves and the have-nots."

"I hear you," said the police officer. "I'll leave you be now, but you may be contacted further about this. One thing you can be sure of is that the local law-enforcement departments will make a genuine effort to figure out who this man is."

"That's comforting," said Coleman.

The officer got in his patrol car and left.

3

The Dilemma

"I'll help you unload your animals," Marlene volunteered, surprising Shane. She normally didn't do that, though she sometimes helped dry his animals off with towels and brush out their fur.

Shane's only son, Rawly, used to join him on the trap line regularly, and was always a big help with the fur handling tasks. But he was in his third year at the University of Oregon now, where he had been properly indoctrinated concerning the political incorrectness of outdoor pursuits like trapping and hunting. He resisted the propaganda for a while, but a liberal gal he was attracted to, first won his heart, then poisoned his mind. Shane hoped and prayed that Rawly would eventually wise up and come back around to the way he was raised. Marlene assured Shane that he would, because, as she put it, "He has too much of your macho-ness in him not to."

After they had all the animals piled up in the garage and began drying them, Marlene said, "It's amazing how insensitive even the police are to the plight of the homeless."

"It doesn't surprise me, really. I hadn't really thought of how much the police deal with them until the officer said what he did.

Maybe if I spent more time downtown around people, I'd see what really goes on. But I'm glad I don't."

"I'm glad you don't either, though the way this section of town has grown the past ten years, I'm beginning to think it won't be long before we're swallowed up and become just like the rest of town."

"What are you saying? That you're finally ready to consider moving way out into the country, where the urban growth boundaries will never reach us?"

"Now that all the kids are through high school, I wouldn't mind starting over." Their youngest daughter was in her first year at Lane Community College, while the oldest was beginning her masters program in marine biology at Oregon State in Corvallis.

"That's the best news I've heard all day," Shane said.

"Speaking of news, I got the sense when you were answering the officer's questions that there was more you weren't telling. You care to talk about it?"

"Actually there is a little more," he admitted, though he knew he wasn't ready to tell her much more. Not yet anyway. "The old man grew up on Lost Creek. He knew Dad."

"The homeless man knew Dad?" she said, as she stopped wiping a raccoon's fur and looked at his face. "He grew up where all of you did?"

"That's right. Of course it was well before my time."

"Why didn't you tell the police that? There's a lot you're not telling me isn't there?"

"I don't know about a lot. Why do you have to be so perceptive all the time, sweetie?"

"God made me this way to keep you in line. What is it you haven't told me? That's part of the reason you didn't want to call the police in the first place isn't it?"

"I can't hide anything from you, can I?" he said, as he stopped drying the fur of the beaver on the table in front of him. While she stared at him, waiting for more, he weighed the idea of spilling his guts to her.

"Well?"

"Dad was Sam's family's mail carrier."

"So you know his real name, I mean his last name? Why didn't you tell the police? I thought I knew you, but none of this is adding up for me?"

"Look, sweetie, when I first told you about Sam this evening, you said how it must have brought back the pain about Dad. Now you see why it did. Not just because he was an old man that died, but because he actually knew Dad."

"I'm so sorry, honey," she said, moving over to him and taking him in her arms. "I miss Dad too. But it must be killing you inside right now, Sam knowing him and dying right there in front of you."

Shane didn't try to speak; he was choked up, not only because of how much all this opened up the wound of his dad's recent death, but also knowing how much Marlene loved him and understood him, and how lucky he was to have her.

After a minute, Shane said, "We better get back to work."

She released him and went back to work at her table, then said, "With him being so much younger than Dad, did he say whether they ever did anything together? Did his parents go to school at Pleasant Hill? Or did he and Dad just know each other because of the mail route?"

"You're asking some of the same questions I wanted to ask him, sweetie. When he figured out I was Buck Coleman's son, he seemed pleased. But he was hurting so bad, he couldn't talk very easily. I wanted to find out so much more from him. And I wanted to go up on the highway and get him some help."

"But you said he had the heart attack while you were talking to him. Was he already sick before that?"

"Yes. I didn't tell you that he hadn't moved the last time I checked my traps there. It turned out he had a heart attack three days ago. He was in bad shape. Hadn't eaten in over three days and had no water the last couple."

"That poor old man," she said, wiping a tear from her right eye.

"It was a lot more complicated than I realized. But why can't you tell the police where he grew up and that he knew Dad? I don't understand?"

"I'm not totally sure myself, sweetie. Part of it has to do with the fact that when I told Sam I was going to get him help, he said he didn't want help. He actually got irritated at the suggestion. He said it was his time to die, and he didn't want anyone else there, or anyone to try to save him."

"But he was only sixty-six. Why would a man want to die so young?"

"He said his life had been very difficult, and he was ready to go."

"But all alone? What about his family?"

"He didn't say anything about his family. Maybe they're all dead. Maybe he had a terrible falling out with them years ago or something. I wanted to ask him about all of that, but he died before I got the chance. So not only do I not know where he lived, I don't even know if his name is really Sam. I don't know how old he was when he moved away from that area or anything."

"But there couldn't have been too many kids in the Dexter-Lost Creek area, right? So maybe we can find out who he is?"

"Trust me, sweetie, there were plenty of kids. If we're lucky, the police will be able to identify him by fingerprints, or in some other way. Maybe they'll get lucky and someone will answer the notice."

"Fingerprints maybe," she said. "But we both know the notice will come up empty. Like just the right person is going to see a sixty-six year-old, homeless John Doe died under a bridge, and put two and two together that it was their long-lost relative. If anyone cared about him, he wouldn't have been under the bridge in the first place."

"Terribly sad, isn't it?"

"It breaks my heart. God rest his soul."

They continued to work and talk, but about other subjects. After the animals were all dried and brushed out, they went inside for the night.

For the third night in a row, Shane tossed and turned. Normally he was so beat from the trap line, or from handling fur late into the evenings, that he slept like a rock. Marlene hadn't known why he had problems sleeping the previous two nights; he had just told her he didn't know why when she had asked. But this third night, she thought she knew the reason. In fact, she didn't have a clue.

Not only was Shane bothered by all that had happened with Sam, but he wrestled with whether he should give Marlene all the details, tell the law what he knew, or possibly talk to one of his friends about it. By 4:30 a.m. he had made up his mind that he would call his life-long friend—at least until several years ago—Hodge Gilbert.

Shane and Hodge both grew up in the Dexter area. Hodge came from a small, well-to-do family and lived in the town proper, while Shane's family lived in a semi-rural area known as poverty row, a quarter mile from Lost Creek. Hodge only had one sibling, a brother two years younger than him. Shane, on the other hand, had five siblings—an older brother and sister, two younger brothers, and the youngest was a sister—until his parents split up when he was in eighth grade. From then on, it was just him and one younger brother. Hodge actually lived with his paternal grandparents, and called them Mom and Dad, because his real dad was a career soldier, and his mom died when he was only six.

Both Shane and Hodge loved sports and were always putting together a neighborhood game of football, basketball or baseball, depending upon what time of year it was. They were both good athletes, but neither made any big mark on Pleasant Hill High School's teams, mainly because Hodge was a year younger than his classmates and small for his age, while Shane was too interested in fishing and hunting—and from his mid-teens on, trapping—to tie himself down to a team commitment.

After graduating high school together in 1975, both young men went into the military service, Hodge Gilbert to the army, and Shane Coleman the navy. After their discharges, they both attended Lane Community College, and stayed tight for a few years after finishing there. But Hodge soon moved away to take a job as a sheriff's deputy with the Multnomah County Sheriff Department in Portland. Shane wanted nothing to do with the big cities. In 1985, he and his new wife, Marlene, purchased their present home, which, at the time, was two miles outside of the Springfield City limits.

Shane worked in lumber and plywood mills, did some carpentry work and worked some grocery jobs over the years. But when mid-fall came around, mother nature always beckoned him back to the ponds, sloughs and streams to trap fur. He was often told he was born over a hundred fifty years too late, and took that as a compliment. He never made a lot of money, just enough for he and his family to get by, but he lived his dream for those four or so months each year when he was his own boss, tromping around in the water and woods.

Hodge, by contrast, fit into the role of cop with some difficulty. In the service he had grown into the stout, five-foot eleven-inch, man he still was. He was always known for having a short fuse, got into one scrape after another, and was called a junk-yard dog by some people. Though he had gained more control of his temper as he got older, the temper and his ill-timed terribly sarcastic sense of humor had sometimes caused him problems with his fellow deputies.

It didn't surprise Shane or anyone else that Hodge had served in three different Sheriff's precincts in his fifteen-year career. He spent the last eighteen months of his career serving as a law enforcement DARE officer at several Portland-area high schools. Some felt he was assigned the high school duty because he had a knack for wrecking patrol cars. But that was just a rumor. He knew he should have been a supervisor by then and finally, out of frustration, quit the force.

From there, Hodge Gilbert took up private investigating, and eventually moved back to Lane County in 2008 with his girl friend. He had hoped to take up with Shane Coleman, like old buds, but found he wasn't interested. Shane, who loved Hodge's ex-wife like his own sister, and in fact had introduced Hodge to her, resented Hodge for leaving her, in 2005, for the younger woman who he still lived with.

But another factor that separated them was that Shane felt Hodge had become the ultimate city slicker over the years and had let his hair down politically, moving away from the conservative values they shared in their younger years. Several years back, Shane had learned through the grapevine that Hodge had actually voted for the state-wide trapping ban the last time the measure made the ballot. That in itself was a death-sentence to their relationship—Hodge voting to shut down Shane's historic frontiersman way of life.

That afternoon, while Shane worked in his fur-shed garage, skinning critters, Marlene brought him the phone, announcing, "It's the sheriff's office."

Shane took the phone and said, "This is Shane Coleman."

"Yes, Mr. Coleman. I have some bad news for you regarding the old man. We were unable to find a match for his fingerprints in the national criminal records files, or the military records system. So we still don't know who he is. Today's Register-Guard has a brief notice, but we don't hold out much hope for any helpful responses."

"That's too bad," Coleman said.

"Are you sure he didn't say anything at all that could possibly help us figure out where he was from?"

Shane looked at Marlene, almost wishing she wasn't in the room. He hated to lie, or rather withhold the truth, but really hated to do it around her.

She was a strong Christian, and they had raised their kids that way, even though he personally wasn't as committed to church involvement as she was. He certainly believed in God. In fact, he often said, "No one could work in God's creation, running a trap line day after day like I do and not believe in, and acknowledge, the awesomeness of a mighty creator." He also often said that was the problem with the liberals. "They are sown and grown in the big cities where they rarely, or never, get to spend time in God's beautiful wild country. If it wasn't for the concrete jungles, America would still be a Christian nation, living the beliefs and principles of our founding fathers."

"I already told the county dispatcher and Springfield Police everything *I could*," Shane answered the officer. Boy he was slick.

"We were hoping maybe since you'd had some time to rest on it, something else would come to mind."

"Believe me, I didn't get much rest last night. And I've done plenty of thinking about it. It's not every day a guy up and has a heart attack and dies in front of you."

"I understand," said the deputy. "If you think of anything that might help, let us know."

"You bet."

They hung up.

"You're really not going to tell them, are you, honey?" Marlene asked.

"Not yet, I'm not. I decided last night, or rather this morning, that I'm going to call Hodge Gilbert about it."

"Hodge? *Why Hodge*? I know he's got the background to help you, but you haven't had anything to do with him in a long time. Not since he supposedly tried to vote your trapping out."

"I know that. But we go back all the way to first grade. I've felt bad all along that I shut him out. But at the same time, I resented him for his politics. How could he have voted for such a narrow-minded, uninformed position? And his messing around on Sheila and finally moving in with that much younger woman. The guy I grew up with and knew for so long wouldn't have done that."

"Her name is Karen, but I know you know that. I understand your hurt, and your resentment toward him, honey. I really do. So why would you choose to talk to him now, about this of all things?"

"He grew up out there too. He was my best friend for all those years. And he knows how to maneuver the system to get information."

"But can it really be that complicated," she said, "figuring out who Sam was? I'm actually all for you patching things up with Hodge. It *is* the Christian thing to do, after all. But I just never considered it would be over something like this. But I guess it could be God's way of bringing you two back together."

"I don't know about that. I just know I need to talk to him about it. And I'm going to."

"You won't get anymore argument from me on that."

4

Hodge Gilbert

By eight that night, Shane had skinned all the animals, fleshed the hides and nailed them out on boards, or hung them on stretchers, depending on the species. After showering, he went out back and called Hodge Gilbert.

"Yeah."

"Hodge. How have you been?"

"I've been over at the courthouse pushing my liberal politics. What's up?"

"Can we leave that stuff alone for now, Hodge? I've missed our friendship. I know we aren't on the same page with some things, but I've been wrong to hold things against you for so long."

"You've always been stubborn."

"Cut me some slack, old buddy. I had a weird thing happen to me yesterday, and I wanted to talk to you about it?"

"Did you find Jesus?"

"Don't be funny. I found him clear back in high school youth group. Same as you."

"So what could be so weird that you would go against your pride to call up your old buddy?"

"A man died on me. I was on my trap line on the McKenzie River, not far from International Paper, when this old man I was talking to had a heart attack and died."

"I'm sorry about that. What's that have to do with me?"

"I'll get to that soon enough. I'm calling on our land line from the backside of the property. I've also got the second cordless phone with me so Marlene can't inadvertently pick it up and hear our conversation."

"So now you're the one sneaking around on his wife, big guy? I guess that's why you decided you could call me. I don't seem so dirty to you now, huh?"

"Would you knock it off, Hodge? I'm out here because of what I have to tell you regarding the old man. I've told Marlene a little about him, more than I told the police. But I haven't told her nearly all of it. And at this point I'm not sure if I will, or even if I should, at least not yet."

"You've got my investigator in gear now. So spit it out already."

"First, I'll tell you what I told Marlene, that the old man knew my dad."

"How did he know your dad?"

"I'll get to that in a minute. All I told the police is that the guy had the heart attack while I was there talking to him, that he told me his name was Sam, and that he was sixty-six years old and homeless."

"It was a homeless man?"

"Yeah. He was living under the bridge in a filthy, old sleeping bag."

"That's sad. And he knew your dad? From where?"

"It gets worse, believe me. Or maybe it gets better. I'm not sure how I should look at it. That's actually one of the reasons I want to bounce it off of you. What I've told you so far is all I've told Marlene."

"Go on."

"He said he was sixteen, living somewhere up Lost Creek, knew my dad from the mail route, and picked in Duncan's bean field in the summer of 1960."

"So?"

"Boy you have been away a long time. Probably filled your mind up with so many other cases, you forgot about this one."

"I'm not following? What do you mean *this one*? 1960? It has something to do with 1960? The bean field? You're kidding me? Ellen Brock? The Ellen Brock case?"

"Now you're with me. Yes, the Ellen Brock case. You remember how scared we were picking out in that field several years later?"

"I hadn't thought about that case since I left the area after college. Did you know the law enforcement departments all suspended that case in 1975, a few months after we graduated? So what does the old man that died yesterday have to do with the Ellen Brock case...? You're kidding, right?"

"The killer?

"The old man who died yesterday confessed to killing her?

"After all these years? A death bed confession?

"And you just happened to come along at the right time? What did he tell you? And why after all these years?

"You didn't tell the police? Why?"

"Boy," Shane stopped him. "I guess your investigator has really kicked it into high gear now, hasn't it? I knew it was a good idea to call you. I *knew* you'd be interested."

"Interested? I can't remember being this interested in a case in years. Tell me what he told you. Why did he kill her? When were you planning to tell the police? What was his name, anyway? Did he live in the area all these years—?"

"Hodge, slow down. Let me catch up with you."

"Geez. I can't believe this. After all these years. It's February 2010. She died forty-nine and a half years ago. Imagine being able to close a fifty-year-old homicide case. It doesn't get any better than that—"

"I know. But it's not that simple."

"Why haven't you told the police what he told you? ...it's not that simple? You got a death bed confession from a homeless man on a fifty-year-old murder, and it's not simple enough to tell the cops?"

"Hodge, you're not thinking like a cop or a private investigator right now. You've let yourself get too caught up in the emotions of the case, that a murder case that hit so close to home for you might be solved. It's not that simple. Slow down. Take some long, deep breaths. I need you to get out of the boy-picking-in-the-bean-field-where-a-nine-year-old-girl-was-brutally-murdered mode, and get back into the career-cop mode. Breathe.

"Believe me, Hodge, I know exactly how you're feeling. More so. When he mentioned 1960 and Duncan's bean field, I was almost overwhelmed with dread and fear. I wanted to jump back in my drift boat and get the hell out of there. To get as far away from the beast as I could.

"But then I told myself there was nothing to fear. I was no longer that boy who was afraid to go anywhere alone. Afraid of being taken and killed by the guy who killed Ellen Brock. The guy they never caught. I was a big, strong man, and the beast was just a shriveled up, dying, homeless, old man. He couldn't hurt me anymore. Or anyone else."

"You're right, Shane. I did get caught up in the emotions. You took me by surprise with this whole thing. I had no idea how much of this has hung inside me for all these years waiting for news like this—"

"Here comes Marlene. Darn it. We're going to have to continue this later."

"You can't do that to me, Shane. You can't leave me hanging like this. Can't you just pacify her in some way and keep talking?"

"Why do you think I've managed to stay married to a beautiful woman like her for all these years. I know when she needs my time, especially my intimate time. She needs me now. Besides, it's getting close to ten, and I have to run my line first thing in the morning. Let's talk tomorrow evening. I'm going to make a quick run, doing the minimum tomorrow. So I'll get back by four in the afternoon and get the fur brushed out. How about if we get together out at the Jasper Café at seven tomorrow evening for dinner? I know Marlene will understand."

"Darn you. If that's the way it has to be. I'm going to have trouble sleeping tonight with everything I have running around inside my head."

"I know, Hodge. I haven't slept much at all the last three nights. Hopefully tonight will be a little better, knowing my old bud's in the know. Talk to you later."

Outside the Jasper Café, 6:55 the next evening, Friday, February 19th, 2010—

"How are you doing, you old fart?" Shane said, as he jumped out of his rig and grabbed Hodge's hand.

"Man it's good to see you," Hodge said, pulling Shane into a full body hug. "I've missed you, buddy. You aren't getting any younger yourself."

Both men got choked up and didn't speak after holding the hug for a few seconds before separating back to look at each other through wet eyes.

Finally, Hodge said, "How'd we let this happen? All these things come between us. Of all my old buddies from back then, you're the only one I kept in touch with all the years, until...you know."

"You're right, Hodge. How did *I let* this happen? Sometimes I'm too stubborn for my own good. I don't know how Marlene has put up with me all these years. She's always been a gift from heaven."

"She sure has. Don't think I don't have plenty of regrets over what I did, and how I let Shiela get away. I guess now's as good a time as any to tell you that Karen left me four months ago for a guy her own age. I'm alone now. Go figure."

"I wish I could say I'm sorry to hear that, but I'm not sure I can,"

Shane said. "Let's forget about our differences and go inside and order some supper."

"Sounds good to me."

After the waitress took the men's orders, and they had both removed their ball caps, Hodge said, "I think you're balder than you were the last time I saw you. I had more hair under my arms when I was seven than you have on the top of your head anymore."

"Yeah, well, you know what they say, 'God gave some guys brains, the rest he gave hair. Speaking of hair, yours is a whole lot grayer than I remember."

"Life and stress have taken their toll. What can I say?" Both Hodge and Shane wore their hair short, and sported mustaches and goatees. "I guess I should be polite and ask how you did on your trap line today?"

"Nothing to brag about. I picked up five beavers, nine nutrias, a couple 'coons, an otter and a few muskrats. We're supposed to get some rain tonight and tomorrow night. That will help get the fur moving."

"So tell me more about the bean-yard beast."

"The old man under the bridge never confessed to killing Ellen Brock."

"What the heck is this all about then, if he wasn't the killer. Geez, but you said—"

"If I could play a recording back of our conversation last night, you would hear that you hardly let me get a word in edge-wise after you got amped up."

The waitress came to the table with a black coffee for Hodge and a chocolate milkshake for Shane.

"You're still sucking up all that milked-down ice cream after all these years, Shane? No wonder you're packing around a beer belly."

"Come off it. You know I don't drink. And my belly is a whole lot smaller than most the guys our age. Give me a break. I'm only fifteen pounds heavy. Just because I'm not the adrenalin junky you've always been. You still have your gym membership?"

"You know I do. Why do you think I'm such a ladies' man?"

"Right. I forgot."

They both sipped on their drinks.

"Now tell me about the old man."

"He said his name was Sam, he was sixty-six and homeless. He worked in Duncan's bean field the summer of 1960 as a sixteen-year-old boy. He said his friend, who had skipped picking beans the day Ellen came up missing, was the one who killed her."

"The guy that died was the killer's friend?" Hodge said, stroking his beard with his left hand.

"That's what he said."

"Do you believe that? Maybe *he was* actually the killer, but just told you he was the killer's friend. Criminals do that all the time. They admit to just enough to try to convince the interrogator that they might have known a little about the crime, but definitely were not the perpetrator. They rarely come right out and confess."

"You're such a good cop."

"Ex-cop, ex-private investigator."

"You're not investigating anymore?"

"Not since Karen left. I've been down in the dumps. I'm not sure if I'll ever go back to it. Being a cop, or a private investigator, puts a guy right in the middle of the seediest way of life, around drugs and druggies, criminals, and prostitutes all the time. Everyone's dishonest, even some of the cops you work with, and you're never sure which ones. Everyone's out to make a buck at all cost, or to get drunk or high, or laid. It gets old. Then you have all the blood and guts, and the nightmares."

"I can't imagine dealing with that stuff all the time. I guess I never put myself in your shoes."

"It's not quite like running your traps, away from all the hustle and bustle of people, doing everything on your own schedule, being your own boss, going where you want to go. When I was up against it, I sometimes thought of you, just floating down the river in your boat, or sitting on a high bank overlooking the water. No cares in the world."

"It's a great way of life, no doubt about it. But you're kidding yourself if you think I don't have any cares in the world."

"Don't spoil my fantasy. You know what the biggest temptation was all the years I worked as a cop?"

"What?"

"The women. It seemed like every time I was dealing with a woman that was guilty of something, she would try to trade a piece of tail for her crime. Even the hookers who I caught in the act with their johns."

"I'm almost afraid to ask if you ever gave in."

"I'm ashamed to admit that I did give in a couple times about the dozen year mark in my career. Sheila and I had begun to have problems. Looking back I've seen that I was the cause of the problems. Shutting her out. You know. For the first ten years of our marriage, when things got heavy for me, I'd use her for talking through. I don't know why I stopped doing that. I think maybe she became too calloused to what I needed to talk about. I think that was her way of dealing with the blood and guts and all the crime."

The waitress brought each of them a Billie Basket, containing a quarter pound burger and a huge pile of French fries, which they had ordered for old-time's sake. After she left they dug into their meals, and continued talking.

"I'm sure it's a catch twenty-two for a cop. The need to get it off your chest with the person you love, but at the same time their need to not have to live the bad stuff with you. And I can imagine how much the spouse worries when the cop's on duty. I've heard the divorce rate for cops is much higher than the general population."

"I don't know what it is, but it's got to be higher. You know I wish with all my heart I could get back together with Sheila. I guess after she divorced me, she tried to be in a couple different relationships. The kids told me she said she couldn't trust anyone after what I did. That tears me up inside, knowing I ruined her. But at the same time, since Karen left, I've had this fantasy that since she *is* still single, maybe someway she and I could get back together."

"I'm sorry for all that, Hodge. I guess I haven't thought about the pain you've gone through during all this. God never gives up on us, does he?"

"What do you mean?"

"He sometimes lets us hit bottom where the only direction we can go is up."

"I haven't thought of it that way."

"Just something to think about."

"Let's get back to the old man."

5

Shane's Dad

"**I've** thought a lot about the old man's claim to being the killer's friend, and the way he explained things. I've questioned whether he might actually have been the killer. Unlike your criminal friends who are always facing jail time, or more jail time, for committing greater crimes than they want you to believe they did, the old man—Sam—was facing death and eternity. I saw myself kind of like the Catholic priest in a confessional booth. Only our booth was under the bridge."

"I see what you're saying," Hodge said.

"If he had actually killed the girl, I'm convinced he would have come clean on that. He was honestly trying to rid himself of the burden of guilt he said he had been under for the last fifty years. He said he had been allowed to live fifty years longer than he had a right to."

"Why would he say that if he wasn't actually the killer?"

"I got the impression that he felt responsible for the killer not being brought to justice, and for the family and public never getting any closure.

"Did he see his friend do it? Or did the friend confess to him? I can't believe the friend would have taken a chance on telling him, can you?"

"You're getting ahead of me again, Hodge. No he didn't see the friend do it, and the friend didn't confess."

"Then Sam must have found some evidence implicating the friend."

"That's right. He found the shirt the girl was wearing the day she went missing; it was in the hay in the friend's barn."

"How old was the friend?"

"Sixteen."

"After Sam died, did you search him for ID?"

"No. I wasn't thinking like a cop or PI. But the police searched him later and found none. Then I got called yesterday by the sheriff's department telling me they didn't get a match for his fingerprints off the national criminal, military, or passport computer databases.

"What did he do with the shirt when he found it?"

"He took and hid it in his own barn until he figured out what he would do with it. He was afraid of his friend, but he also thought the friend wouldn't have deliberately killed the girl. He thought about talking to someone, but never did. A day or so later he confronted the friend with his suspicions. The friend denied any involvement and told Sam never to bring it up again to him or anyone else, or he would regret it."

"And I bet Sam figured if he killed the girl, there was no telling what he was capable of."

"Exactly."

"And Sam was smart enough not to tell him he had found the shirt. Did he take the shirt back to where he found it?"

"You were a cop and investigator too long. He thought about telling someone, but then worried that his own fingerprints might be on the shirt, that he might be suspected, or that the authorities would think he was lying about the friend to save his own butt."

"And obviously no one ever found the shirt."

"Right. Sam said he went back to his friend's barn some time later, but the shirt was gone. Obviously the killer had recovered it and destroyed it."

"What if he didn't destroy it?" Hodge asked. "Maybe the murder was sexually inspired and the boy kept it for a reason."

"Are you suggesting that after all these years the shirt might still be somewhere waiting to be found?"

"I just said what came to mind. Only a fool would believe the boy didn't destroy the shirt after his friend suspected him, even if he had originally kept it for a sexual memento. You said the boys worked in the bean field. I'm sure they and everyone else were questioned. The fact that the boy wasn't in the field the day the girl went missing could either exonerate him entirely, or implicate him, depending on a lot of things. Did Sam say anything about whether his friend was ever seriously considered a suspect?"

They both finished the last of their French fries, and continued to sit at the table after the waitress took their empty baskets. Hodge sipped on the coffee that the waitress refreshed periodically, and Shane drank ice water.

"No. He died before we got to that. He died before he could answer so many of the questions I had for him. I wanted to know if he or the killer continued to live in the Dexter-Lost Creek area very long after the murder, or if it was possible the killer still lived out there, or in Lane County anywhere. Or whether he was even still alive. Every time I probed into any of that, including asking the killer's name and where he lived, Sam found a way to avoid answering. I wanted so bad to get the killer's name, but in the end I didn't even get Sam's full name or where he lived. I'm not even sure if Sam is his actual name either."

"Why do you think he eluded your questions?"

"He said God brought me to that bridge before he died just so he could ease his own guilt. Not to stir anything up for anyone else. I've wrestled with the whole thing, whether pursuing it would do more harm than good. I was hoping you could help me answer that."

"I understand your dilemma, though I don't share your caution," Hodge said. "I'll tell you right now that we can't just leave this case be. Sam is dead. It's no longer his concern. That he could keep such a dreadful secret for his entire adult life in order to protect the killer or even himself, whatever his reasons, means nothing to me. In fact, as an ex-cop, it only makes me more determined to get to the bottom of this."

"But what about the potential heart break for the surviving relatives of both Ellen Brock and the killer? Or them having to sit through a trial?"

"Look, Shane, with it being a fifty-year-old case, chances are good very few relatives still live in the area. Do you know off hand if any of them do? We know she was the youngest of the Brock kids, and we know that—"

"I guess now's as good a time as any to tell you a few other things surrounding this case."

"What's that?"

"My dad always believed he knew who the killer was."

"Why didn't he go to the authorities with that? When did he tell you that?"

"When I was an older teenager, I asked my dad about the case several times. He would always explain things just the way we heard them in the bean field, and how I had heard them on rare occasions around our supper table, or from neighbor kids, at least the stories that were accurate. As you may remember some of the stories were pretty far fetched, but they sure scared the hell out of us back then. Remember the one that described the Brock girl getting her arms, legs, and head hacked off and buried around the corners of the bean field?"

"Yeah, now that you mention it, I do remember that one," Hodge said. "Wasn't she found in one of the sloughs running through the property, naked, but not dismembered?"

"Half naked, actually, from the waist up. At least that was the general consensus. Supposedly the police never released that information, since it was an unsolved homicide case. Do you remember how the older teens would taunt some of the younger kids when they were in the outhouses if their moms or older siblings weren't with them, beating on the walls with rocks and saying, 'This is Ellen Brock's killer come to get another?'"

"Or hide in the bushes and jump out when kids came by, shouting, 'Ellen's ghost!'"

"It's amazing how cruel kids can be."

"Or funny."

"Getting back to my dad. After I got out of the service, I asked him about the case because Tommy (Shane's oldest brother) had recently told me that Dad actually knew who the killer was. And that he was still living in the area."

"What'd your dad say?"

"He said it was true. He said he never told me that when I was a kid because I *was* a kid. But he was open about it later."

"Obviously he never told you who he knew the killer to be."

"Actually, Dad didn't say he was positive about who the killer was. It was Tommy that said that. Dad said he was pretty sure who it was. And now that Sam said the age of the killer, it confirms what Dad told me. Dad said he believed it was an older teen that lived up Lost Creek and was a picker in the field at the time."

"How would your dad have known that anyway?"

"Him being the mail carrier, and a very observant person to boot, he picked up a lot of information. And who knows what he saw. Maybe he saw the kid driving his dad's truck at the wrong time of day for someone supposedly home sick from picking that day. I never thought to ask him that when he was alive. He probably wouldn't have told me anyway."

"But if the cops questioned everyone, why didn't they figure it out? If you're dad did see *that kid* in the truck the day the girl went missing, wouldn't he have told them that? Geez I wish your dad was alive right now."

"I can't answer any of that. And the truth is my dad may not have been right about who it was. Maybe he was just right about it being an older teenage boy who lived up Lost Creek."

"Was your dad questioned in the case?"

"He said the police did question him because as the mail carrier they thought he might have seen or known something. Remember, the kid Dad suspected was also questioned by the cops, just like the rest were. For all I know Dad did tell them who he suspected and why; but I got the impression he didn't."

"Did you ever ask your dad if the person he thought killed the kid still lived in the area at the time you asked him about the case?"

"Yes. Dad said, he did still live in the Dexter-Lost Creek area."

"When was the last time he told you that?"

"About 1990."

"Chances are, if he was still living in that area as late as 1990, he's still there today—unless he's died since then. Maybe Sam knew that too, and that's why he didn't seem to want to answer that question for you: because the killer still lives in Dexter or up Lost Creek."

"So what do we do, find out who all the sixty-five to sixty-seven-year-old men are that live out there and search their properties for the shirt?" Shane asked.

"You're on to something with the ages, but you just as well forget about finding the shirt. Even if by some miracle we found the shirt, the DNA evidence would undoubtedly be compromised after all these years. But he never would have been stupid enough to not destroy the shirt."

"I agree. Oh, I wanted to tell you one other interesting detail that you may or may not remember. I worked for Ellen Brock's father in the hay season of 1972 hauling hay."

"You did? I don't think I ever knew that. That must have been a little awkward, knowing that his little girl had been murdered."

"It was weird. I felt sad for him. He was a nice old guy, in his sixties then. My neighbor and I did all the bucking and stacking, while old man Brock drove the pickup."

"If he was in his sixties then, he would have died a long time ago," Hodge said.

"He did. In 1986. His wife died a few years later. I read their obituaries in the Register-Guard. The obits caused me to feel a little grief, especially seeing the part that said, 'a daughter, Ellen, preceded the parents in death in 1960.' Seeing her name in print made it more real."

"Well, you've given me plenty to think about. Let's get back together in a few days when I've put together a plan on how we should go about investigating this thing. I'm assuming you want me to kind of take the lead?"

"That's one of the reasons I called you in the first place: for your investigative expertise. Do you have any contacts with the local police?"

"Of course I do," Hodge said. "A few guys we went to high school with work in the various departments."

"I knew Leroy Patterson was a sheriff's deputy, and that Martin Steen used to be one of the local game officers with the state police. Are there others?"

"Gary Turner is on the Springfield Police Force, and Steen is actually an OSP captain now working out of the Springfield office."

"Leroy might be some help to us," Shane said. "He and I always got along good. He and Jerry Weathers were best friends in the class behind us."

"I know that. Just because I lived in the big city all these years, didn't erase all my memory of our days at P. Hill."

"With your politics, I wondered."

"I don't think you really know what my politics are. But let's stay off that for the time being. I'm not in the mood to fight right now."

"I thought you were always up for a good fight."

"I finally grew up. At least give me that."

"I'm sorry. Let's connect tomorrow night."

On the phone the next evening, Saturday—

"You're never going to believe this, Hodge. I got a call from the sheriff's department a few minutes ago. Some forty-something-year-old woman came into the county morgue and identified Sam after reading the notice in the paper."

"No way."

"I'm not kidding. She said she met him on the streets several years back and shacked up with him for quite a while."

"So what did she say about him? Did she confirm he was from Dexter-Lost Creek?"

"That's part of the problem. She said he was from Southern California."

"I don't believe that. Everybody's from Southern California. How did she know that? In fact, why did she even come into the morgue? She couldn't have figured out who he was from the little information they printed."

"She could, and did. She read the 'sixty-six year-old homeless man who said his name was Sam' part, and knew it was her ex. She said his name was Sam Hostick. That he grew up in the country outside of Ramona, California, and came to Oregon when he was in his late thirties."

"Do you believe that, Shane?"

"Which part?"

"Any of it. That he was from SoCal, that she was his ex, that this would mean everything he told you was hogwash?"

"I'm just as frustrated as you are, Hodge. But what was I supposed to say to the sheriff's deputy? That she had to be lying, or had some wrong information? That I hadn't been totally candid with them about what I knew about him? That he was actually from Dexter and was party to a fifty-year-old unsolved murder, but that wasn't important enough to tell them?"

"You're right. And now your not telling them is coming back to bite you in the butt, isn't it?"

"I guess so. Maybe I can still tell them. What if you got a hold of Leroy Patterson, and warned him that the woman may not be telling the truth."

"I could do that, but he's going to want to know what my interest is with the old man. How much should I tell him?"

"I feel like we just slipped under the wheels of a semi."

"Does what she said really matter enough to get Patterson involved yet? Let's assume *she is* telling the truth about being with him, and about where *he said* he was from. At least someone who was involved in his life at some point missed him and cared enough to identify him. That ought to make you feel a little better, just knowing that he wasn't just a nameless old man who no one ever cared about."

"It does make me feel better in that regard," Shane said. "But I still think you should talk to Patterson."

"I didn't tell you this before when we were talking about Patterson being on the force. I'm not exactly Patterson's favorite guy."

"Why's that?" Shane said with irritation in his voice.

"He was sent up to Portland to gather some information one time on a case, and he and I had a run in."

"I guess that figures," Shane said, shaking his head. "You just can't keep from fighting with people, can you?"

"I'm sorry, Shane."

"Is there any way to patch things up with Patterson? I think he could be a good resource somewhere along the way on this, even if we don't enlist him right now."

"I suppose I can try to make things right. But I'd really like to get in contact with *that woman* first, just to find out if she knows anything about this case. You said he never told anyone what he knew, but what if he did? What if he actually said something about the case to that woman?"

"You've got a good point, Hodge. How about if we go down to the morgue and see if we can get any information about her? Surely they would understand my interest, under the circumstances."

"You're right. Call down there right now and see if we can come in."

At first, Shane only got a recorded message on the non-emergency business line, saying to call back during normal business hours. But after calling back several times and not leaving any messages, someone actually picked up. Unfortunately, the morgue wouldn't be open until Monday morning at 8:30.

Back on the phone with Hodge Gilbert, "Darn it. We can't get in until Monday morning," Shane said. "I run my line tomorrow and handle fur Monday, so at least I won't be stuck on the line then. How about if you meet me at my house at 7:30 Monday for some breakfast, then we can go to the morgue from there?"

"I'll be there."

In bed at the Coleman home, a little later—

"Sweetie, I got some news today from the sheriff's department."

"Something about Sam?"

"Yeah. Some woman in her forties read the notice in The Guard, went down to the morgue and identified him."

"You're kidding?"

"No. It turns out, according to her, that his name is actually Sam Hostick, and she had lived with him for a few years, several years back. They met on the streets."

"That's great. At least we know that he mattered to someone, and she cared enough to identify him. I'm so happy for him. Did you learn anything else about him or her?"

"No."

"Well at least knowing someone missed him should soothe your mind."

"It does and it doesn't."

6

The Woman

"**I don't** understand."

"I've been holding out on you, sweetie. Please forgive me."

"I knew you weren't telling me everything you knew about Sam," she said. "But I knew you would eventually."

"You're such a gift from God to me, sweetie. I don't deserve you. Other women would have jumped out of bed, furious that I hadn't told them everything I knew. Not you. You're love for me and your patience shows itself again and again."

They hugged and held each other for a minute, kissed a little, and then sat up with their backs partly against the head board, so they were semi-facing each other. Shane knew their love-making was going to be extra special when he got done explaining things. And that he would get the best night sleep he'd had in over a week.

"Sam made a death-bed confession to me. He knew he was dying and said he believed God had brought me under that bridge so he could unload his heavy burden of guilt."

"So he must have been a Christian."

"I don't know about that, but from the way he talked he obvious-

ly believed in God. He said God had judged him for not telling what
he knew about a murder that happened when he was sixteen. A
nine-year-old girl was murdered in a Dexter area bean field in
1960."

"A girl was killed in a bean field in Dexter?"

"Near Dexter, off Wheeler Road. It was the same bean field my
brothers and sisters and I used to pick in. The one I took you to one
time—Duncan's."

"She was killed in the same field you picked in?"

"Yes. Of course it was five years before I started picking there. I
was only three when she was killed. But Dad was the bean farmers'
mail man at the time she was killed."

"Why didn't you ever tell me about that before?"

"When the kids were young, and I took all of you over there to
show you where I worked in the summers when I was a kid, I didn't
want to scare you or them with the knowledge that a local girl had
been murdered there. I know kids today, who watch all that gore on
television, are probably desensitized to the horror of a crime like
that. But since we never let the kids watch that kind of stuff, I didn't
want them to know. They would have had nightmares. I had nightmares about it when I was a kid. I didn't want that for them. And I
didn't want you to have to worry for the kids' safety like so many
mothers did who knew about the murder back then."

"I'm glad you didn't tell us about it then. You're right, I would
have worried."

"The kids nowadays know nothing about the way things were for
us back then. There haven't been any bean fields for kids to pick in
for over twenty-five years. But it was a huge thing in the Willamette
Valley when I was growing up here. Thousands of kids picked
beans each summer. But Ellen Brock was the only kid I know of
that was ever murdered in one."

"And it was in the field you later picked in. All this time, and
you never told me. So Sam said he knew who killed the girl?"

"Yes. It was one of his best friends, another sixteen-year-old boy. The friend supposedly stayed home sick the day the girl went missing. Her body was found a couple weeks later. Sam knew the friend did it, because he found the shirt the girl was wearing in the friend's barn."

Shane then told Marlene the same things he told Hodge about Sam and the murder case, and agreed to keep her up-to-date on anything he learned. She expressed her concern for his safety if the killer was, in fact, still alive and living locally.

She said, "If you were an old man and had lived all your life in the same area where you killed a little girl when you were a teenager, and someone started poking around asking questions about the case after all these years, *what would you do?*"

"Yeah, I know. We'll have to be careful. We can't have him finding out what we're doing, or things could get ugly one way or another."

After they finished their conversation, the Coleman's united in the act of marriage and then fell off to sleep in each other's arms.

At the Lane County Morgue, Monday morning—

"You released Sam's body to a woman who merely claimed that she was his ex?" Shane said.

"Yes we did. You have to understand how it is with the John and Jane Does that come in. If no one claims them, they cost the county thousands of dollars to bury. We can't cremate them because you never know who might come along years later and want to exhume them. Besides it takes the person's family members' permission to cremate someone. We're always thrilled when one of them is claimed because they rarely are. Less than five percent."

"So any Tom, Dick, or Harry can come in here and tell you they have a connection to the body your holding, and drive away with the stiff?"

"It's not quite that simple, though sometimes I wish it was. The person has to fill out a form giving certain information, and then they have to pay a minimum $300 to cover our transport costs. In some cases it might cost considerably more."

"The woman who identified Sam Hostick paid $300 to take him?"

"That's right. And she filled out the information form to our satisfaction."

"Can we see the form?"

"Of course not. That's privileged information. Unless, of course, you are related to Sam—and you already said you weren't."

"Why didn't you wait several more days to give his relatives a chance to inquiry about him?"

"Look, Mr. Coleman, it's not like our John or Jane Does are hot commodities, like a fine house and property, or a nice car, where the seller will get multiple offers. Of the five percent that get claimed at all, less than ten percent of those ever get a second inquiry. You have to look at this from our position."

"I see your point," Shane said.

"Is there any chance you could just give us the woman's name and the street she lives on?" Hodge said. "I'm a private investigator, so I know how to keep you out of it."

"Why is that old man suddenly so important to you guys anyway?"

"Let's just say we think there may be more to Sam than meets the eye."

"If I give you the name and address the woman gave me, you won't ever reveal where you got it or why?"

"Of course not."

"And will you let me in on your great secret when it plays out?"

"You can be sure of it."

"Alright then. Just a minute." He opened a file drawer, pulled out a sheet of paper and said, "Desiree Lebron, 1578 West 6th Street, Apt 26, Eugene."

Both Shane and Hodge scribbled in their three by five spiral notebooks, thanked the coroner's assistant, and then Hodge said, "Can you give us a physical description of her?"

"She was mid-forties, dark complexion, almost east Indian dark, with very long, thick black hair. Quite attractive actually."

"Thanks," they both said before leaving.

They immediately drove over to the sixth street apartments at the address given them—Whitmon Manor Apartments—and walked to the second floor.

Shane knocked on the door of apartment 26, but got no answer. He knocked a couple more times, but still nothing.

"We couldn't have gotten that lucky—for her to be here," Hodge said. "Let's go down and see if we can get any information about her from the manager.

"They're not going to tell us anything."

"How long have you been a private investigator, Shane?"

"You've got me there."

Hodge had Shane go wait in the truck, while he went to the manager's office—

"My sister, Desiree Lebron, isn't answering her door," Hodge said to the apartment manager. "I came from Nevada and was supposed to pick her up to go see our mother in Portland. Would you happen to know when she'll be back, or would it be possible for you to let me in to her apartment?"

"You're her brother who she was supposed to meet?"

"That's right."

"And what number was the apartment?"

"Twenty-six."

"She checked out of that apartment this morning. It's a furnished apartment, so people come and go pretty regularly."

Just then, a blue Pontiac backed out of a parking spot across and down from the manager's office, then drove past them.

Hodge saw that the driver was an attractive, dark-skinned woman, with long, dark-black hair. The manager also saw her, but said nothing. Hodge acted like he didn't recognize her and said, "Well, if she calls asking about me, would you tell her I stopped by and ask her to call my cell number." He hustled down the sidewalk and around the corner to Shane's waiting truck and jumped in.

"Get on it. She just went that way." Hodge pointed behind them to the street on the right.

Shane did a quick U-turn, running up on the curb to complete it, and drove off in the direction the Pontiac had gone. The apartment manager was still watching; Hodge hoped she had no way to call Desiree.

"There she is," Hodge said. "Let's follow her. Something's up for her to move out in such a hurry."

"She moved out?"

"That's right. If we had been any later, who knows when or how we could have found her."

"I wonder if she has Sam's body in that car."

"I sure wouldn't bet against it. If she picked it up Saturday, it's got to be thawed out by now, and maybe starting to stink."

"She's turning up the I-105 on-ramp."

"Good, that'll make it easier to stay with her" Hodge said. "No traffic lights to deal with."

They continued talking as they trailed the Pontiac by two hundred feet.

A few minutes later, she turned south onto Interstate 5, then several miles later took Hwy 58 east.

"She's headed out toward Dexter."

They followed her past Pleasant Hill, then a few more miles east, where she crossed the bridge over Lost Creek and immediately turned right onto Dexter Road.

"This is getting interesting."

She then drove two miles, stopped at the Dexter Market and went in, while they parked across the street at the Buckhorn Tavern. Five minutes later, she came out of the store carrying a sack containing some food and drink.

"She's definitely a looker, isn't she," Hodge said.

"Makes you wonder how she ended up on the street and with an older guy like Sam."

"She may have made that up. I can't wait to talk to her."

"Maybe we should get over there and catch her before she gets back on the road," Shane said.

"Yeah, ask her to pop her trunk open, or ask if we can sit in her car for a minute to see if anything stinks. You can tell her you were the one that found Sam on the river and *were just* going to leave him rot, *but* your conscience got the best of you. And *now* you're just following his body around to see that it gets a proper burial."

"Funny. You still have that same killer sense of humor, don't you?"

"That's one of the reasons I made a good cop. I try to put a lighter side on stuff. Let's just follow her. We've got her plate and vehicle description. I forgot my camera in my rig, or I'd take some photos of her."

"Mine's in the glove compartment," Shane said.

Hodge reached in, grabbed the digital camera, and quickly snapped a few photos.

"I wonder if she has any photos of her and Sam together."

"We can ask her that, and tell her we're representing some of Sam's long-lost relatives who believe they have a claim to his estate."

"Now you're the one being funny," Hodge said.

"What if he was actually *rich* and just lived as a pauper out of his guilt for keeping the Ellen Brock secret all these years? Maybe he really did have a lot of money, and she knew that."

"We could write a book with all the possibilities on this thing."

They followed Desiree east through Dexter, past the Catholic Church that Shane attended as a young kid, then turned south on Lost Creek Road. Just past the railroad fill, she turned right and dropped off to the bottom of the steep hill, and drove the winding road a quarter mile to Rattlesnake Road, crossed it and stopped on the right side of the road across from an old house on the left with the remains of a burned down barn nearby. They pulled off and watched from a distance.

They both remembered playing in that barn several times when they were kids, back when some cute girls lived there. Neither said anything about the girls, however.

Then finally, Shane said, "Give me my binoculars on the floor under your seat." Hodge reached underneath his seat, grabbed the binocs, and handed them to Shane.

"She's just sitting there across from the burned-down barn looking in the direction of the barn. I wonder why that place interests her."

"I don't have a clue," Hodge answered.

After a couple minutes, she drove up the driveway to the old farmhouse, parked her car, walked to the front door, and knocked. Through the field glasses, Shane saw an old woman answer the door. She and Desiree exchanged several sentences, with each of them motioning toward the barn once.

"She's got to be asking about the barn." Shane said. "That barn intrigues me. Is it possible Sam once lived at that place? Maybe he hid something in the barn."

"Maybe the girl's shirt. Maybe he wasn't being straight with you when he said he took the shirt back, and that he never saw it again. Maybe *he* was really the killer after all. His whole story about the friend could have been what he convinced himself of from way back, just after he did it. Maybe that's how he lived with it. Maybe that's how he managed to live in the same community all those years, like your dad said."

"I don't believe that. You even agreed with me that he wouldn't have confessed to anything unless he was going all the way. His death-bed confession had to be the truth."

Desiree turned and walked away from the house, back toward her car. After she got in, Hodge said, "You better get turned around in a hurry and pull your pickup down by the creek back there so she doesn't see us if she comes back out the way she drove in."

Shane quickly maneuvered his green, 2000, three-quarter-ton Chevy around and into a road leading back into some brush.

As it happened Desiree turned left on Rattlesnake Road and headed west, back toward Eugene.

"Follow her." Hodge said. "Let's hope she doesn't take us on a wild goose chase."

"That's for sure," Shane said. "I've got a pretty good pile of fur I need to get to before it gets too much later."

They followed her into the little town of Goshen, at the junction of Interstate 5 and Hwy 58, where she parked at a large *brown* house that looked like it was once a church. She went inside.

"Why don't we drive up there and have a talk with her right now." Shane suggested. "We could waste a lot of time on nothing. I really need to get back home and work on the fur."

"You're right, Shane. Let's talk to her right now."

7

Desiree Lebron

They knocked on the old church's door, and a skinny, artificial blond-haired woman, about five-foot-four, in her early forties, with a dark-skinned, pock-marked face answered. At once, both men thought, *druggie.*

"We're here to talk to Desiree Lebron," Hodge said, guessing Desiree probably wasn't a stranger to this place. Dressed casually, both men looked like plain-clothed cops.

"Desiree," the woman at the door said, as she turned away from the two men. "A couple of handsome, rugged men are here and want to talk to you," figuring a little flattery might go a long way in keeping her out of trouble.

Twenty seconds later, Desiree came to the door, stood next to the druggie, and said flirtatiously, "Yes, I'm Desiree. What can I do for you big guys?"

"I'm Shane Coleman, and this is Hodge Gilbert. I'm the guy who was with Sam when he died at the river last week, and Hodge is my friend from way back."

"You were with Sam?"

"Yes."

"Why are you here, and how did you find me?"

"How about if you follow us over to the Goshen Café for some coffee, and we can talk in private about it?" Hodge said, not wanting to say anymore in the druggie's presence.

After sizing them up, she said, "Okay. Let me get my purse."

A few minutes later, at the Goshen Truck-Stop Café, as they each sipped on coffee—

"So how did you find me, and why?" Desiree asked.

"Actually, we followed you."

"Are you cops or something?"

"Something," Hodge said.

"Why would you follow me, and what's this have to do with Sam? How long have you been following me anyway?"

"Since you left your apartment complex."

"What's the big deal? Was I set up or something?"

"What do you mean?"

"With the notice in the Register-Guard?"

"No. That wasn't a set up. But it surprised all of us when you responded," Hodge said, hoping maybe she'd figure he was somehow connected to the sheriff's department, but knowing better than to falsely impersonate a deputy. "Most the time the John Does are never claimed."

"Please don't refer to Sam as a John Doe. He was much more than that to me."

"If he was so much more, then why was he just left to die alone under that bridge?" Shane asked. "When I found him, he was out of food and water, and had no ID."

"He wasn't *just left*. He left me," she said, "Let's don't beat around the bush. What do you want with me?"

"I like that approach," Hodge said. "I'm not the beat-around-the-bush kind of guy. You picked up Sam's body. Let's start with that. Is it still in your trunk?"

"You're kidding right?"

"Why don't you tell us how you're connected to Sam."

"Like I told them at the morgue, Sam was my ex-lover and roommate. We met on the street about nine years ago. I liked him a bunch right from the start. He had a great sense of humor and he genuinely cared about me."

"Why did he leave you then?"

"We were together for a little over four years, about half of that time living along the Willamette River. But that was fine with us. We stayed away from all the losers down there—as much as we could anyway. Not all the transients living on the streets or in the wild are bad people. I'm not. And Sam sure wasn't. I haven't lived on the streets since Sam and I got an apartment together."

"Why did he move away from you, and end up back out there?"

"He said he didn't deserve me. No matter what I said to try to change his mind about that, or him moving out, he was too stubborn and wouldn't listen. I went looking for him several times over the years, down where homeless people would be. I found him twice and begged him to come back and live with me, but he wouldn't do it. He told me I needed to move on with my life and hook up with a good man closer to my own age. The last time I saw him was over three years ago.

"I never knew what happened to him after that. I thought he might have moved out of the area, or died. So I was shocked to see the notice—my Sam, the right age and everything." Tears trickled down her face. She wiped them, and continued. "I thought it couldn't be him, even though I knew it had to be. It's not like there are *a lot* of homeless guys his age named Sam around Eugene-Springfield."

"What were you looking for today when you drove out to Lost Creek?"

"Soon after we met, when it was clear that we were a couple, Sam showed me these small tattoos in his arm pits." Both men looked puzzled, and thought, here comes a new one. "He actually shaved the hair so I could read them. The left pit had five numbers, and the right pit had the name of a road."

"You're kidding, right?" Hodge said.

"Sam told me that when you put the two tattoos together they made up the address of where he lived on Lost Creek." Both men's mouths dropped open; they couldn't believe it could be this simple.

"Then why did you tell the county people he was from Southern California?" Shane blurted out, but then realized his blunder when Hodge gave him a dirty look.

"Because everybody is from Southern California, and I didn't think it was necessary for those people to know otherwise."

"You're a smart lady," Hodge said. "So you knew all along that he was from Dexter-Lost Creek?"

"Of course I knew. I even went out there looking for him once after he left me, thinking maybe he went back there."

"Did you go to the same house?"

"No. I didn't know where to go, other than somewhere up Lost Creek."

"You didn't have the address?"

"No. We were living on the river when he showed the numbers to me. I didn't think that much about it at the time. I actually thought his armpit tattoos were cool."

"Why would a man get tattoos in his armpits?" Shane asked.

"You can find tattoos anywhere nowadays," she said. "Not just on the outside of the body. Anywhere a tattooist can reach. Same thing with piercings."

"That's more information than I wanted," Shane said. "And I thought the tongue rings were bad."

"So you went to the house today, because you read Sam's tattoos after you picked up his body?" Hodge said.

"Yes."

Both men knew there was more she wasn't telling, but were afraid she might clam up if they pressed it.

"What if I told you there never was a Sam Hostick that lived anywhere around Lost Creek or Dexter?" Hodge said, taking not only Desiree by surprise, but Shane as well—though he tried hard not to show it. He guessed Hodge was using one of his investigative techniques.

Desiree looked back and forth between Hodge's face and Shane's hoping to pick up a clue that he was just joking. She wondered, is he toying with me? Or is he implying that I'm lying?

"That's not true," she finally said. "Where did you come up with such a blatant lie?"

"Trust me, it's not a lie. Perhaps you're the one who's lying?" Then not wanting her to get defensive, he said, "We know you're not lying, given that Sam gave Shane the same name."

"So you're just messing with my head, right?"

"No. I'm not messing with your head, though I know it's confusing. It is to us too."

He included Shane as if he knew the same thing. Shane was indeed confused, but rather because he had no idea where Hodge was going with this. Shane felt a friendship love and respect for Hodge well up inside him right then, listening to the way he worked for his information. How had he let this man's friendship get away from him for the last several years?

"I checked the postal files. The only Hosticks ever on the rolls out there didn't move into the area until 1987, and none of them were named Sam, Samuel, or Samson. How do you account for that?"

"The files have to be wrong."

"Trust me, they're not. So what has to be true is that this so-called Sam Hostick was actually someone else altogether."

"But I trusted him. He was one of the greatest guys I ever met."

"I'm not trying to take any of that away from you, Desiree," Hodge said. "No doubt he was exactly the person you thought he was, and grew up out there like he said he did. But for whatever reason, he used the alias Sam Hostick instead of his real name."

"I wish I knew why," she said.

"So what did you do with Sam's body if it's not in your car?" Shane asked, his curiosity finally overcoming him.

"Right after I picked it up, I contacted a local funeral home and arranged to bring it right over to them."

"Which one?" Shane asked.

"You don't really expect me to tell you that, do you?"

"What difference does it make?"

"That's what I'd like to know," she said. "What difference does it make to you guys where his body is now? If you cared that much, or had any claim to it, you would have picked it up before I did." All of them knew they wanted to see the tattoos for themselves.

"Are you going to have a funeral for him?"

"No. I'm just going to have a preacher say a few words over his grave when all's said and done."

"Where's he getting buried?"

"I haven't decided yet."

"Did Sam ever tell you if he picked beans when he was a teenager?" Hodge said, fishing.

"He said he hauled some hay and worked for farmers doing various other jobs. Why?"

"We're just trying to get some background on him."

"What for?"

"We can't tell you that now," Hodge said, "but maybe later. Why don't you give us your cell number and—here you can have my card." He pulled a business card out of his left shirt pocket and handed it to her.

"Private Investigator," she said scrutinizing the card. "I figured as much. What's this about anyway?"

"Like I said, I can't say."

"You want information from me, but you won't tell me why. Do you take me for a fool?"

"Anything but. But you don't have a need to know."

"Neither do you. I've got to run now," she laughed. "I've got your number, so if I think of anything that might be helpful, I can call you." She quickly got up and walked out of the café.

In Shane's truck driving away from the café a couple minutes later—

"Do you think she was blowing smoke about the tattoos?" Shane asked.

"No telling. But anything's possible," Hodge said. "I bet you wish you had searched the body after Sam died, don't you? You could have satisfied your hairy-underarm fetish. Imagine the thrill you would have had when you discovered the tattoos." They both cracked up.

"You're terrible. Did you really look up Sam Hostick in the postal files?"

"No. But I will later today. Of course the postal roll records in a lot of places only go back to the mid-seventies, when computers were first used on a wide-spread basis in the postal service."

"So he may actually be Sam Hostick who grew up in that area?"

"I'd bet my right nut, he's not."

"How can you be so sure?"

"The transients rarely use their real names, even with each other. Most of them don't trust anyone, because they figure everyone else is just as dishonest as they are. Besides that, most of them don't want to be found by any relatives, because they blame the relatives for why they're homeless in the first place. Most homeless people have what I call the 'victim mentality.' They see themselves as victims of circumstances."

"Aren't they?" Shane asked.

"Indirectly most of them are. But many of them made the bed they're sleeping in—or, more accurately, the one they don't get to sleep in."

"Being a cop sure gave you a different way of looking at things, didn't it?"

"No doubt about it."

"Is that what changed your politics?"

"I'm not ready to go there with you yet. We're doing fine right now. Let's don't ruin a good thing," Hodge said, his voice showing a hint of the pain he was still carrying over their broken relationship.

Inside the Goshen house—

"What was that all about?" asked Riva, Desiree's drug addict sister, when Desiree walked through the door.

"They were just trying to clear up a few questions regarding Sam."

"And I was afraid they were undercover cops looking to nail us for the drugs. At least we know they're not on to that."

"Oh, you can be sure they know what's going on," Desiree answered, not saying what she was thinking—that only a fool wouldn't know Riva was a drug addict. "I thought I lost them when I took Lost Creek Road."

"Obviously you didn't. Now I have to worry that they'll turn me in."

"Take a chill pill, Sis. They've got more important things to deal with than a drug addict."

8

The Sisters

The Colemans sitting in their living room late that evening, Monday, February 22—

"Shane, I've been thinking about what you said, that Hodge wants so much to get back together with Shiela."

"I knew you'd be moved by that."

"Why shouldn't I be? With God, all things are possible."

"Come on, spit out what you've been thinking," he said.

"I always liked her so much. When we used to get together with them, it was always fun. Back then they really seemed to love each other deeply. Then as the years went by, things seemed to be strained between them, you know, before he left her for Karen."

"So what are you saying, that you want to play matchmaker?"

"You did it the first time. But I guarantee you, if they have any chance now, it will take a woman's touch. A special woman's touch. A woman who can feel Shiela's pain, cry with her, and pray with her. A woman who can bridge the communication gap between her and Hodge."

"And that would be you?"

"Me, with a lot of prayer behind me. The way he's hurt her, God will have to intervene and heal her heart to allow her to be able to forgive him and open herself up to him again. It won't be an easy thing for her. But I think it would be worth it."

"I hope so. I think Hodge is ready to acknowledge the terrible mistakes he made. The question is: can she ever forgive him?"

"I'm going to call her tomorrow and run this by her. Tell her what he said and all. She'll need time to think about it. How much longer are you going to be on the Bellinger to Hayden Bridge run?"

"I'm going to pull the line tomorrow, and set below Dexter on the Willamette River the next day. I'll have to get the rest of yesterday's fur skinned when I get off the line tomorrow, which should be by no later than 2 pm."

Once again changing the subject, Marlene asked, "Do you believe that woman's story about the tattoos?"

"I don't know. I've never heard of anyone doing that before. Hodge is going back up to the house with the burned-down barn tomorrow to get the address and talk to the occupants. There aren't any other places close to that one. I got the impression from Sam that he lived right near the friend that killed the Brock girl. His property and the friend's both had barns. Of course, in all these years, things could have changed a lot up there. I know when I was last up Lost Creek, over five years ago, some of the old places had been torn down and new places built. I couldn't even remember where some houses used to be.

"I spent a lot of time fishing that creek during my teens. I knew all the best holes. Some stretches of the creek didn't have much even back then, but the runs that did were exciting. Dad said that I wouldn't have believed the number of trout that were in the creek when he was a teen, back in the thirties. After I got out of the navy, I fished a few times and didn't catch much. The fishing never did come back after that. It breaks my heart... the memories. That's all they are anymore—just memories."

"Maybe we should move completely away from Lane County?

Some place with few people and lots of fish."

"I never thought I'd hear you say that. This summer we'll start looking. What do you say?"

"No argument here."

Over the phone the next evening, Tuesday—

"How'd you do on your line today, Shane?" Hodge asked.

"Not bad. I pulled all my traps and will be setting below Dexter tomorrow. You get anything accomplished on the case?"

"This morning I got online and managed to get into the postal service files."

"You hacked your way in?"

"You didn't hear it from me. We PIs have our ways of getting information."

"How do you do that without someone backtracking you."

"Very carefully. But when you're good, it can be done."

"Were you right about there being no Hosticks?"

"The only Hostick was a woman named Adel that lived on Rattlesnake Road, in the late seventies, early eighties. Other than that, no Hosticks. But like I said earlier, the postal roll records only go back to 1975 in the Dexter area. But—"

"But you used your talents to get that information somewhere else?"

"Yes. I went down to the Lane County Courthouse and looked the Hostick name up on the land owner records."

"Well?"

"Only Adel Hostick. Then I looked at the plat map for the piece where Desiree stopped and got the name of the land owner during the late fifties and early sixties. It was a couple named Virgil and Beverly Minton. After that, taking us up to 1974, the property was owned by the Helbers; we both already knew that."

"I'm sure you couldn't get any information from the property owner records on whether the Minton's had any boys the right age."

"No, I couldn't. But I got that information by checking the vital records. The Minton's gave birth to four kids between 1948 and 1962. All girls. Unless they adopted Sam, he never lived on that property."

"It would have been too simple if he did, wouldn't it?"

"Yeah, but that's what makes these cases fun—having to get creative."

"In the afternoon, I went for a drive up Lost Creek. I drove by the house Desiree stopped at and got to thinking."

"You were thinking she was feeding us a line of crap," Shane said. "That she figured out she was being followed and stopped there deliberately to throw us off."

"She wouldn't have known she was being followed because of Sam. She probably would have thought it was about drugs."

"She's obviously a very savvy woman. That's why she was able to make up that story about the tattoos so fast."

"I don't think anyone could make up a story that unique that fast. I think she slipped up somehow, and then had to cover her butt. The more I've thought about it, the more I believe there actually were tattoos and they may still be a key to solving this mystery."

"You're kidding, aren't you?"

"I'll just keep it on the back burner. While I was up Lost Creek I made the acquaintance of a few younger teen boys. I've decided I'm going to enlist their help in the investigation."

"How's that?"

"We're going to survey all the houses and people from the railroad fill upstream. Find out who lives where, how old the adults are, ask how long people have lived up the creek, and a number of other things. I figure it'll take the boys a couple weeks. Then we'll take any information that might help us in this case and take it to the next level, by you and me going back to certain houses. Of course, to avoid being obvious, we'll have to sit and listen to some stories that won't get us anywhere and maybe even bore us to tears. No one said being a PI was all fun and games."

"Can't you get the same information from the courthouse?"

"I could get some of it, but it would take a lot of time and I still wouldn't get some of what I want. Besides it will be fun for the boys, playing investigators."

"Are you paying them?"

"Of course. Five bucks for each filled-out form, divided two ways. I'm having them work in pairs. They'll all have Census maps showing where every house is, and they'll all have the same survey form."

"I wish I was that age again. That's good pickup money for little work," Shane said. "What are you giving as the reason for the survey?"

"That it's for a book that a writer is putting together on the history of the Lost Creek community."

"You're slick. Most people want to be in books in some way. But how can you justify lying to people and using boys to do a survey for a book that you know will never be written?"

"But *I am* going to write a book."

"Who are you kidding?"

"What, you think I can't write a book?"

"I'm sure you could probably write a book. But we both know that's just the line to get you in with those people."

"You're wrong, Shane. I fully intend to write a book about this case when we're done."

"Even if you do, we're telling people that the book will be about the history and memories of the people of Lost Creek Valley. That's still being deceptive."

"I don't see it that way at all. A girl who lived near Dexter was murdered by a teenager who lived up Lost Creek, and it was his friend, who also grew up on Lost Creek that opened the case back up. I could include many details, including testimony from your dad and numerous other people that lived out there over the years."

"I have to concede," Shane said, "I guess *you are* legitimate. That makes me feel better."

"I'm figuring we'll run on to a number of people who will remember your dad as the mail carrier, so we'll use your connection to him whenever we can. What years did your dad deliver out there?"

"1949 to 1973."

"We're bound to get some good out of that. Well, I better let you go. I'm sure your woman needs you again tonight. You are one lucky man."

The next evening, Wednesday, at the Coleman's dinner table—

"Honey, I invited Rawly to bring his girlfriend over for dinner Friday night. I knew you wouldn't mind."

"I wouldn't mind?" Shane said, immediately getting elevated. "She's a liberal, anti-everything that I believe in."

"You don't know that."

"I know she's poisoned my son's mind, and taken away his manhood."

Getting irritated, Marlene said, "Can she come over or not?"

"I guess it'll be alright. Maybe I can convert her."

"You never know. But please don't go overboard applying pressure. The last thing we need is for you to alienate her."

"Maybe if she sees what she'd be getting into if she ever married Rawly, she'll decide it wouldn't be worth it."

"We both know no one marries or doesn't marry someone based on the parents."

"It was a good try, though, wasn't it? Maybe we should invite Hodge over at the same time. Then the liberals wouldn't be outnumbered."

"You're awful."

"Did you ever get a hold of Shiela?"

"As a matter of fact, I did. She has some serious reservations about giving Hodge another chance."

"That's no surprise. But is she willing to consider it?"

"She said she'd have to give it a lot of thought, talk to the kids about it, and pray."

"When do you plan to talk to her again?"

"I'm going to let her call me when she's ready to talk about it. And of course I'll be praying."

"You're a wise woman, sweetie."

"What's going on in yours and Hodge's little investigation?" Marlene asked.

"Hodge went back out to Lost Creek today and enlisted some local boys, young teens, for our survey. He and I are going to hook up tomorrow evening to take a look at the questions he's come up with."

"If nothing else, you'll probably get some interesting stories, and may even learn a thing or two about Dad that you didn't know."

At the Goshen druggie house the same evening—

"As my baby sister, Riva, I'm going to let you in on something that I never told you. But you have to promise me you won't tell anyone else, okay?"

"I won't."

"You know the other day when I went to the café to talk with those two guys?"

"Yes."

"They caught me off guard, and I gave them some information I shouldn't have."

"About Sam, or the drugs?"

"About Sam. Would you stop worrying about the drugs," Desiree said, scowling. "No one cares that you're a drug addict. No one except me, that is. Promise me that *you will* follow through with that drug rehabilitation program I have you set up for next week. I want things to be like they were when we were kids. Before we got into the drugs and everything else. Before Mom and Dad were killed. You're all I have, and I'm all you have."

"I promise," Riva said, while pulling a cigarette out of its pack. "So what do you want to tell me?"

"When Sam and I were together he showed me some tattoos he had in his armpits."

"In his armpits? A guy?"

"Yes. One time he shaved the hair under his arms and showed me the tats. One pit had five numbers and the other had the name of a road."

"You're kidding? What was that all about?" She put the cigarette in her mouth with her left hand, lit it with the yellow BIC lighter in her right, and sucked in a long drag.

"He told me that together they were the address of the place where he used to live up Lost Creek."

"That's hilarious, but cool," Riva said, coughing smoke out with the words. "He really was good to you."

"Yes, he was," Desiree answered, her eyes watering. "He was better to me than you know."

"How's that?"

"Not only did he tell me the tats were his old house address, he told me that he had hidden thousands of dollars inside the walls of the old barn at that place."

"No way. Thousands?"

"Yes. Tens of thousands."

"And you slipped up by saying something about the house to those two guys?"

"Yes. I thought I lost their tail long before I got to the house, but at the café they asked me what my interest was with that house. They saw me park across from it for a couple minutes, and then I drove in and talked to the occupants."

"They saw you at the house? What'd you tell them?"

"About the tats. That they were Sam's old address."

"Surely you didn't say anything about the money?" Riva said, while twisting her stringy hair with her right hand.

"No I didn't tell them about the money."

"Maybe they already know about the money. Maybe that's what they were really after."

"I doubt that."

"We've got to get back to the barn before they do," Riva said, sucking on her cigarette like it was a milkshake.

"The barn's gone."

"No way!" she hacked. "There's no barn? It's been torn down?"

"It burned down several years ago. The charred rubble is still laying there."

"We're out tens of thousands of dollars?"

"Yes."

"I almost wish you hadn't told me about it now."

"I know. Now I almost wish Sam hadn't told me about it back then."

"Why didn't you ever go get the money after you and Sam broke up?"

"I loved him. I wasn't going to steal his money. And besides, I didn't have the address."

"You didn't write it down when you were together?"

"Why should I, I loved him and thought we would always be together. I trusted that we would get the money when he wanted us to."

"Sometimes you can be so smart, and other times you can be so naïve."

"It's not being naïve, it's about honesty—something foreign to you, especially when you're hurting for a fix."

"So you got the address after you picked up Sam's body?" Riva said, ignoring the return put down.

"Yes."

"The tats were the reason you picked up the body in the first place, weren't they? You weren't motivated by love, but by greed. You knew the tats were your ticket to all that—"

"Stop it! That's a bunch of crap. I loved Sam deeply. If I never got any money, it wouldn't have mattered. I was going to see that he got a decent burial."

"How did you pay for that? Is he buried?"

"I paid on credit, figuring if the money was still in the barn, some of it would go to paying that. If the money wasn't there, then I'd pay it off myself. He was buried yesterday."

"Where?"

"At an old cemetery outside of Crow."

"Crow? Why clear out there?"

"Because he would have wanted to be someplace like that. It's up on a nice hill, overlooking a valley. It's beautiful. I'll take you out there sometime."

"It sounds nice. I'm sure he's happy there."

"Those guys at the café told me Sam Hostick wasn't Sam's real name."

"How would they know that?"

"I don't know, but they were pretty certain of it."

"What do you believe?"

"I don't know. He was Sam to me and always will be."

"So that's what you have his grave marked, 'Sam Hostick?'"

"Actually it says, 'Samuel Hostick.' If I ever find out for sure it wasn't his real name, and I learn what the real name is, I'll add that to the marker."

"What did you put for dates?"

"Just the dates I knew to be true. His birthday was February 2nd, 1944."

"He died two weeks after he turned sixty-six?" Riva said, "He was too young to die."

"The street life can be hard. You know that yourself."

"I don't ever want to end up back out there."

"Then do the drug treatment."

9

The Liberals

In Shane Coleman's garage the following evening, Thursday—

"Hodge is here, honey," Marlene Coleman said.

"Thanks," Shane answered. "Send him out here,"

"Are you sure?"

"Of course I'm sure. We have to face off sooner or later. It's time I put the man back in him."

"It's your call."

A minute later, Hodge walked through the door that led from the utility room into Shane's fur-shed garage. He closed the door behind him and then scanned the room.

On the far side, next to the outside door, was a small pile of un-skinned animals that Shane hadn't worked yet, containing a couple beavers, a raccoon, and a few nutrias. To the right of that, in front of the car garage door, were two big stacks of dried round beaver hides, along with piles of dried nutria, and 'coon hides. Hanging from pipe poles in the ceiling were dozens of nutria, 'coon and muskrat pelts, along with a few otters, all nailed out on various-size stretching boards. Along the right wall were seven half-sheets of plywood with beaver hides tacked out on both sides of each.

To Hodge's left, taking up the rest of the room, were a fleshing beam, various fur handling tools and knives, buckets partially filled with flesh or meat, and two tables—one covered high with skinned furs from yesterday's catch, and on the other Shane was nailing out a large beaver hide. Hodge also noted there were a number of dried otter pelts piled on the top of cupboards on the far side of the tables.

"Looks and smells like you've been busy," Hodge finally said.

"Some men have to work for a living."

"You won't get any argument from me. I never did think fur trapping was for a lazy man. When I passed Marlene on the way out here, she gave me a look that said, 'good luck.' I can't imagine why."

"Me either. Back when I first got started trapping in high school, you used to be curious about it."

"Who wouldn't be? It was part of America's history."

"A huge part," Shane said. "And here I thought I was going to use you for a warm up to tomorrow night's dinner."

"Why, what's happening then?"

"Marlene invited Rawly to bring his liberal girlfriend over."

"Oh. So you thought you'd practice your best arguments on me—the liberal."

"Why not?"

"Maybe I'm not nearly as left-wing as you seem to think I am. We were bound to have this conversation, so now's probably as good a time as any. We'll just get it all out on the table. Then when we're done, we can clean the mess up into some of your buckets over there." He gestured toward them. "That is, if either of us is still standing."

"I guess I've asked for that, haven't I? I want to start things off by telling you how sorry I am that I let our differences, and my hard feelings destroy our friendship."

"I accept your apology, and return mine. I'm sorry I let you down by chasing other women and ditching out on Shiela. She sure as hell didn't deserve to be treated that way."

"It does me good to hear you say that. Confession is the first step toward reconciliation."

"Where are you going with that?"

"Only time will tell," Shane said. "But neither of us wants to be old homeless Sam on our death bed before we make amends for the wrongs we've done. Why waste anymore of our lives, holding grudges, or not trying to make up with people who have wronged us or who we've wronged?"

"Almost sounds like a sermon."

"Sermon or not, it makes sense, doesn't it?"

"More than you know," Hodge said. "Being alone these past months has given me a ton of time to think. Time to think about, and look at, where my life has been, where it is, and where it's going. I haven't liked what I've seen."

"Remember how we used to go down to Lost Creek every day when we'd get home from the bean field, meet the other guys and the girls and have a ball?"

Instantly neither of them was in the garage anymore.

Their minds drifted back in time, each to a slightly different memory, to a time when they were just kids without any cares or worries. They were running and jumping off the bank into the six-foot-deep swimming hole behind the Dexter Market, building rock dikes, dams, and channels to control the flow of the water. Believing their childhoods would never end.

After nearly a minute, Hodge said, "Remember how we used to gather up crawdads from under the rocks in the shallows and boil 'em up in a number ten can, right there on the bank of the creek?"

"Or the time we experimented with skinny dipping to find out what the big deal was?"

"Yeah, then the older Holloway girl walked up on us, and said, 'If you ain't got no more to show than that, you're wasting my time.'" They burst out laughing. "Sometimes I wish I could just go back to that time in my life and start over. There's so much I would do differently."

"Maybe you wouldn't," Shane said. "Maybe you'd do everything the same."

"I hope not. I do know that I wouldn't want to be a kid growing up today. All this technology has robbed most kids of so much of what we did back then."

"And so much more of the population lives in cities anymore."

"Can you imagine you and me growing up in the city. Yet that's what I did to my kids. Made them grow up in a city. Not just *a* city. *Portland.*"

"At least you lived on the outskirts where it was only twenty minutes to the woods."

"Small consolation, considering I rarely took them there."

"Did I ever tell you I was baptized in Lost Creek," Shane said.

"No. Where?"

"Right below the Highway 58 bridge, back when the long, deep swimming hole was still there. I was home on my second leave from the navy in mid-November, 1975."

"You got baptized in November?"

"Yeah. I'm still shivering."

"What a fitting place for you to do it. You always loved Lost Creek like no one else I knew."

"The creek was alive to me. Whenever I was there, it was like I was with my maiden. I still love her. I just rarely visit her anymore. Marlene knows it, but I think she understands." Then, thinking now was as good a time as any, Shane said, "Knowing how much I love the outdoors, and particularly trapping, why did you vote against trapping?"

"Did I tell you I voted against trapping?" Hodge said, immediately feeling his face flush.

"No, but just after you left Shiela for Karen, I heard by the grapevine that you voted right along with the rest of the uninformed liberals to shut it down. To shut me down."

"I don't remember anyone being in the voting booth with me."

"I heard you told a group of people at a party one night that the days of the trapper are long past and anyone still doing it is living in the past. And when one of the liberals in our graduating class brought hunting and trapping up at our thirty-year reunion—which you avoided—my name was mentioned. Someone spouted off, 'Your old buddy, Hodge Gilbert, even voted to ban trapping. That ought to tell you something.'"

"I may have let my sarcasm go too far sometimes when I was drinking and said something that could have been misconstrued. But believe me, that's all it was—sarcasm. I *did not* vote against trapping. I may not personally take any interest in it, but I think people who want to do it, have a right to. Just like any other outdoor pursuit."

"Hodge, I should have taken Marlene's advice a long time ago when she said to just go to you and talk about the things that were bothering me. Find out if everything I had heard was true, and level with you. She told me I shouldn't let any of it ruin our friendship. But you know me, I chose to avoid conflict and let it fester."

"Maybe there was a reason we never ironed it out before. If I hadn't lost your friendship when I lost Shiela, and now Karen, maybe I never would have hit bottom. I forgive you, buddy. Let's just leave it all behind us now." Hodge reached out his hand to Shane, who took it and shook.

"If I was a drinking man," Shane said, "I'd say let's pop one open and celebrate. But how about if you hang out here for a bit while I work a little longer, then we'll go in and have a root beer float."

"You know I could never turn down a root beer float. We can suck on those while we're looking at the survey form I put together. How much longer are you going to be trapping this year?"

"I'm on my last stretch now. And I'm only going to check it three times."

"That's good. I'm going to get the boys started tomorrow. We can start some of the follow up the week after next, if that works for you."

"That'll work. I'll be on the tail end of the fur handling by then. I'm anxious to get my feet wet in this investigation."

"That's what I wanted to hear."

Friday Evening—

Shane pulled his truck and trailer up outside his house at dark, an hour later than expected. When Marlene came out to meet him, she was more than a little upset.

"Shane, the kids will be here in twenty minutes. Why are you so late?"

"I put in a bunch of new sets," Shane said. "Plus I had a good catch, which slowed me down even more."

"You should have been done out in the shed, and getting into the shower before now. Now they're going to be here before you even get the boat unloaded."

"Lighten up, Marlene. I'm not on the liberal young lady's time schedule."

"I can't help you unload the animals tonight. I'll end up smelling like beavers."

"There's no need to get all worked up about it. I don't need your help. You can go back in and finish with supper. Let me get this boat backed in now."

During the meal, an hour later—

"This broccoli casserole is wonderful, Mrs. Coleman," Kindra, the girlfriend, said. "Everything is."

"Thanks, honey," Marlene said.

"Did Rawly tell you I'm a fur trapper?" Shane said, bringing attention to the elephant in the room.

"He mentioned it," Kindra said, not opening the door for further discussion.

Rawly and Marlene looked at each other across the table, each suddenly feeling more tense than they already were. Marlene had half-hoped maybe the subject could be left alone this first time, but she knew Shane well enough to know better. He was proud to be a trapper and wasn't going to let anyone make him feel guilty about it—certainly not a young liberal in his own home.

"My dad was a trapper, and so were my grandfather and great grandfather; Rawly used to trap with me a lot too. He's pretty good at it."

"I haven't trapped in a long time," Rawly said. "Not since I started college two years ago." He hoped Kindra had enough sense to not push her politics now.

"Would you pass the salad please, Shane," Marlene said, pleading silently with her eyes for him to let it go.

He passed the salad by way of Rawly, then said. "My family has always been proud of its trapping heritage. I understand you don't know much about trapping?"

"Is that what Rawly said?" Kindra answered.

"In so many words."

"Actually, when I was young, one of my brother's friends trapped a few muskrats. But that was years ago. Since then I've learned how wrong trapping is. And I don't really approve of hunting either."

Shane's face immediately flushed red. Rawly and Marlene knew the cap was about to burst, but prayed silently that Shane would somehow not take the bait.

Shane wisely took another bite of his casserole and chewed slowly, knowing this was a make or break moment in history—at least his family's history. If he gave into his anger through his words, not only would he alienate Kindra—not that he cared much about that for himself—but he would put a huge wedge in his and Rawly's relationship. And he definitely wouldn't get lucky with Marlene at bedtime. He was smart enough to know that a naïve, young man like Rawly would always take the side of the woman of his affections.

"Have you spent a lot of time out in nature, Kindra? Or studied a lot about how life works among animals out there?"

"I enjoy watching birds and squirrels, and going for hikes," she said. "But I have to admit that I haven't studied animals a lot, other than through the wonderful literature put out by The Humane Socialist Society of the United Colonies (HSSUC), and Predatory Persons for the Ethical Treatment of Animals (PPETA)."

Rawly prayed his dad wouldn't say something like, *so you've been brain-washed by two of the most notorious animal rights groups in America, and then you brainwashed my naïve, skirt-chasing, testosterone-laden son as well.*

"An old lady once thought she would put me on the spot by saying, 'How can you consider yourself a Christian when you trap all those animals?' You know what I said to her?"

"What?"

"I asked her if she had ever read the Old Testament. She said she had read it many times. So I said, how do you explain all the animals that God *required* His people to raise for the sole purpose of being sacrificed to Him. Just for His pleasure and to appease His people's guilt."

"I heard something about that. But isn't that one of the reason's they call it the *Old* Testament?"

"You're obviously a bright young lady, Kindra. And you're right that in the New Testament God no longer requires animal sacrifices because He made His Son the final complete sacrifice. But then He said man was now free to eat any and all animals, without the restrictions of the old covenant. I could expound on all of what the Bible teaches about animals, but my point is that God created animals for mankind. He created them to be used, enjoyed, and eaten by man. He didn't create them as equals to man. The problem in our society today with the whole God-man-animal situation is that many people no longer acknowledge God *as God*. And they consider man to be no more important than an animal. In fact, they say *he is* an animal."

"I guess I hadn't looked at it like that."

"I don't want to belabor my point, but you need to understand that life out in the wild is not a box of chocolates. It's a brutal dog-eat-dog world. Animals are constantly killing each other for food, and sometimes just for sport. Nature will regulate wild animal populations either through predation, disease, or starvation. The land can only carry so many animals. Any hunter or trapper who does those two activities ethically is being a good steward of a natural resource. The great thing about man being involved in the death of an animal is that he gets the benefit of using the animal's body. He doesn't get to do that when animals die from disease or starvation, which often happens when animal populations are too dense."

"You're making good sense," Kindra said. "But there's a lot more I would like to discuss about my reasons for being against trapping, such as the methods used."

"I'd love to talk about that stuff with you," Shane said. "But how about if we do it another time, and go on to some other subject now."

"That sounds like a great idea," Marlene said, suddenly feeling relaxed.

"I agree," Rawly said. "Kindra, why don't you tell Mom and Dad about the singing group you toured with last summer."

"You toured in a singing group, honey? We'd love to hear about it," Marlene said, winking at Shane, indicating that it was still his lucky night—like most every other night.

10

The Survey

Speaking to the six boys, ages twelve to fourteen, the next day, Hodge said, "Boys, did all of you get the signed permission slip from your parent allowing you to help us out with this survey?"

"Yes," they each answered, while handing their slips to him.

As he handed each of them a survey form, he said, "Go ahead and read the survey carefully. If there are any questions, I will answer them when everyone is finished reading. As you can see, it's simple and straight forward."

Lost Creek Valley Survey

Person's name-

Age-

Address-

Phone number-

Email address (Optional)-

1. How long have you lived in the Lost Creek Valley?

2. How long have you, or any of your relatives, lived in the area?

3. Did you farm? What crops?
4. Did you, or any of your relatives, ever work for local farmers in the Lost Creek, Dexter, or Trent areas?
5. Doing what for farmer?
6. When did you (or your relatives) work there?
7. Do you have any stories or memories about the valley or its people that you would consider sharing with us at a later time?
8. When would be the best time to contact you (Days of the week, time)?

Thank you for your time. Your help with this project is appreciated.

Two minutes later, Hodge said, "Do any of you have any questions?" A couple of boys asked some questions, which Hodge answered.

"When you guys are doing the surveys, it is important that you are polite, and that you get as many of the questions answered as possible. Make it clear that you are doing the survey to get information for a book that a writer is doing on the history and memories of the people of Lost Creek Valley.

"Here are your maps, pens and survey envelopes." He handed them each a map similar to what the U.S Census Bureau uses. "Each team has a different area shaded in on its map. That is your area of coverage, so there won't be any confusion and we will get to each house. Make sure you circle each place you visit and put a box around the circle if the person was home and you completed the survey there. We need as many of these surveys filled out as possible, but don't pressure anyone to answer anything they don't want to. You are to write the person's answers down on the survey form yourselves, then read the answers back to the person to make sure you heard them correctly. Think of yourselves as newspaper reporters gathering information for a news story.

"Some people will probably try to tell you a lot more than the question asks for. If they start to do that, tell them the writer or his representative will contact them later to talk in more detail. Tell them the writer is having you boys do the survey to cover the basics only.

"You will notice that one of the envelopes is marked, 'Blank Survey Forms,' while the other one says, 'Completed Survey Forms.' If no one is home the first time you go to a house, try to go at a different time when you go back."

"Is all of this clear?" Hodge asked.

"When will we get paid?" one boy said.

"I will pay you in cash each time I meet with you, about every third or fourth day."

"How will you be able to keep track of how many surveys we each completed?"

"Use your head," another boy said. "He'll know by how many surveys are in your completed survey envelope."

"Oh," the first boy said, "I guess that *was* a dumb question, wasn't it?"

"That's alright, son," Hodge said. "What is your name?"

"Goon," one kid answered for him. The other boys laughed.

"Paul."

"Well, Paul, the only dumb question is the one not asked. When I was your age, they called me goon too." All the boys laughed. "It comes with the territory of being a kid... Okay, I've got each of your phone numbers. I'll be in touch to collect your surveys and pay you. Now get on your bikes and get to work."

One week later, Friday afternoon, March 5th, at the Coleman's dining table—

"Those boys are going to town for us," Shane said, as he thumbed through the filled out surveys. "You sure saved us a lot of work."

"I've learned a thing or two about this stuff over the years," Hodge said. "They're about half way through based on the number of houses marked on the maps. What do you think, any information in there we can use?"

"Definitely. I didn't think there would be this many old-timers still living up there. Not that there are a lot, but I guess I thought we'd be lucky to get half a dozen people in the whole valley that had been there since before 1960. Here we already have ten surveys like that, and half of those are people who would have been kids in 1960."

"Josh Standifer was in our graduating class," Hodge said.

"Here's Kent Simons. He was in the class of '69, same as my oldest brother. I think he even picked beans in Duncan's bean field. But I can't remember for sure. It would have only been during my first year or two there. He and Tommy used to fish together quite a bit. He could be a huge help to us, either way. I only wish my dad was still alive. He used to hunt with Kent's dad, 'Doc,' when they were in high school together. I wonder if Doc is still alive."

"Maybe he lives with Kent, and Kent just didn't mention it. Maybe he's too senile to be of any good to us."

"We'll find out. I bet my dad would have remembered all these old-timers. But I'm sure he would have told us we were asking for trouble doing what we're doing."

"That *is* a possibility, I have to admit it now," Hodge said. "I didn't want to tell you that before because I didn't want anything to dissuade you. But I know nothing will stop you now. You're as crazy about all this as I am."

"You've got that right, old buddy," Shane said.

"Let's meet at the Jasper Café for breakfast at eight tomorrow morning, then we'll go make contact with some of these people."

After breakfast the next morning, they each drove their vehicles across Jasper Bridge, parked Shane's truck in the parking area to the left there, then rode in Hodge's SUV to Rattlesnake road. As they made the right hand turn to the south onto Rattlesnake Road, Shane said, "Remember the morning we were on our way to school and came upon the wreck that had just happened here?"

Hodge chuckled. "I couldn't forget something like that if I tried. The right front fender of Mark William's little Dodge Dart was folded up against the left front fender of Bill Eastman's Ford pickup; neither was willing to yield when they turned onto the highway."

"You know they were racing to school, don't you?"

"I heard that, but neither of them ever confirmed it."

"Maybe not to you. Williams told me, he and Eastman had just got off the phone with each other five minutes earlier. Eastman had said, 'I'll beat you to school.'"

"Why didn't Williams just pull into the lane beside Eastman?"

"He said there was oncoming traffic, so he had to pull clear across."

"Imagine explaining that to your parents or the police."

On Lost Creek Road, just past the Rattlesnake Road-Lost Creek Road junction, Hodge turned his vehicle down a long gravel drive-way on the left, leading to an old house near the edge of the woods. The old widow, Bertha Williams, had lived in that same house since 1949. Over the phone she had said, "I gave birth to my first two kids right here in this house, 1950 and '52."

The short, chubby, old woman answered their knock, wearing an ancient shin-length dress, half covered by a pink apron. "Come on in," she said.

Hodge and Shane followed her into the small, cozy living room, which smelled like Shane's grandma's house always used to smell—like something had been baked recently. Hodge took a seat on the couch, Shane sat in a chair across from him, and Bertha sat down in an old wooden rocking chair between them.

"Which one of you is Buck Coleman's boy?"

"I am, ma'am, Shane Coleman. This is Hodge Gilbert. He grew up in Dexter also. He's been a social worker for years. Myself, I've mostly trapped fur and worked in lumber mills."

"Your dad was quite a trapper, as I remember. Back in the fifties everyone knew everyone out here. Times have sure changed since then. Your dad was my mailman for over twenty years."

"Twenty-five, actually. That is, if you've lived here since 1949."

"Twenty-five it was then. Let me get you boys some coffee and cookies," she said, getting up and heading toward the kitchen.

They both grinned, and Shane said, "I could get used to this."

"One of the perks of PI work."

She returned with a cup of black coffee for each of them, and a round, eight-inch china plate covered with cookies.

Shane said, "Those aren't molasses cookies are they?"

"Oh yes they are."

"They're my favorite. The old lady that lived next to us in Dexter when I was a kid made them three times a week for her grandkids that lived with her, and all us neighbor kids. It was a shame when she died of a stroke; we didn't get the cookies anymore." All three of them laughed.

While eating a few cookies apiece, Hodge and Shane asked Bertha several questions and listened to her tell about a number of interesting things that occurred in the valley over the years. Hodge recorded the conversation on his cell phone, and they both scribbled notes on their miniature spiral notebooks.

Finally Hodge got to the point, "Bertha, did anyone in your family ever pick beans at Duncan's Bean Field?"

"My oldest daughter, Cathryn, picked there with a couple of her friends and their mother for a full season and part of another."

"Do you remember what years?"

"I could never forget," she said. The men quickly glanced at each other, anticipating what was coming next. "She started there in 1959, and then picked part of the season in 1960. I pulled her from the field when the tragedy occurred."

"The Ellen Brock murder?"

"That's right. Ellen was a year younger than Cathryn. The sweetest little girl I ever saw. We had her over night a couple times, the last time only a few weeks before she died. I can still visualize her laughing and swinging on our play set out back. After they found her, I used to have nightmares in which my own kids would end up chopped to pieces like one of the reports said happened to Ellen."

"That had to be terrible, as a mother, to have something like that to worry about," Hodge said. "Shane and I picked in that bean field ourselves for several years beginning in 1965. We heard stories about the murder pretty regularly during the time we picked there."

"Then you know they never found the killer. A lot of people said it was probably some hobo just passing through the area; the bean field was only a mile from the railroad. Myself, I always thought it was more likely someone who lived local. Maybe even one of the older teenagers that lived near the bean field."

"It's funny you should say that, because my dad always believed it was a local boy too," Shane said. He knew immediately, from the stern look Hodge gave him, that he shouldn't have said that.

"He did? Being the mail carrier, he probably knew more than a lot of people about a lot of things that went on around here."

"Well, we're going to have to run now, Bertha," Hodge said, deliberately looking at his watch so she could see him do it. "We've got a few other people we're supposed to talk with up the creek. But we will definitely come back."

"I sure enjoyed talking with you guys. I hope I was of some help. I'll clue you in to the best source of information in the valley. An old widow named Bessie Rogers."

"Bessie Rogers?" Shane said. "Is that the same Bessie Rogers who was Roland Roger's grandma?"

"Yes. He's just one of her fourteen grandkids and ten great grandkids. She turned ninety-two last summer; but she's still sharp as a tack. And she still keeps up on everything. She's the valley gossip."

"Where does she live?"

"Just down from the Mt. Zion Church, across the creek. They still have the original cedar log bridge going to their place. Her husband died fifteen years ago. Her daughter and son in law, who live up Rattlesnake, check in on her a few times a week."

In Hodge's SUV, pulling out of Bertha's driveway on the way to their next stop—

"I'm sorry I said anything about my dad thinking the killer—"

"That's okay. Just be more careful next time," Hodge said. "We have to sit back and just let people tell us whatever they want to about the case, without telling much of what we know or think. Later, when we go back to certain people, we'll probe deeper and maybe tell some of what others in the valley recall, without dropping source names, of course. Then we can ask each person their opinion about what the others have said. It's kind of a ping-pong game. We have to bounce things back and forth. If we say too much, or appear overly interested in certain details of the case, someone is bound to put two and two together. Then if by some chance the murderer is still living in the area, and gets on to what we're trying to do, things could get ugly."

"You mean dangerous, don't you?"

"That's a possibility."

"At what point would you bring the police in on it?"

"I don't know yet. Probably not until I'm confident we have it solved."

"Why wait that long?"

"You haven't been around much, have you?" Hodge said. "No offense intended. Whenever you get the police involved, some people have a way of clamming up. Especially anyone who's had a negative interaction with the cops. And who hasn't?"

"I see your point," Shane said. "By staying with the pretense of writing a history book, we can keep from raising suspicion."

"That's the idea anyway."

"So are we going to go right to the best source, Bessie Rogers?"

"Not hardly. Not yet, anyway. If she's the gossip Bertha made her out to be, all we would accomplish by talking with her is to ensure that the wrong ears hear the wrong things. Women like her can really stir the pot, and they always add enough of their own spices to attract a lot of attention.

"You have a good point."

After leaving Bertha's, the men stopped and visited with four other long-time residents from their list and picked up some useful information, along with some interesting history. All of the old-timers either knew Shane's dad personally or at least knew he was the mail carrier.

11

The Simons

On the phone that evening, Saturday, March 6th, from the Goshen church house, talking with her sister at the Multnomah Drug Rehabilitation Center—

"Riva, it's great to hear your voice," Desiree said. "How did your first week up there go?"

"It's great to hear your voice, too, Sis," Riva answered. "I'm glad I came. It's been a rough week, with all the withdrawals. But not nearly as rough as it could have been according to everything I've heard from the staff and other addicts who have tried detoxing by other methods. Everybody here says their Neuro-Transmitter Restoration Therapy is the best way to get off drugs."

"I knew we made the right choice, getting you in there."

"I'm pretty well through the worst of it now. The food up here is excellent, and they give me lots of time to rest."

"That's great."

"I started getting one-on-one counseling and doing group sessions two days ago. I've made some new friends, including two women and a guy that are from Eugene. After I complete this thirty-day program, I'll continue to meet in an out patient support group in Eugene a couple times a week. I really think I'm going to make it."

"I know you will, Sis. I'll be here for you."

"I love you, Desiree."

"I love you too, Riva. Hang in there."

Sunday afternoon, as they parked Shane's truck at the home of Kent Simons—

"There's an old man sitting on the front porch," Hodge said.

"I hope it's Kent's dad," Shane said, basking for several seconds in the warmth of the early-March sunlight coming through his open pickup window. "I haven't seen either of them in over twenty years. Last time I saw Kent I was fishing the very upper end of the creek. He said he hadn't fished up there in years and was very disappointed at how few fish there were anymore. I felt the same way. The only thing left now are the memories. But boy they are great memories."

Shane opened the dilapidated wooden gate and saw that much of the cement walkway, leading to the porch, was choked with ivy bushes that encroached from either side of it. He looked around the front of the ninety-year-old, two-story farmhouse and observed that the grass, weeds, trees and shrubs, were all in dire need of attention. Brown paint was peeling away from the outside of the house. He remembered this place being perfectly trimmed and nicely painted in the past. The way it looked now, he wondered why it hadn't been condemned.

The Simons' place was on the west side of Lost Creek Road, which ran west of Lost Creek from just north of the old Kittan place to just upstream of Gaines Falls. Across from the Simons, the creek veered east over two hundred yards away from the road and stayed behind all the houses for the next mile or so. The deepest hole anywhere on the creek was across from the Simons' place.

In mid-June, when the creek's water was finally warm enough to swim in, the fifty-yard-long pool, which was twenty feet across, ran twelve feet deep on the north side, right up against the bedrock wall that lined that side of the creek. Over the years, the swift winter and spring currents had run up against the rock wall and dug out the deep hole. The second deepest hole on Lost Creek was at Gaines Falls, several miles upstream. Shane had fished through both holes many times during his teen years, but only swam in each a few times. He and Hodge had done most of their swimming in their favorite holes miles downstream.

Old man Simons, "Doc," was known as quite an archer in his day. Both his boys, Kent and the oldest one, Ed, also loved bow hunting, back in the seventies, before it was so popular. All the men in the Simons family were tall, at least six-foot-four, and thin. Kent played backup center on Pleasant Hill's team the year Shane's older brother was a senior.

When they reached the front porch, Shane was pretty certain that the old man had to be Doc Simons, though he looked even skinnier than he remembered him. "Is that Doc Simons?" he asked.

"Yes," the old man answered, peering out at them through his coke-bottle thick glasses, as he sat on an old wooden rocking chair. "Who wants to know?"

Shane and Hodge both chuckled silently. "It's Shane Coleman, one of Buck Coleman's boys. Buck was your mail carrier years ago."

"I know who Buck Coleman is. Which one of his boys are you?"

"I'm the second oldest. My oldest brother graduated from high school with your son Kent in 1969."

"Come on up here, Coleman." Looking up at Hodge through squinted eyes, Doc asked, "Who's your friend?"

"This is Hodge Gilbert. He grew up in Dexter also." Doc shook Hodges' outstretched hand.

"I don't remember that name, but that doesn't mean anything. My memory isn't what it once was, at least not with names. What brings you up into these parts?"

"We're here to talk with Kent. I guess he didn't mention that we were coming."

"I guess not," he said. "Kent," he yelled through the screen covering the front door opening. "Kent, Buck Coleman's kid is here to talk to you."

Kent came out and shook both Shane and Hodge's hands, as Shane introduced Hodge. "You guys have a seat there on that bench." He pointed to a six-foot-long, decrepit wooden bench to their right on the thirty-foot-long by eight-foot-wide front porch they were standing on. Kent took a seat in an old wooden rocking chair to the left of his father. Hodge stepped over to the bench and sat down.

"It was sure a surprise to hear from you, Shane," Kent said. "Sorry to hear about Tommy."

"Thanks. Vietnam finally got him. Pancreatic cancer. They said it was probably caused by Agent Orange."

"I heard that at our forty-year reunion last summer. I loved your brother. Boy was he a good fisherman, just like your dad. Is your dad still alive?"

"No, he died two years ago."

"Sorry."

Changing the subject, Shane said, "We're sure glad to get to talk to you. I couldn't believe it when the boys had a survey filled out by you. And it's a real pleasant surprise to find your dad still alive and well after all these years."

"He's a stubborn old goat. We're not ready for him to give up the ghost yet."

"Hey, watch you're mouth, son." Doc said.

"Kent, you're one of the few people in the world I would trust with the information we have. But as Tommy's childhood best friend, I know we can trust you. And I know we can trust you, Doc, as my dad's old best friend."

"You're going to write a book about the history up here?" Kent said. "What could be so secret that you would introduce it like that, Shane?"

"Actually, Hodge is going to write the book, but it's going to focus more on a certain aspect of the history. Hodge grew up in Dexter not far from me. He and I were best friends all the way up. He was a cop for fifteen years, and has been a private investigator since leaving law enforcement."

"You really have my curiosity up now," Kent said.

"Mine too," Doc added.

"Do you remember the Ellen Brock murder at Duncan's bean field in 1960?"

"You're kidding me," Kent said. "You're investigating that after all these years?"

"There's been some new information in the case."

"Are the cops involved?"

"No, actually, they're not. And for the time being, we don't want them involved. Or anyone else."

"What new information do you have?"

"I met an old man on the McKenzie River a few weeks ago when I was running my trap line. It turns out he knew who killed Ellen Brock. He and the killer used to be neighbors."

"He knows who killed her? Is the killer still alive?" Kent asked.

"If he knows who killed her, why hasn't he gone to the police in all these years?" Doc said.

"Why did he tell you?" Kent added.

"The old guy died while he was telling me about it. He was a sixty-six year-old homeless man living in his sleeping bag under a bridge near the Springfield International Paper Plant. He knew he was dying and wanted to get it off his chest before he died."

"So why didn't he go to the cops with his information?" Doc asked.

"Did he give you the killer's name?" Kent said.

"I'll get to that," Shane said.

"Was the homeless man from the Lost Creek area?" Kent said.

"I had the same questions," Shane said. "And unfortunately, I got very few of them answered before he died. He said I could call him Sam, but we're almost certain that was not his real name. I'll explain that and everything else."

"This is better than reading Sherlock Holmes," Doc said.

"Yeah, *we get to play* Sherlock Holmes," Hodge said.

Shane went on to explain everything they knew so far, including the part about Desiree, then said, "Obviously, if the killer still lives in the area, or knows someone in the area and somehow gets wind of our investigation, it would throw a wrench into things."

"You don't think your little historical survey could tip him or someone that knows him off?" Kent said.

"No," Hodge said. "There are no questions on it that even hint at the Ellen Brock case. Even our questions about working for local farmers are way too general to give anything away. Consider that the guy has lived fifty years without anyone fingering him. The case has been suspended for the last thirty-five years. As long as we maintain a low profile, don't say anything we shouldn't to the wrong people—like Bessie Rogers—and work the local history angle, we'll be alright."

"How can we help?" Kent said.

"First off," Shane said, "We were wondering if you ever worked in Duncan's bean field?"

"Yes, I did," Kent answered.

"I know my brother Tommy didn't start picking there until 1963. He picked at Bloud's before that. So he wasn't working there when Ellen was murdered. What years did you work at Duncan's?"

"I started there the same year Tommy did. I only picked there three years. I also picked at Bloud's with Tommy before that."

"I know Ellen was the same age as you and Tommy. Did you know her?"

"She was in my first grade class room. I teased her a little on the playground like all of us boys did to all the cute girls. I'm sure you guys probably did the same thing at that age."

"Of course," Shane said. "When I was an adult and asked Tommy about Ellen, he said he remembered her being a playful girl, but he was too shy to ever strike up a conversation with her. And he never had the same teachers she had. He said she was killed the summer between their third and fourth grade."

"I never talked to her either," Kent said. "What is it that you guys want me to do to help with this case?"

"I'm still not clear on that," Hodge said. "I'm thinking maybe we could use you as a filtering system for information. You said on the phone that you lived here off and on over the years and that you moved back here a couple years ago to help your dad, right?"

"That's right. I stayed here off and on a few times over the years when either of my two marriages were in trouble and after the divorces. I know the place looks like hell right now—"

"You don't have to explain that to us," Hodge said. "Things happen, divorce can tear a man up. Believe me, I know first hand."

"The inside of the house looks a lot better—" Doc said.

"It's alright. We don't care about the house," Shane said. "All the wealthiest people around, with all their house maids and land-scapers, will never be the people I always knew the Simons to be. Why do you think I've leveled with you on all this? Because you're good people. The best people."

"You're definitely Buck's boy," Doc said. "He never made a ton of money, but he was always a good, honest man who knew what was most important in life."

"Thanks," Shane said. "I miss him dearly."

"We've got a couple more people up the creek to talk to today, so we've got to get going," Hodge said. "Here's my card if you need to get in contact. We'll check in with you periodically."

In bed that night at the Coleman's—

"Marlene, we ran into Dad's best friend from high school up Lost Creek today," Shane said.

"Who was that?"

"Doc Simons. Ronald 'Doc' Simons. He got the nickname when he was a medic in the army in World War II, and it stuck after he returned home."

"I bet seeing him made you miss Dad."

"You know it. He's eighty-seven. Still seems to have a pretty clear head, though I think he may have some short-term memory loss. His youngest son, Kent, is living with him right now. Kent graduated from high school with Tommy. They used to fish together all the time. Hodge and I decided to bring both Kent and Doc in on the whole investigation."

"Isn't that kind of risky?"

"Not at all. You never met any nicer folks than the Simons. There's not a bad apple in the bunch."

"I'm happy for you, honey, getting to talk with all these people from yours and Dad's past. I bet it brings back a lot of good memories."

"It sure does. I guess I didn't know just how well thought of Dad was by his patrons and the community. When you're a kid, you take your dad for granted. He moved away from Dexter in the mid-seventies, when I was in the navy, and neither of us ever lived there after that. Over the years, whenever I happened to run into someone I knew when I was hunting, fishing or trapping out that way, they'd always ask how Dad was."

"I miss Dad," Marlene said. "Hold me, honey."

Shane took Marlene snuggly in his strong arms and thanked God for giving her to him.

Three nights later, Wednesday, March 10th, over the phone—

"Shane, I've been doing a lot of thinking about the things Desiree said. I've come to the conclusion there's more to the tattoo story than meets the eye. We've got to have a look at those tattoos ourselves."

"How do you propose to do that when we have no idea which funeral home Desiree worked with, *if* in fact she did, or even if his body was buried locally. And *what if* they cremated it?"

"You heard what the guy said down at the morgue. A body can't be cremated without next of kin signing."

"And Desiree isn't next of kin."

"So his body has to be buried somewhere, and I'm guessing locally. There wouldn't have been any reason for her to transport it out of the area, especially since she had no idea anyone would care about it besides her."

"But she would have had Sam buried after we talked to her. There wouldn't have been enough time before that."

"There was still no reason for her to take Sam's body out of the local area."

"So tell me why you're suddenly so hot on the tattoos," Shane said.

"If the numbers on the tattoos actually were connected to the address where Sam once lived, and the house with the burned barn wasn't it, then something doesn't add up. I'm thinking maybe Sam used some different numbers."

"Like a code?"

"Exactly. If he did that and was smart—which from the little I've gleaned from you and Desiree about him, he was *plenty* smart—he *would have* used the address of an *actual* house, with a barn, for the basis of his code."

"Why would he need to make things so complicated?"

"Think about it. Why have an address tattooed on your body in the first place?"

"Why put a tattoo of anything on your body in the first place?" Shane said. "Did you ever get a tattoo?"

"Not hardly. I'm macho enough without crap like that."

"You sure are."

"I believe Desiree slipped up when she told us about the tattoos, but I think Sam was sharp enough not to tell her his code," Hodge said. "Think about it. If you hooked up with a homeless gal, even if you loved her to pieces, would you have enough doubt about her to prevent you from giving her your deepest secrets?"

"I don't trust any of them much now."

"Sam told you he never told anyone else about his friend killing Ellen Brock, right? If he didn't tell her that, then why should he tell her about the tattoos if they led right to his old house? I've been thinking there's more to his barn than he had a chance to tell you?"

"You think the shirt may still be in his barn, that he didn't return it to the killer's barn like he said?"

"No. He had to have returned the shirt, or his friend soon would have discovered the shirt missing from the hayloft and realized the reason Sam suspected him of killing Ellen in the first place was because he found the shirt. The killer would have gone right to Sam demanding he turn the shirt over or he would kill him, knowing the shirt tied him directly to the crime."

"But wouldn't the killer have figured Sam must have found the shirt or he wouldn't have had a reason to question him about the girl?" Shane said.

"I doubt it. The killer would have figured Sam would have told him he found the shirt if he had."

"That's true."

"I think the killer, especially being so young, just felt his guilt very heavy and would have lived with the constant fear of being discovered. Because of the guilt he felt, he would have thought others, including Sam, sensed his guilt—kind of like when you get embarrassed and feel your face getting warm. You think everyone will notice. He undoubtedly saw himself as having this beacon of guilt that constantly flashed a subliminal message, saying, "I killed her. *You all know I killed her.* Why do you make me suffer knowing that I know you know I killed her? Why won't any of you admit it? What are you waiting for?"

"I never thought of that. Geez, Hodge, you really understand the criminal's mind."

"I hope you aren't implying anything with that, old buddy."

"Of course not. I'm just really impressed. So the killer felt *the beacon* had tipped Sam off, rather than the shirt?"

"That's my guess. Let's assume Sam was being candid with you on everything he told you. Everything he had a chance to tell you. I believe if, in fact, he was paid off, he would have gotten around to confessing that as well."

"But he died first."

"That's right. Even though he might have told you about any payoff money—if there was any—he never would have told you where his old barn was, because that would have narrowed down where the killer lived back then. And maybe still does, or nearby."

"So one reason Sam never told anyone about the crime, was because the killer was actually paying him money all those years for him not to tell," Shane said. "Yet it's possible he never spent any of the money because his conscience wouldn't let him spend blood money."

"And after any amount of time passed, especially after Sam became an adult, if he had gone to the authorities, he could have been viewed as an accomplice of sorts. Or at the very least he would have figured they'd get him for obstruction of justice. And you can be sure the killer pointed that out to him. It's even quite likely that as they both got older, maybe in their thirties or forties, the killer leveraged Sam's guilt as a way to stop paying him."

"So Sam doesn't give up the killer's identity to me, because he knows he took his money all those years to keep his mouth shut. But he still needed to get the burden of what he knew off his chest before he died. Maybe Desiree did know about the money?"

"If there was—or is—money and Sam told her anything about it, I'm sure he never would have told her where it came from and why. And if he did tell her about the money, I suspect it would have been when he was high or drunk."

"Boy your theories are amazing, Hodge. If they're correct, if there was blood money hidden for years in Sam's old barn, and he did use a code for the address, why can't we just figure the code out from the address of the house Desiree stopped at?"

"That's like believing you can use a newspaper article as the basis for your investigation, Shane. If you want to know you're on solid footing right from the start, you go right to the original source, not the reporter. We have to find where Sam is buried and look at those tattoos ourselves."

12

Sam's Grave

"Do you have any way of determining where he was buried?" Shane asked. "It would have been nice if we could have gotten on this two weeks ago."

"Yeah, we should have got on it earlier. But we didn't, so we'll have to take it from here. Besides, maybe Desiree contacted the cemetery to tell them to watch for grave robbers. The fact that we haven't attempted anything before now is probably a good thing. Desiree probably figures since we haven't gone back to the house in Goshen looking for her by now, she has nothing more to fear from us."

"I don't know. She seemed too sharp to let things go that easy."

"I know that. I was just checking you out. You have some good investigative instincts in you. Did you know that?"

"Hey, I'm a trapper and hunter. I know how to analyze what I see and hear. I know how to track. And I think before this whole thing is over we might be using my outdoor skills more than we think," Shane said.

"You've obviously been considering the possibilities, haven't you?"

"Let's just say, I've put myself in the killer's place to try to think of how he might think and react if he learns the case is being investigated."

"What have you come up with?" Hodge asked.

"I'm sixty-six years old, I've lived a normal life, except for a terrible thing I did when I was a teenager. I can't bring the girl back to life, nor can I ever erase the pain I caused her family. I've already lived with the guilt and remorse of the whole thing for fifty years. What good is it going to do for me to go to prison, or get the death penalty, now?

"And then a couple of gung-ho, ex-Dexter kids decide its time to make me own up to, and pay for, my fifty-year-old crime. What are my options when I can see they don't intend to give up until they have me behind bars for the rest of my natural life, *or executed*?

"I can leave the area and go live where no one can find me. Or, I nip the investigation in the bud by shutting up the investigators. I figure that since the cops aren't involved, there's a reason for that. They don't want the cops involved. But why? In the end, it doesn't matter, other than it makes my job of eliminating them easier. If I handle it right, no one will ever trace it back to me, and I can go on living my life like I always have."

"You've come to the same conclusions I have, Shane. I knew all the risks when I got involved, but it's not like I really have anything to lose. Not like you. Shiela is gone and she's never coming back. If I were her, I wouldn't either."

"You never know what God might bring about, Hodge. Love is a powerful thing that can be re-kindled at the time when you least expect it. I know how much you and Shiela used to love each other. I wouldn't give up on that just yet."

"What are you saying?"

"Just that. Don't give up. If love is still buried somewhere in Shiela's heart, who knows what God could do with it."

"I'll believe it when I see it."

A week later the boys had completed surveying the Lost Creek Valley; Hodge and Shane had followed up with several more of the locals, but still had more contacts to make.

By cell phone—

"Shane I've figured out where Sam is buried."

"How did you manage that?"

"I have my sources."

"I'll say. Where is he?"

"The Crow Cemetery. Can you go out there with me Friday night?"

"Yeah. Have you been out there yet to confirm he's there?"

"What do you take me for an idiot? Of course I've been out there. Did I ever take you poaching where I didn't already know there'd be deer?"

"You never took me poaching. Did you poach deer?"

"I was messing with you, buddy. Lighten up."

"I guess I deserved that. Are we going to dig him up on Friday?"

"Yes. I'll have the tools and the light."

"They don't have any security out there?"

"Of course not. It's just an old country cemetery that picks up maybe four *new* bodies a year. There can't be more than two or three hundred people buried there. It's on a mostly grassy hill surrounded by deciduous trees, and it has a long private driveway through a fir forest. We'll park my truck in the woods on one of the side roads and hike up to the cemetery after dark."

"That sounds simple enough."

"Come ready to dig hard and fast."

"No problem there."

"Be at my place at 5:30."

Friday evening, March 19th, 7:30—

"You weren't kidding about the cemetery being on a hill," Shane said, breathing hard as he climbed the steep grassy incline, carrying two shovels—a square blade and a round tip.

"I thought you were in shape with all that trapping," Hodge said.

"Age must be catching up with you, huh?"

"Trapping the river by boat is a different kind of exercise. I haven't humped any hills since the fall deer hunting and mushroom picking seasons."

"I hear you."

Near the top, coming from the north, Hodge said, "We'll stop hear to rest and listen for a minute to make sure the coast is clear.

"No argument here."

A minute later, "Let's go," Hodge said, sounding like the army sergeant he once was.

When they were half-way around the west edge of the cemetery, Hodge said, "Here it is," as he pointed his mini-maglite at the ground. "The temporary marker is right in the center."

Shane stepped up beside Hodge, pointed his own miniature light at the ten-inch-square marker, and read, "'Samuel Hostick, February 2, 1944 — February 17, 2010.' I wonder if the permanent marker will say anymore."

"Who knows? She probably ordered something like, 'My beloved, Sam. I miss you. Why didn't you give me the money before you kicked the bucket? I could sure use it about now. Rest in peace.'"

"That's terrible."

"What I feel even worse about is that he isn't going to get as much *rest* tonight as he usually gets." They both laughed.

"I wonder where Ellen Brock is buried," Shane said.

"Probably in the Pleasant Hill cemetery."

"Tommy and my mom are both buried there. I sang, 'Spirit Song,' when we had our family graveside service there for Tommy."

"Tommy was a good big brother to you."

"I still remember the day he left for Vietnam. When we got back in the car at the bus station, Dad broke down bawling. I had never seen him break down like that before. Of course, Mike and I cried right along with him."

"Wasn't your dad in on the Normandy assault on D-Day?"

"You've got a good memory, Hodge. You know he never told me any of the details until after I went to see 'Saving Private Ryan.' I cried silently sitting in the theatre imagining Dad going through that. Afterwards, I went over to his place and told him I'd seen the movie. I asked if that's how it really was.

"He said, 'No movie could accurately portray the true horror of that assault. I thought we were in hell. German machine guns firing non-stop from their bunkers high on the sea wall, chopping us to pieces. Artillery shells exploding all around us, body parts flying every which way.'"

Hodge and Shane both stood silently for half a minute, staring blankly at Sam's marker.

Shane finally said, "I don't know why, I've always liked walking around in old cemeteries, looking at the various gravestones, reading the names and dates, wondering what each person's life was like, and how they died."

"It's sobering, isn't it?" Hodge said. "A person can be full of life and laughter, like the class clown, or a shy, quiet wall-flower. But when it's over, they all end up out here, just the same."

Shane started singing, "To everything, turn, turn, turn. There is a season, turn, turn, turn. And a time *for* every purpose under heaven."*en

Hodge joined him, singing, "A time to be born, a time to die..."

Finally, Hodge said, "We better get to work." They each turned their headlamp on and put their mini-maglites in Hodge's backpack on the ground, before putting their gloves on.

Hodge removed the marker and set it off to one side, then said, "Help me roll up this turf." They each pushed a shovel under a corner to lift it, then grabbed the grass and sod and rolled it up the long way, finally pushing the cylinder of grass a few feet away from the edge of the plot.

Then they each went to work shoveling dirt out onto one side. Shane said, "This is a whole lot easier than it would be a year from now."

"No joke."

When they had dug the dirt free down to a couple feet, Hodge suddenly stopped, and said, "Do you hear that?"

They both froze.

"Someone's coming," Hodge said. "Grab the other shovels, I'll get the pack."

"I knew something like this would happen," Shane said, quickly gathering up the other two shovels and following Hodge in the opposite direction from where the voices were.

They ran to the scrub oak trees thirty yards away and laid down on their bellies, facing Sam's plot, with their headlamps turned off, listening and watching.

"I see a flashlight beam," Shane said. "They're coming directly toward Sam's plot."

"Damn it," Hodge said, as they both listened to a male and a female voice talking back and forth. "It sounds like a couple of older teenagers. He probably has plans for her."

"They're sure taking their time, they must be reading gravestones," Shane said. He hit the illuminate button on his watch, and said, "It's 8:15. With it being Friday, they could be up here all night."

"The marker!" Hodge said. "If they find Sam's marker, they'll know he's buried there and come to the wrong conclusions about what's going on."

"What conclusion would be wrong?"

"I've got to go get that marker." Hodge immediately sprang up and dashed out, crouching as he approached the grave. He spotted the marker, picked it up and ran back to Shane.

"You barely made it. They can't be more than twenty yards from Sam's plot now."

They continued to wait, nervously.

"They've turned," Shane finally said. "They're headed down slope, away from his grave."

"Maybe we'll get lucky and they won't come back."

The voices grew faint, but still audible. They began hearing less talking and more giggling. They guessed the young couple was messing around. After ten minutes, the voices began to grow louder again. "Darn it," Shane said, "it sounds like they're coming back our way."

Five minutes later, the couple was only fifteen yards from the hole, when the male voice—that of an older teen—said, "Look there," as he pointed his light directly across Sam's grave. "What do you think is going on with that?"

The teenagers walked right up to the grave and peered inside.

"I've never seen the ground crew dig up part of a plot and leave it. They always just do it all at one time," the young man said.

"Maybe this wasn't done by the ground crew," the older teen girl said. "Maybe some of the relatives of the person they're going to bury here are doing it. Maybe they got *a better deal* on the plot price, by choosing the self-service option."

"That's funny. They don't do that. At least I don't think they do."

"Maybe there's a marker around here that will tell us who's going to be buried here."

They shined their flashlights all around the immediate area of the grave, but found nothing.

"If I didn't know better, I'd say this digging was done sometime today," the young man said. "Maybe even just before dark. I think we better tell someone about this tomorrow."

"Why not tell my parents tonight," she said. "See what they think."

"Margie, it's Friday night. Let's take advantage of it and not have our night ruined by your parents calling the cops, or having us bring them back up here."

"I guess you're right. Let's go down to your barn then. We can put on some music and have some fun."

"I'm up for that."

"Don't get any ideas," she said, "You know I'm saving myself for that special day."

They continued their conversation as they slowly walked back out the way they originally arrived at the cemetery.

When they could no longer hear the couple's voices, Hodge and Shane returned to the grave and went back to work. Hodge said, "We better hope we don't have anymore interruptions. I don't want to have to come back later to re-dig this."

"Yeah, and after the kids report what they found, people are going to be watching this cemetery," Shane said. Then changing the subject, "If we don't get anything else out of this evening, I have to say it was great to hear a young woman stand up for herself, and not give herself to that guy."

"You can't read too much into that, Shane. A girl might use that line to keep one guy off her, then give it up to the next one."

"I think she sounded too convincing."

They continued to shovel dirt for another couple feet down and finally began hearing their shovels hit against the top of the casket. They switched to the square tip shovels and then finally to a wisp broom to brush all the dirt off the top. Once they had cleared the sides enough to reach the latches, they each unfastened two of them.

"Are you ready, Shane?"

"You say that like you've done something like this before."

"I have. Alright, pop the top."

As soon as they opened the two halves of the lid, an unpleasant odor escaped and filled their nostrils."

"That's disgusting," Shane said. "I thought embalming prevented odors."

"It does to some extent, but I seriously doubt Sam was embalmed. There wouldn't have been any reason to embalm him. It would have been an unnecessary expense."

"Let's get him up out of there."

"I've got his shoulders, you get his legs. Now lift," Hodge said. "Geez, Sam, for an old guy who hasn't eaten in a month, you're sure heavy."

They both grunted as they lifted Sam's body up and over the side of the hole opposite the piled dirt, and set him on his back. Residual air escaped from his lungs causing a slight groan. "Sorry Sam," Hodge said. "We'll try to be more gentle when we put you back to bed in a few minutes." They climbed out of the hole and knelt beside him.

As they shined their head lamps into Sam's sunken face, Hodge said, "I bet he looked healthier the first time you saw him on the river."

"That's an understatement."

"Let's get his shirt and jacket off, and get a look at those armpits."

"Did you bring a razor?"

"I'm sure *he hasn't* grown any hair since Desiree shaved him."

"I forgot about that."

Hodge raised Sam's torso upright and held him there, while Shane went to work unbuttoning and removing his jacket and shirt. Once his clothes were off his upper body, Hodge laid him back on the grass, and stretched his arms straight out, perpendicular to his body.

"Get your pad out, Shane." Hodge stretched the skin under Sam's left arm tight and said, "Write this down, 54374." He then changed sides and stretched the skin under the other arm, "Lost Creek Road." Hodge then pulled his little spiral notebook out of his front shirt pocket and opened it to the page with the address of the house and burned-down barn where Desiree had stopped.

They compared the addresses, "They match."

"We could have saved ourselves this hassle if we had just gone with the original house number," Shane said.

"But we wouldn't have had this much fun, and we never could

have been positive it was correct. Now we know it is. Let's get his jammies back on and put him back to bed."

After Sam was comfortably back in his box, and it was sealed, the men immediately began shoveling the dirt back in on top of him, stopping periodically to walk on the dirt to pack it down. Shane said, "Imagine if those kids had shown up while we had him laid out there with his shirt off."

"Our options would have been slim and none," Hodge said. "Maybe old Sam would have helped us out by suddenly sitting up and saying to them, 'I'm Ellen Brock's killer coming back for another.'" They both died laughing.

Ten minutes later, they were done covering the grave. They quickly rolled the grass back over the dirt, replaced the marker, picked up the tools and hustled off the hill.

13

Blind Date

On the phone the next day with her sister in the Multnomah Drug Rehabilitation Center—

"Riva, you only have nine days to go. Are you excited?"

"Sis, I can't even tell you how excited I am. I feel like I have my life back. How I ever let myself get in so deep, I'll never know."

"Now that you're on the tail end of your treatment, I'll tell you that I'm *not* convinced Sam's money is gone."

"But you said it was in the barn, and the barn burned down."

"That's all true," said Desireee, "but I don't think that was Sam's place."

"You mean you misread the address on the tattoos?"

"No. I got that right. But the more I've thought about it, the more I think the tattooed address was bogus. It had to be."

"Why would Sam have had a false address under his arms? That makes no sense."

"If you had thousands of dollars hidden somewhere, and you were a homeless man like Sam, who really trusted no one but himself, would you have told your new street girl friend about that money, and given her the address where it was kept hidden?"

"No. But I don't think there really is any money," Riva said. "If there was, why would he have been homeless?"

"Oh, I'm sure there is money. Sam mentioned it too many times, drunk and sober."

"What do you plan to do then, search inside every wall in every barn up Lost Creek until you find it? He could have picked it up anytime after he left you and moved it, or spent it. You're chasing a rainbow."

"I don't believe that. There's got to be a way to figure out where he lived. Someone out there had to have known him."

"You've got a dead sixty-six year old man, who was homeless for many years, who goes by the name Sam Hostick—which is undoubtedly a false name—and you're going to be able to find just the right person who knows who he is and where he once lived. I don't see it happening, Sis."

"Maybe not. But I've got plenty of time. There can't be that many houses and people up there."

"They're sounding the dinner bell," Riva said. "I've got to run. Will you be here next Sunday morning for my graduation?"

"You bet I will. You're doing great, Riva. Keep it up. I love you."

"I love you too, Desiree. I can't wait to see you. It seems like it's been forever."

Early evening at the Coleman's on Jasper Road, Sunday, March 21—

Hodge rang the doorbell. Shane answered the front door and invited Hodge in. After he stepped in, took his light jacket off, and tossed it over the back of the couch to his right, Shane said, "Marlene has cooked up an excellent lasagna, bread and salad dinner for us. I have someone I want you to meet.

Hodge looked at him, quizzically, and said under-his-breath, "You didn't say anything about this being a blind date."

"That's because I didn't know until this afternoon if it would come together," Shane said.

Whispering to Shane, Hodge said, "I wish you had asked me first. My heart's not up for something like this again so soon."

"I know you well enough to know you'll rise to the occasion and at least be polite."

Just then, Marlene walked out from behind the divider separating the living room from the kitchen, with the blind date following right behind her.

Hodge couldn't believe his eyes. The woman was gorgeous, five-foot-three, with green eyes, a perfect complexion, and wavy, full, shoulder-length, blond hair.

"Shiela." He broke into tears, unable to speak. Neither of them was sure what to do. Shiela was very nervous and had no idea what to say. Shane nudged Hodge toward her, while Marlene put her arm around Shiela's back and nudged her as well.

Finally, Hodge took two normal steps to close the remaining distance, and opened his arms up wide. Shiela took the last step, and they embraced. Hodge wept freely, while Shiela's tears were much more controlled. She had been badly hurt by his infidelity and the divorce.

"I'm so sorry for what I've done to you, Shiela—for what I did to us. Please find a way to forgive me. I'm not asking you for another chance. I'll never deserve that. But I beg for your forgiveness. You were God's gift to me, God's lamb for me to protect, to love, and to cherish. And I did love and cherish you for a lot of years, but then I let myself fall into temptation. I drifted from God, and then I drifted away from you and the kids. Please forgive me."

Shiela said nothing as she stood with tears trickling down her cheeks onto the front of Hodge's shirt.

Marlene winked at Shane, and then gave him a thumb up. He winked back, and mouthed, "I love you, sweetie." She returned the gesture. Then they came together and hugged and kissed.

It didn't take Hodge long to notice that Shiela's body was tense. He understood, and couldn't blame her. He prayed silently, "God, only you can repair the damage I've done to her. Please give us another chance. I promise I'll never again let you or her down in our relationship."

Finally, Shiela pulled gently away, and stood beside Hodge. She put her right hand in his left and led him to the couch, where he took the clue for them to sit down together.

Shane and Marlene snuggled into the nearby loveseat.

Hodge felt like he was in heaven. His whole body was warm, his heart was racing, he was overwhelmed with love for Shiela. Yet, at the same time, he felt a devastating grief over what he had done to her. He told her again, "Shiela, baby, I'm so sorry. Will you please forgive me?"

She chanced a look at his face, but couldn't look into his eyes. She said, "I forgive you, Hodge. Not in my own strength, but in God's. You can thank Marlene for helping me to get to this place. She and Shane have prayed every day for a month that God would somehow give me the grace to forgive you and to think about what we once had. I know He is the author of reconciliation. But I'm not ready to reconcile yet. You have to understand that. But *I am* willing to be the vessel that God can heal. Right now, I can't make any promises."

"That's all I can ask for, Shiela. For you to forgive me and give God the chance to work out anything else according to His will."

The four of them sat silently, holding hands, for a couple minutes. Then Marlene invited everyone to the table for dinner. She had the plates arranged so she was next to Shane and Shiela was next to Hodge. She knew that would be easier for Shiela than having to sit directly across from him. Her heart needed time to heal.

They all enjoyed the Italian dinner, with the men mostly talking to each other, while the women did the same. It was a start. That's all Shane, Marlene and Hodge could hope for.

On Lost Creek Road, the next day—

"That's Desiree's car ahead of us," Shane said. "I wonder what she's doing back out here."

"Did you think she was going to just disappear?" Hodge said. "If Sam told her there was lots of money, maybe she got to running the same things through her head that we have. And came to the conclusion that, as much as Sam loved her, he never would have given her the address to the *money barn*."

"So now we have competition for finding the house, but for entirely different reasons. Maybe we should come clean with her on why we're interested in Sam."

"I've thought about that. But it's hard for me to see how she would benefit us. We hardly know anything about her."

"That's true."

"Another thing that would keep me from being candid with her is that druggie lady she was with. I'm thinking they may be related, probably sisters."

"Since we're in your SUV this time, she won't recognize us if we keep back a ways. Why don't we follow her and see where she goes."

"That's a good idea."

A mile up the road, Desiree pulled her little car into the Lost Creek Market on the right. Instead of driving by when he reached the market, Hodge suddenly braked hard and swung right in next to her.

"What are you doing, Hodge? We didn't want her to see us."

"I just came up with a better plan. Watch and learn."

He hopped out of his vehicle and walked up to the front of the store. Desiree was messing with her hair, and hadn't paid any attention to who was in the SUV next to her. When she looked up and recognized Hodge, she fumbled with her keys trying to get them back in the ignition, giving Hodge the time he needed to get to her open window.

"What's your hurry, Desiree? You look like you've seen a

ghost."

"Why are you following me?" She immediately spotted Shane sitting in the vehicle beside her, and gave him a dirty look.

"We're not following you. We just happened to notice you on the road ahead of us. What are you doing out here again?" Hodge asked. "I know you don't live out here."

"What I'm doing here is none of your business. What are *you* doing out here again is a better question?"

"We're following up on surveys we've taken of the people who live out here."

"You expect me to believe that?"

"It's the truth. I'm writing a book on the history and people of Lost Creek Valley. I grew up in Dexter. So did Shane."

"Is that why you were interested in Sam before, because you knew he had connections to Lost Creek?"

"You could say that. While we've been interviewing people we've heard some interesting stories. You want to know about one of the *most* interesting?"

"Whether I do or not, I'm sure you're going to tell me."

"We had a few people tell us there was a man that lived out here that used to hide his money in the walls of his barn when he was younger. Supposedly he didn't trust the banks. He went by Joe or something like that. Well one day the barn—where all his thousands and thousands of dollars was hidden in the walls—caught fire and burned to the ground."

Desiree felt like she'd been stabbed in the heart, but tried her best to hide it.

"Old Joe was so torn up about it, that he just kind of gave up, went and lived on the streets after that."

"Why are you telling *me* that story?"

"Old Joe sounds kind of like your old Sam. You think there could be any connection?"

"How would I know?"

"But I'm sure you have some compassion for old Joe, losing all that money and ending up on the street, don't you?"

"Who wouldn't feel bad for him?" she said, inserting her key into the ignition and starting her car. "I've got to go now."

"I thought you needed something at the store."

"If I did, I forgot what it was."

"Here's another card." Hodge handed her a business card. "If you think of anything that might be good material for my book, please give me a call. Have a great day."

She backed her car into the road and drove away in the direction she had come from.

Hodge smiled at Shane, then went into the store and picked up a couple sodas and candy bars. When they got back on the road, headed farther up the creek, Shane said, "What was that all about?"

"From the way she reacted to my old Joe story, I'm convinced her motivation for being up Lost Creek is to find Sam's house and barn, so she can get his money. She's concluded the same thing I did, that the address on Sam's body was bogus. I'd bet my life's savings on it."

"What, all ten dollars? So why did you handle it that way?"

"I decided the best way to deal with her was to take her straight on. Let her know we know what she's doing."

"That sounds like the junk-yard-dog Hodge I grew up with. But what makes you so sure she's after Sam's money? "

"When you've spent twenty-seven years in law enforcement and private investigating, reading people the way I have, you get a good feel for when you've hit the right nerve."

"Do you think she bought your line about writing the book?"

"Maybe. But I guarantee you she's not going to waste any time getting back out here."

"Why do you say that?"

"She's too smart to give up on that money without checking out every barn in the valley. Even if she finds out some old Joe's barn burned—like the one at the bogus address—she's too obsessed with getting her hands on Sam's money to believe it's been destroyed."

"I think you're right. I think she picked Sam's body up out of greed, rather than compassion," Shane said.

"Since she now knows we're out here getting information for a history book on the area, I expect she may try to use that for her angle when she talks to people. She'll probably tell them she's helping research the book, then ask about Sam Hostick, and maybe say he could have used a different name back then. She'll focus only on the places that have *old barns*, and tell the owners she's fascinated by their barns—from a historical perspective, of course. She'll undoubtedly have her camera and flash plenty of photos of the old barns to appear genuine."

"It seems you've got her nailed, Hodge."

"One way or another, she'll try to find that money. What concerns me is if she gets specific about Sam's age, or shows any pictures she might have of him."

"If she talks to the wrong guy, she may endanger herself without realizing it."

"That's what worries me. She could blow this whole thing sky high, and end up dead in the process."

"It almost sounds like we're going to be forced to tell Desiree about Ellen Brock and Sam's confession just to keep her safe."

"It's a catch twenty-two, isn't it," Hodge said. "One way or another, she's definitely going to complicate our investigation."

"So what are we going to do?"

"We'll let it ride for right now. If she starts talking to anyone we've talked to, or will be talking to, we'll get a good feel for her tactics. We can base our response on that."

"Have you begun trying to figure out Sam's code on that address yet?"

"Not yet. I took Saturday off from the case, and you know where I was last night. I can't thank you and Marlene enough for bringing Shiela and I together. I just hope it was a positive thing for her."

"What's a best friend for?" Shane said. "I think you just need to be patient. In bed last night, Marlene said she got some real good vibes about things from Shiela. She said she's not going to push it with her, or even ask what she thought. She's just going to let Shiela open up about it on her time. When you've been hurt as bad as she was, you can't be rushed. God will do the work. Just be patient."

"I will be."

14

The Bean Field

At the church house—

After her confrontation earlier in the day with Hodge Gilbert, Desiree Lebron didn't believe for a minute that his and Shane's interest in Sam was simply because of some supposed Lost Creek Valley history book. There was more they weren't disclosing, and that story about old Joe and his money was a smokescreen that proved they must know something about the money. She was certain of that. There was money to be found, or they wouldn't be up there themselves. She knew Hodge told her that story in hopes she would believe the burned barn at Sam's tattooed address was the same barn where he hid the money—that Sam was Joe and had lost all the money in the fire. She wasn't buying it. No way she was going away that easy.

She sat down in her living room with a tablet and went to work writing out all the different combinations of addresses she could get from the numbers tattooed under Sam's arm. If she still had her computer, she could have used that. But she didn't mind. She had always been a doodler.

She had already confirmed that all the addresses up the creek began with 54, so only the last three digits had to have been written using some kind of code. She knew there were only 998 other possible combinations for those three numbers. Of those 998 address possibilities, at least two hundred had to be actual addresses, based on the number of addresses the lady at the Dexter Post Office said were being used up the creek right now. Too bad she wouldn't give Desiree any of the people's names or addresses.

She started with 001, 002, 003, and so on.

That evening Hodge hacked his way into the Dexter Post Office computer records and copied to his computer the list of current names and addresses of every address in the Lost Creek Valley. He did the same at each five year period going back to 1976. He then entered those addresses into his special computer program that analyzed and compared number sequences to find patterns.

In less than five minutes, his computer gave him sixteen addresses that compared favorably in a definite sequence to the last three digits of Sam's tattooed address— 374. If Sam used some form of sequencing relationship to his real address to come up with the tattooed address, then Hodge had things narrowed down to just those sixteen addresses. Of course if Sam didn't, none of the sixteen meant a thing. Now he would drive to those addresses and look for barns. The addresses without barns would be eliminated.

He thought if there was money to be found, and he found it, the killer's fingerprints might be on it. Certainly Sam's would be. He cussed himself for not taking Sam's fingerprints when they dug him up. Then he consoled himself that since Sam obviously was not embalmed, and his face was all sunken in, the skin on his fingertips would have been too shriveled up to take good prints from anyway. Finally, he remembered they had fingerprinted him at the county morgue.

As Hodge thought further, he doubted the killer would have been stupid enough to handle the money bare handed. Even if he left fingerprints on the money, at some point he would have had to work in a government job, been in the military, got a passport, or been booked by law enforcement for his prints to be on file in a computer somewhere. Of course if all that came together, the prints would be an excellent way to determine his identity. Not that any of that would prove his guilt, or even be used, in a court of law. On the other hand, if they learned the killer's identity, finding him would be much easier.

As the evening progressed, Hodge began thinking maybe he had let himself become too focused on the address where the money might be. In reality, the more important consideration was where Sam lived when he was sixteen. Sam had told Shane that he lived *near* the killer. Figuring out where Sam lived in 1960, and learning what kids lived close by needed to be the priority.

The next day, Hodge picked Shane up at 9 a.m. sharp, and they drove back out to the Dexter area. On a lark, Shane said, "Why don't we swing down to the old Duncan place to see if the old lady is still alive? My dad pointed out Bud Duncan's obituary to me about ten years ago. I haven't been down to the old bean field for probably fifteen years, back when I trapped a few beaver and fox there. Mrs. Duncan was in good health then, but he wasn't doing so good."

"I remember Bud always had that big, shiny silver tooth in front that made him look like he was always smiling," Hodge said.

"Yeah, we called it Bud's Beacon, remember that?" They chuckled.

"I'll never forget it. I always hated it whenever Mrs. Duncan checked our rows after we finished them to make sure we picked clean enough. I never thought either of them was especially friendly."

"But they weren't unfriendly either. I think them being our bosses is what made it so uncomfortable to be around them."

"Yeah, unless we got over two hundred pounds that day. Then I felt vindicated."

"How many times did you ever get two hundred pounds?" Shane said. "You were always too busy fighting and knocking down bean vines."

"My last year I cleaned up my act some and made it over two hundred several times."

"You probably conveniently forgot that my last two years I got over two hundred pounds most days. Even topped three hundred a few times, when the beans were really thick because we got to them later than we should have, and we picked until late in the day to finish up the field."

"Those were some fun times. Kids today rarely work in the summer. Back then it was a way of life."

They came around the last corner of the paved road and spotted the old farmhouse on the left. Straight across the driveway was the long open shed—now empty and run down—where the Duncans used to park the tractors, the wooden crates, and the flatbed truck used for hauling the beans to the cannery in town."

As they drove up to the house and parked, Hodge said, "I haven't been back down here since high school."

They both got out of Hodge's pickup and sucked in the warm early-Spring morning air. Though the bean vines had been gone for thirty years, somehow they each thought they winded them. "Man does this bring back a flood of memories," Hodge said. Suddenly, his eyes started watering, taking him and Shane by surprise.

"I know how you feel, Hodge. When I first came back here to trap, I was often overwhelmed with the memories. I sometimes wish we could just go back to being kids out here again."

"Remember the old pop machine they had in there?" Hodge pointed underneath the carport adjoining the farm house. "Glass bottles. I think they were twelve ounces."

"My oldest sister got us started collecting the metal lids that we would get from the holder where everyone popped the lid. We made armies with the different colored caps."

"Remember the champion bean fights?"

Pickers used to find a strong U-shaped bean—usually they grew twisted around the main vines—and save them to challenge other pickers' fighter beans. The opponents would face each other, hook their two beans together, grip their beans between their fingers, and pull in opposite directions. The bean that didn't break in two was the champion. The winning picker would then challenge other champions until his bean finally broke.

"Oh yeah. I had a champion one time that won a dozen fights before breaking. That had to be close to the record."

They walked up to the farmhouse door by way of the short concrete porch and knocked.

A gray-haired woman around sixty answered. It obviously wasn't Mrs. Duncan.

"I'm Shane Coleman and this is Hodge Gilbert. We used to pick beans out here—"

"Your dad was our mailman," she said before Shane could say anymore.

"Are you the Duncan's daughter? Are you Belva?"

"Yes. How did you remember my name after all these years? You look too young to have picked here when I was a kid."

"You were our row boss for a couple years."

"When was that? I was row boss off and on a few different seasons."

"It seems like it was around 1969 or 70."

"That would be right."

"Is your mom still alive?"

"Yes, but she has Alzheimer's real bad. We finally had to put her in a nursing home."

"I'm sorry to hear that. She must be in her mid-eighties by now."

"Eighty-four to be exact."

"Are you living out here?"

"No. You just happened to catch me on my once a week trip to check on the place."

"So it's still in the family?"

"Yes. But I could never live out here again. Too many memories. Good *and* bad, but *mostly* wonderful."

"Would you mind if we walked the place, just for old times?"

"Of course not," she said. "Make yourselves at home. Weren't those some great times—picking beans, cutting up, just being kids?"

"They sure were. We'll leave you alone now, and go see what kind of memories we can stir up."

"Have fun."

They walked away from the house, without speaking, down the old dirt road that ran along one side of the slough toward the lower bean field—the one always known as, "the late field," because the beans were planted later to spread the crop out. When they had rounded the first bend and got the blackberry bushes between themselves and the house, Hodge said, "You couldn't do it, could you?"

"No, I couldn't. Nothing could have been gained if I did bring it up. She's got to be the same age, a year or so either side. They were probably playmates. After all these years, why bring up something that would have been so painful to her? Imagine not only losing one of your best friends and playmates, but having her killed on your own property. The way I feel right now, I'm wondering if bringing any of this up at all, digging into this, is the right thing to do."

"I hear you. But we're already in this deep."

"But would solving the case be worth it? We'd put a man behind bars, who lived an otherwise normal life—if it's the guy my dad believed it was. And we would open up some very old wounds for Ellen Brock's relatives."

"You don't believe if he's still alive, and has lived like he didn't do it all these years, he should still have to pay for his crime?"

"I'm not sure. Part of me would like to catch him, tie him up and torture him for all the pain and fear he caused so long ago. The other part says, listen to my dad. He was just a kid. It probably wasn't cold-blooded murder. There may have been a good explanation for what happened. I don't know what to do."

Hodge suddenly stopped walking, and said, "Well I'll tell you right now, I'm seeing this case through whether you do or not; maybe that's the cop in me."

Shane stopped a few feet ahead of Hodge, turned and faced him. "Darn it, Hodge. Why do you always have to be the one to settle everything? If things aren't black and white, then by golly, junk-yard-dog Hodge Gilbert will make them that way."

"Settle down, Shane. You know that's not fair. Yes, it used to be that way. But I grew up. You're the one who called me in on this. And *now* that you feel all emotional for the old farmer's daughter, we suddenly have to just drop the whole thing. I'm not buying it. Don't you think it would mean a lot to the family, even to the whole community, to finally get some closure? To know that their beautiful, playful, wonderful, little girl didn't just happen to get murdered one day in this bean field, and nothing was ever done about it. That her killer got off scot-free. *That beast* caused me to be afraid more times than I can count. Sure, most the time, we didn't think about it. But when we did, it could scare the hell out of us. That beast restricted mine and your activities many times, because of our fear. He restricted the activities of hundreds of people. But he got away with it. After being down here, I'm even more convinced that I'm going to nail that bastard. He's got to be made to pay for what he did—whatever that means."

Then backing off a bit, Hodge said, "I understand not saying anything about it to Belva Duncan today. I'm with you on that. Why bring it up when it won't help our investigation. But once we find the guy, we have to let the chips fall where they may. I'd bet that most people who experienced pain like Belva did will, at first, be stunned and glad to hear that the killer has finally been found. Then they'll probably immediately relive some of the emotions they felt years ago—the pain and fear. But in the end, they'll come back around to being glad the case was finally solved. Trust me on that.

I've seen it before—not with a fifty-year-old case of course—but with several cases that weren't solved for quite a few years, then finally were."

"You're right Hodge. I know you are. It's just that being down here, seeing Belva, all of it—it just stirs me so deeply. Part of me wants to just go back to where I was the week before Sam confessed to me."

"I understand, old buddy. But you can't. You know that as well as I do. You know you're in too deep to not see it through now."

"We could still turn it over to the police."

"I guarantee if we do that, if the killer is still in the area, he'll figure out what's going on before they ever have enough to arrest and charge him. He'll run, and that will be that."

"Why do I believe you're right?"

"I am right, and you know I am. Let's walk the rest of the place then call it a day. Maybe you can tell Marlene about Belva and everything you felt down here."

They continued walking toward the "late field."

As they walked down into the dip where the road crossed between two adjoining sloughs, just before it reached the late field, Hodge said, "Remember the old hand water pump that used to be up around the corner to the left under that maple tree?" He pointed to the tree that was still there only much bigger than it was when he last saw it thirty-eight years earlier.

"It was still there when I trapped here fifteen years ago," Shane said.

"I'll beat you to it, Shane!" Hodge said, as he took off sprinting up out of the dip. Shane, always the faster runner of the two, instantly broke into a sprint himself, but couldn't overtake Hodge in the short distance up around the corner.

"It's still here!" Hodge shouted as he rounded the bend in the road. "I wonder if it still works."

"It did fifteen years ago. I don't see any containers around to prime it with anyway."

"I've got to see if it still works, Shane."

As they caught their breath, both of them looked around in the edge of the blackberries that encroached on the area around the pump that used to be wide open.

Shane walked over to the base of the old maple and started kicking around in the leaves with his feet. "What do we have here?" he said, reaching down to grab something. "An old quart jar." He picked it up, dug some rotten leaves out of the inside of it, and said, "I'll be right back."

He immediately ran back around and down into the dip they had just come through, and tromped some high grass down to get access to the water in the slough.

Two minutes later, he was back at the pump with the full jar which he immediately dumped into the top of the pump hoping to prime it. Hodge began furiously pumping the handle up and down causing the pump to squeak. In a few seconds, they heard the old familiar sound of water rushing up the pipe and out the spout.

"Amazing," Hodge said, as he continued pumping to flush the rusty brown water from the pipe.

After well over a minute, Shane said, "I think it would take longer than we want to get that cleared up enough to drink, old buddy. Let's walk the rest of the place."

Hodge reluctantly quit pumping, while Shane placed the jar, that he had filled in Hodge's last couple strokes, upright on the ground next to the pump. Then they continued their nostalgic tour.

15

Split It

Two days later, in mid-afternoon, Shane and Hodge were pulling up the long gravel driveway of one of the addresses on Hodge's sequential code-list and came face to face with Desiree driving out from the place. She immediately stopped her car in the center of the driveway. Shane drove his truck up to hers, and stopped with his front bumper four feet from her car's front bumper. All three of them got out and met in front of their vehicles.

"How much longer are you guys going to harass me?" Desiree asked.

"Were not harassing you," Hodge said. "I suppose you're just out for a leisurely afternoon drive."

"What's it to you? I can't seem to go anywhere anymore without you two following me."

"Why don't you stop playing games with us, Desiree," Shane said. "Admit what you're really doing out here."

"I'm trying to learn more about my Sam. His dying really hit me hard, made me want to find out what kind of a life he lived before we met. Check out his roots."

"Save the BS for the idiots, Desiree," Hodge said. "We know what you're doing out here. We're doing the same thing. And I think it's time we pool our efforts."

"I don't know what you're talking about."

"Look, Desiree," Hodge said. "We all know you're after Sam's money. We are too. How about if we work on this together? If there really is any money left, when we find it, we split it three ways."

"Even if there was any money, and I was trying to find it, I definitely wouldn't split it with you two when I did find it."

"So you'll risk taking nothing if we find it first?" Shane said.

She hesitated, mulling over that possibility, then after several seconds, said, "If there is any money, you guys don't have any right to it. I was Sam's lover, his girl."

"So why did he leave you? And if he wanted you to have his money, why didn't he just give it to you when you were together?"

She knew he had her there. "He said that sometime in the future, we were going to use the money for a large down payment on a nice house and live happily ever after."

"Do you take us for fools, Desiree?" Hodge said. "Maybe he said that sometime when he was drunk or high—"

"Don't talk like that about Sam."

"We're sorry for your loss," Shane said, trying to diffuse the situation. "Neither of us questions what Sam meant to you. Or what you meant to him at one time—"

"We just as well tell you now," Hodge interrupted, "that we know of at least one other guy who is also very interested in Sam's money. And you need to know, he will go to any measure to get it."

"Any measure?"

"Any measure meaning just that."

"How do you know about this other guy?"

"We can't tell you how we know about him, or what we know, other than we know he's already murdered at least one person. He's very dangerous. We don't want to see you get hurt or worse."

"And I'm supposed to believe you've been following me around to protect me."

"You don't get it, do you? This is not some fantasy wonderland where Alice runs into scary obstacles along the way, but everything works out perfectly in the end. If you don't stop what you're doing, you're likely to get yourself killed. I can't say it any plainer than that."

"I guess you can't," she said. "So why should I trust you? Maybe you're just trying to cut out your competition. You already told me you guys were up here gathering local history to write a book. Now you want me to believe something else—"

"We *are* gathering local history, and Hodge *is* going to write a book," Shane said. "Sam's money is something we learned about in this process, and so is the other guy."

"Tell me more about the other guy."

"We can't do that."

"If I agree to split the money with you it will have to be fifty-fifty. The two of you get half, and me and my sister get the other half."

"We're smarter than that, Desiree. Why should we agree to a split like that? Your sister isn't entitled to any money. I assume that druggie woman at the old church was your sister."

"She isn't a druggie anymore. In fact, she's in her final week at a drug treatment center in Portland."

"And you want us to shout, hallelujah! Then give her a fourth of Sam's money so she can be sure to stay clean," Hodge said.

"You've got one hell of a mouth on you, don't you?" she said. Then looking at Shane, said, "How do you put up with him?"

"We grew up together," Shane said. "You get the bad with the good. You should know that, considering your sister's situation."

"It's fifty-fifty or no deal."

"Okay," Hodge conceded. "But you have to agree to leave well enough alone. Let us handle things. If you don't, you may not be around to collect your half."

"Alright," she said. "It's your game then."

Hodge and Shane got back in their truck, and backed it off to the edge of the road, allowing Desiree to drive past. She drove out to Lost Creek Road and, once again, headed home.

As she drove away, Shane said, "Do you think she bought any of it?"

"Maybe some of it," Hodge answered, "But I guarantee you, she has no intention of splitting any of Sam's money."

"I guess we don't have to wonder if there really was any money anymore, do we? You were smooth on getting that out of her."

"Just call me greased lightning." They laughed. "We can't make the mistake of underestimating her."

Shane drove the truck within sight of the ranch from where Desiree had come. "That barn's definitely been around awhile. We can add this place to the list of possibilities."

Hodge drew a star next to the address on his list.

"Why do you think she was here?" Shane said. "You don't suppose—"

"She's an intelligent lady. She probably came up with her own list of likely addresses. Maybe she even used a program similar to the one I did. We know nothing about her background. Maybe she's a computer whiz. I doubt Desiree Lebron is her real name. It's time I do a background check to see what I can learn about her."

"Have you talked to Patterson yet?"

"No. He was always a little egotistical," Hodge said. "The last thing I want to do is make him think I need his help for anything. Besides, you talk to one police officer, and somehow they all get wind of it. I want to stay away from the law until we have things figured out. Let's turn around and go to the next address on my list. We'll come back here later."

"Did any of the addresses on this list of sixteen match any of the places from the survey that we followed up on, or still need to follow up on?"

"Seven. All of them farther up the creek."

Hodge and Shane stopped by the Simons' place while they were in the area and gave Kent an update. Doc was taking a nap. Kent said he had been driving all around the Lost Creek area in the afternoons in hopes of bumping into some of the folks he used to know. He even ran into Bessie Rogers and got an earful. In fact, he wrote down a few things she said that he thought might benefit the investigation. He shared some of that information with Shane and Hodge while they were at his house.

That evening, in the Coleman's living room, while snuggled up in the blue love seat watching Grey's Anatomy on their thirty-inch television—

"That Desiree woman is going to get herself killed if she isn't careful," Shane said.

"You don't mean that, do you, honey?"

"Yes. She's going about things the wrong way. We've talked to several people already who have asked if she was part of our history survey."

"What'd you tell them?"

"The truth. That she's just trying to learn about some old guy from her past. Hodge did stretch the truth a couple times."

"He's still the same old Hodge. I take it you two are getting along well."

"We have our moments, just like we always did. He can be pretty obnoxious sometimes. If you'd have heard what he said to Desiree today, you would have slapped him."

"What was that?"

"Just a put down about her almost-rehabilitated druggie sister."

"I can imagine. You don't really believe Desiree is in danger do you?"

"Yes. If she inadvertently runs across Ellen Brock's killer and asks the wrong questions, or he realizes that *her* Sam is his old high-school buddy that knew he was a murderer, and thinks he could have told her... You're a smart woman, what do you think?"

"My gosh. This is sounding more like a murder-mystery movie all the time."

"Let's hope the only murder in this one is the one that happened fifty years ago."

"Are you and Hodge in any danger?"

"Life is dangerous."

"Don't give me that, honey. I want to know if you guys are in danger. Would he hurt *you*?"

"Hodge has been a cop and private investigator too long to screw this case up. He knows what he's doing. As long as we do things his way, we've got nothing to worry about." He lied. In fact, Shane had been worrying more and more as he realized what he might do if he was in Ellen Brock's murderer's shoes.

"I sure hope you're right," she said. "By the way, I've got some good news for you."

"Shiela?"

"You're pretty smart. She called me today and has decided to move to Lane County. She said that was the next step if she was going to give hers and Hodge's relationship a chance. She's going to rent her house out, then rent a place somewhere around here."

"I want to call Hodge up right now and tell him."

"A typical man. Gets to first base and immediately wants to go for a homerun. Please, Shane honey, wait and bring it up casually when you guys are together. And don't give him too much hope. I'd hate to see him get hurt like he hurt her. She needs time."

"You're right. As a man, I can't understand how it must be for her. I just want to get it all fixed and back to the way it once was so we can all hang out together like we used to do."

"I know that. Just be patient. I believe it will get there in time."

16

Vietnam Vet

While the Coleman's were cozily watching Grey's Anatomy, Kent Simons was on a covert night-time mission, following up on something Bessie Rogers had said to him. Something he didn't tell Hodge and Shane. He had sat on the sidelines long enough. If Ellen Brock's killer was still alive and living in the Lost Creek Valley, he couldn't just let Tommy Coleman's little brother and his buddy have all the fun. Little did he know, he was taking a big step toward getting someone—maybe himself—killed.

Just up Lost Creek Road from the Eagle's Rest Bridge, which crossed over Lost Creek, lived Cambell Ritchey, who graduated from Pleasant Hill High School in 1967, the same year as Kent's older brother, Ed.

Cambell's house sat back in the Douglas fir forest, a quarter mile west of Lost Creek Road. It was actually more a shack than a house, built out of rough sawn lumber back in the nineteen-thirties, it was maybe 800 square feet. It had no running water and the only bathroom was a single-seat outhouse, fifty feet south of the house itself. The outhouse was deliberately built in that location to take advantage of the prevailing northwest winds, which normally carried the unpleasant odors emanating from the outhouse stack downwind away from the house.

There were two hand water pumps on the property: one at the kitchen sink, and one just outside the back porch. There was also an elevated one hundred gallon water tank up against the north side of the house next to the gravel driveway. But it was rusted out on the bottom at one end. Any bathing was done by sponge from the kitchen sink, or in the old stand alone bathtub on the left side of the ten-foot-square back porch, which was on the west side of the house. The bathtub was covered with dried green and black slime. It hadn't been used in years.

When Kent reached the house, he peered inside through the dirty glass of the four-foot-wide, living room window on the south side of the house. The wind was uncharacteristically out of the south, and he immediately picked up the foul stench coming from the nearby outhouse. He didn't know how anyone could still live like it was the pre-nineteen-forties, without taking advantage of modern-day conveniences like hot running water and a flushing toilet. Of course, the homeless people living along the local rivers would have been happy to have a place like Cambell's.

In his junior and senior years, Cambell Ritchey was the star first baseman and a good pitcher on Pleasant Hill's Emerald League champion varsity baseball teams. He was a tall, thin, left-handed thrower and batter, about six-foot-two, one-sixty. He had always been a big hit with the girls because of his excellent sense of humor. He was also best friends back then with Kent's brother Ed. All that was before he went to Vietnam.

He was drafted into the army right out of high school, left for basic in early July, and arrived in Vietnam the first week of January 1968, just in time for the Tet Offensive. Two months into his tour in Vietnam, on March 16th, he was involved in an incident that changed his and several dozen other American soldiers' lives forever, not to mention the tragic impact it had on thousands of

Vietnamese people.

As Kent did his best to see through the film on the window, Cambell came out of the kitchen and sat down in the living room on an old, beat up, cushioned rocking chair next to a lamp stand with a burning oil lamp on it. Kent knew if he sat there for more than ten minutes without getting up, he was probably taking the right dose of his medication, and it would be safe to try to talk to him.

When Cambell started slowly rocking the chair, Kent looked at his watch. It was 7:37 p.m.

As he waited, he looked at his watch two more times. When it had been fifteen minutes without Cambell getting up, he eased away from the window and walked to the front door and knocked.

Thirty seconds later, Cambell opened the door.

"Cambell. It's Kent Simons, Ed's little brother."

"I know who you are. I'm not always screwed up. What do you want?"

By the light of the full moon, Kent noticed a little tremor in Cambell's left hand as he held it up against his belly. The same hand that once delivered a mean screw ball to right handed hitters.

"Can I come in? I'd like to talk to you."

"Come on in. The place is a mess. I don't have a lot of energy most the time. You understand. It's the meds."

"You don't owe me any apologies, Cam (the nickname he'd gone by since junior high)."

"Take a seat, if you'd like." He gestured toward a worn out couch to the left of the rocking chair and lamp stand. Cam returned to the rocking chair and sat down. There was no other furniture in the room, though several old twelve by sixteen portraits of people hung in disarray from the long wall across from the couch and chair. With the dim light in the room, Kent didn't recognize Cambell in any of the photos. He suspected the people in the photos were probably Cambell's parents, grandparents and other older relatives.

Kent also noticed a few different piles of various magazines lying on the floor on either side of the rocking chair: Soldier of

Fortune, Vietnam Warriors, Reader's Digest and several other titles.

They both sat without speaking for over a minute, which didn't seem to bother Cam. Kent got the impression they probably could have sat all evening without speaking, and it would have been fine with Cam.

"An old friend stopped by the house a couple weeks ago," Kent finally said. "Actually it was the younger brother of one of my friends in high school. I'm sure you remember Tommy Coleman; he played outfield on your baseball team. It was his brother Shane."

Cam's face seemed to light up for a few seconds upon hearing Tommy's name, then returned to its normal deadpan expression. Looking at Cam's face in the dim light of the oil lamp, Kent thought he looked too old for his years. He had several days' worth of beard growth that bordered a long narrow scar on his right cheek. The scar ran from the bottom edge of his ear lobe clear across to just below the right corner of his mouth. Cam also had a scar on his neck that started a few inches down from the right angle of his jaw and stretched to just below his Adam's apple, almost like he might have tried to slice his own throat at some point. Kent had often wondered if he got the scars in combat.

Cam's greasy salt and pepper hair was shoulder length, and had never been much shorter than that since he grew it out after being discharged from the army. As Kent sat there a few feet away from him, he could smell Cam's body odor, but that was no surprise. He rarely ever cleaned himself up.

When Cam didn't respond to Kent for far too long for Kent's comfort, he wondered if his mind was even in the room.

Then suddenly, Cam jumped up from his chair to a standing position and shouted, "Cease Fire! Cease Fire!" startling Kent. He didn't know what to make of it. He knew it must have something to do with Cam's combat experience and his ongoing mental condition. Kent had never talked with Cam about Vietnam because he didn't want to cause him anymore problems than he obviously already had.

Cam received a medical discharge under honorable conditions in early 1969, after spending months in an army psych unit state-side. His tour in Vietnam was cut short because of his breakdown. Since returning home he had been in and out of the Roseburg Veterans hospital many times over the years—one time he was there for almost two years. Fortunately for him, in the old days, one of his brothers used to room at the house with him and kept it in pretty good shape. In the last few years, his doctors had tried some new medications on him with good results. He hadn't been an inpatient at the Vets hospital now for over three years.

When Kent had looked at the completed surveys that Shane and Hodge showed him, and the Census maps showing each house had at least been visited, he knew the boys had lied about stopping at Cam's house. He suspected they probably lied about a few other houses as well, but he said nothing about it, figuring Shane and Hodge knew as much.

None of the neighbor kids had come close to Cam's place in years. Supposedly, back in the late seventies and early eighties, several kids had turned up at home with unexplainable multiple minor flesh wounds—like they had encountered some kind of light concussion explosion. Of course, since the perimeter of Cam's property was clearly marked with "No Trespassing," signs, the kids never told their parents where they incurred the injuries. Rumors in recent years said Cam no longer booby trapped his place. But no kid was willing to find out.

Cam stood erect in front of his chair for nearly a minute, his hands shaking, without speaking. Then in a monotone, he said, "It was Lieutenant Calley, sir. He gave the orders." Now Kent knew. He had often heard rumors that Cam may have been involved in the much-publicized My Lai Massacre that occurred on March 16, 1968. But this was the best evidence that the rumors were more than that.

Kent said, "Cam, are you alright?"

He didn't respond.

"Cam, are you okay?"

Cam suddenly came back to the present, and turned toward Kent, shook his head slowly, and said, "It was the voices and sounds of combat in my head again. This has been going on for years. Not all the time. Sometimes they had me so heavily sedated that I'm not sure my brain was even functioning. And other times I'd go months without any problems." He sat back down in his chair, without sitting all the way back, obviously still tense. "Just this week, they've come back loud and clear."

"It must have been terrible, whatever it was that happened to you over there, Cam. Would it help at all to tell me about it?"

Cam got a little antsy in his chair for a minute without answering, then seemed to settle down.

Finally Kent asked him a second time, "Would it help...?"

"Maybe it would. They tried for years at the VA to get me to talk through it, but I couldn't. It was too painful. I don't know. Maybe that's what I need to do. Just tell you about it. Maybe that would help get it out of my head. I don't know."

They both sat silently for what seemed like a long time, but was only a few minutes. Kent wasn't going to press the issue, yet he was very curious.

Then Cam started talking, "Three days before my nineteenth birthday, in March 1968, shortly after the Tet Offensive, my company—Charlie Company—was ordered into a series of hamlets in the Son My Village where the Vietcong (VC) were supposedly holding up in force. Our company had suffered numerous casualties, including half a dozen KIA's (killed in action), from mines and booby traps over the previous month, even though we'd had little-to-no direct contact with the enemy. Everyone was on edge.

"We were ordered to go in and kill all guerilla (Vietcong) and North Vietnamese soldiers and *suspects*, which included women and children, and all the animals. We were to burn the village and pollute the wells." Cam began to get worked up, his voice got louder. He rocked back and forth in the chair. "The officer said,

'They're *All* VC. Now go and get them. Who is the enemy? Anybody that's running from us, hiding from us, or even looks like the enemy—shoot them.' So that's what we did.

"My platoon, the 1st, led by Second Lieutenant William Calley, entered the My Lai 4 hamlet and immediately began shooting at suspected enemy positions, but received no return fire. Still we kept shooting. We shot several civilians, then we began attacking anything that moved. Old people, young people, kids and animals, it didn't matter. We killed them with our machine guns, grenades and bayonets." Cam was crying and shaking now.

"The men in my platoon went crazy. We gunned down unarmed men, women, children and babies. We shot families that huddled together for safety in huts or bunkers. Anyone who came out with their hands held high, it didn't matter. We murdered them all. Beat them with our rifle butts, stabbed them with our bayonets. Bodies were strewn all over the place. Men, women, children, babies. Dozens of them, hundreds. I can't get the scene out of my mind."

"Finally a few soldiers began yelling, 'Cease Fire! Cease Fire!' But the shooting and slaughter continued. Lieutenant Calley even grabbed the machine gun from one soldier who refused to shoot anymore people, and gunned down several civilians himself.

"The crying and groaning of the injured… I can't. I can't get it out of my head. Soldiers searching for the wounded and killing them with their machine guns and bayonets. God forgive us. God forgive me."

As Cam sat on the front edge of the rocking chair, with his head in his hands, weeping, shaking, Kent sat silently on the couch nearby—stunned, numbed by the horror of what Cam experienced. He finally understood why Cam had been so screwed up all these years. He felt compassion for him. He wiped a couple tears off his own cheeks with his fingers.

There was no way he would talk to him about the Brock girl tonight. Maybe not ever. Yet, based on what Bessie Rogers had told him, he believed Cam might know something that would help them find the killer. But not tonight.

After five minutes of sitting, waiting for him to say something, Kent got up from the couch, and stood next to Cam. He put his hand on his shoulder and said, "I'm sorry. I'm sorry for all of it. I'm sorry I put you through that."

Several seconds passed, then without looking up, Cam said, "It's okay. I'm glad you did. I've lived that experience over in my head hundreds of times, maybe thousands. It was good to finally get it out."

"I hope so. I'm going to get on home now, Cam. But I'll be back to see you soon. We can talk then."

"I'd like that, Kent," Cam said, much more relaxed than Kent could remember ever seeing him.

When Kent got home, Doc was watching a movie. "Where have you been, son?"

"I drove up the creek. Stopped by Cambell Ritchey's place."

"What'd you go there for? He's been worthless since he came back from Vietnam."

"Dad, your war wasn't the only one that screwed people up, and you guys were heroes. Imagine having people react to everything you tried to do in Europe the way they did to the Vietnam War and its vets. You never had the media or politicians working against you, like they did."

"I know, son. I shouldn't have said that about Cambell. As good a boy as he always was growing up, it had to have been some bad stuff he went through to mess him up that bad."

"You know some of the rumors we've heard over the years that he might have been involved in the My Lai incident? Well he was, Dad. He told me about it tonight. It was just as brutal as we'd heard. And he was right in the thick of it."

"He killed children and babies?"

"He never used the word, 'I', but said, 'we,' referring to his platoon. The situation wasn't as black and white as the media made it out to be. At least it may not have been from a soldier's perspective. His company had taken a lot of casualties by mines and booby traps recently and were really wound up. You can imagine how that would have been."

"That's the hell of war. No one who hasn't fought in one can grasp how terrible it was for the soldiers."

"In Vietnam they never had any frontlines like you guys had in World War II. The enemy could be anywhere. The people they were fighting for could be the enemy. And the enemy could be a normal farmer during the day and kill you at night. That would make you suspicious of everyone. I'm glad I never had to go over there."

"I'm glad neither of you boys went to that war."

(See novel endnote regarding this fictional chapter.)

17

Bessie Rogers

Friday, March 26th—

Hodge picked Shane up at his house at nine in the morning on the way out to Lost Creek.

"What do you say we stop by to have a little chat with Bessie Rogers this morning, Shane?" Hodge asked. "I've been dying to talk to her, but knew it'd be best if we got to others first."

"I'm up for it," Shane said. "I'll probably even get to learn something I didn't know about my dad."

"I'd bet on it, if she's half the windbag people say she is."

They knocked on Bessie Roger's door and waited. Pretty soon the door opened and a very old woman answered, while talking on her cell phone.

"I'm gonna have to run now, I've got two strapping young men at my door. I'll chat at you a bit later. Don't forget to tell Marilyn what I told you I heard about Eileen's grandson. She'll get a real kick out of knowing that."

Hodge and Shane looked at each other, and thought, whose idea was it to come here?

"What can I do you handsome young hunks for?" Bessie said, winking.

"We're doing a history on the people of Lost Creek Valley," Shane said. "You completed a survey for some boys working for us a few weeks ago."

"I wondered when you would get around to interviewing me. I've been looking forward to chatting with you. I'm ninety-two years old. I'm kind of a walking history book myself. Why don't we go sit on my back porch for this? I've got a wonderful view of the hills back of here."

They followed her through the old house, out the back door to the large porch, and took a seat next to each other in the old stationary wooden chairs grouped in a semi-circle facing the large chicken house and adjoining wooded hills. They could almost sense the rumors that got started out here, and only hoped the ones she told about them after they left were at least *mostly* true.

The men immediately heard the cackling of hens, and then heard one squawk. "Sounds like one of your hens just laid an egg," Shane said.

"You must have grown up around chickens. Most people wouldn't know that."

"We had some when I was in junior high and high school," Shane said.

"It looks like you had quite an operation here at one time, ma'am," Hodge said.

"Yes we did. But I keep less than two dozen hens anymore. Just enough to keep the memories alive. Every other day I sell a dozen and a half eggs to the Lost Creek Store. Can I get you some coffee? I already have some made."

"Sure. Black please," Shane answered for both of them.

A few minutes later, she returned with a tray carrying a pot of coffee, three cups and a plate of cookies.

"I brought you some of my home-made peanut-butter cookies."

"My favorite," Hodge said.

After filling all three cups with coffee, and taking a seat across from them, Bessie said, "Now what are your names?"—Like she hadn't already heard.

"I'm Shane Coleman and this is Hodge Gilbert."

"Yes, Shane Coleman. You're as handsome as your dad was. He was my mail carrier for years. His older brother took me out a few times right after high school, a few years before he went off to fight the big war. (Shane hadn't told Hodge any of that, nor that the reason his uncle had quit dating her was because she never seemed to stop talking.) Sorry to hear of your dad's passing."

"Thanks," Shane said, while Hodge choked on a cookie.

After sipping some coffee to wash the cookie down, Hodge pulled Bessie's completed survey from the brown manila folder on his lap, and looked it over.

"You said on here that you and some of your relatives worked picking beans for some of the local farmers," Hodge said, as Shane wasted no time grabbing a cookie and going to work on it.

"That's right. We picked in four different fields over the years. The last one I picked in was just down the road from here—the Schmitts. Of course no one's had any pole beans for years now. When they changed the child-labor laws, they ruined things for the farmers and the kids, at least in Oregon. Why are you guys so interested in the farming?"

"Shane and I both used to pick beans and strawberries in the summer ourselves. We think it's a shame that something that was such a big part of our childhood is only history now.

"I'm with you there. Wait 'til you get to be my age, nothing will be like it once was."

"You said here you once picked in Duncan's Bean Field, but you didn't say when."

"It was from 1957 until that little girl was killed. Ellen Brock. A couple of my fourteen grandkids picked there in the seventies." They weren't about to tell her they knew her grandson Roland

Rogers, and that he was three years behind them in school. The last thing they wanted to do was get her sidetracked.

"That's where we picked too, only later. We heard all about Ellen. A few other people we've talked to have mentioned her. What can you tell us about that story?"

"I wish it was *only a story*. She was the sweetest little girl. All three of my kids were out of high school by 1960, and weren't picking beans anymore. It was horrible. Her body was found about a week before the season ended. I quit picking the day they found her. I didn't have the stomach to stay out there. A number of other pickers didn't finish out the season either. Until they found her, there was always the hope that maybe she was still alive and would somehow turn up.

"The authorities had searched all over. They even had boats searching the river from the back of the farm clear downriver several miles, in case she had gone into the river and drowned. In a lot of ways that would have been far better than what happened to her."

"No one told us about the river search. If you don't mind me asking, do you—or did you ever—have an opinion about who killed her, or why? Could the killer have been someone who lived local?"

"Do you men have children?"

"Yes, we both do," said Shane. "They're all out of high school now and going to college."

"Then you must know how heartbreaking the whole Ellen Brock thing was to her family. Ellen's mom and dad attended the same church we did. Her death really shook their faith. The dad actually became quite bitter over it. Imagine the guilt he felt as a father over his little girl being killed. She was wearing his favorite shirt the day she came up missing, 'Daddy's Angel.'" Bessie wiped several tears from her cheeks with a tissue.

"You don't have to tell us about this if it's too difficult," Shane said.

"No, it's okay. My gosh, it's been fifty years ago. But thinking about the father and that shirt…"

"But he had no reason to feel guilty. He didn't pick in the bean field, did he?"

"It's not that. No, he didn't pick there. It's the guilt he felt knowing his little girl was killed, and as her father he didn't stop it from happening. Put yourself in his shoes."

"I know what you're talking about, Bessie," Hodge said. "As an ex-cop, I've seen plenty of fathers blame themselves for bad things happening to their kids—especially their daughters—because they felt they should have protected them from *all* danger. But we all know that's simply not possible, and that it's rarely the father's fault."

"Mothers feel that too, but maybe not as powerfully as a father."

"Do you have any theories about who killed Ellen?" Hodge asked.

"I always believed it was someone local."

"Why?"

"I can't give you a good reason, other than my mother's intuition."

"Do you think she was killed by a man, or could it have been a teenage boy?"

"It could have been either."

"Could it have been a boy that worked in the field?"

"No. All the boys that worked down there that year were good kids. None of them would have done something like that." The men glanced at each other. "The police questioned all of them too. They questioned everyone who picked there. And hundreds of other people in the area."

"You said you went to church with the mother. Did she pick beans there?"

"No. Ellen picked with her aunt and two older siblings. I was good friends with her mom, though. Nothing could be worse to watch your friends go through than when their child is murdered. It's bad enough when kids die in car wrecks, or from some disease.

But none of that can compare to when they are murdered. The mother was never quite the same after that, as you might imagine."

"Do you know if any of the kids that used to pick in the Duncan's field in the years you picked there still live in the area?"

"Let me think about that," she said. "There probably are a couple. I'm not sure. The ages and years all blend together after you get to be my age."

She sipped on her coffee, while she searched her memory. Hodge and Shane looked at each other with a look that said, you mean there's something she doesn't keep up on. While they gave her a few moments to think, they munched on cookies and drank their coffee.

Finally, she said, "I hadn't thought about the time frame in a long time, but the old postmaster grew up on the creek here sometime around those years. So did his cousins, the Ritchey's. I don't know, maybe I'm getting my time periods confused. Yeah, I'm sorry, I think I am.

"I know the one Ritchey boy served in Vietnam. He came back with his head all messed up. People have stayed away from him since then. He has spent a lot of time at the Vets hospitals. When that My Lai Massacre incident came out all over the news and in the papers about the time the Ritchey boy got discharged, some people in the area said they thought that's where he may have got his head messed up. That rumor was never confirmed, but it would have made sense. American soldiers slaughtering all those Vietnamese women and children. For what? That generation of men couldn't measure up to the men I grew up with that won World War II."

"I don't mean any disrespect, ma'am," Shane said, "but my older brother was a marine in Vietnam in 1970 and 71. No matter how bad the media may have made our soldiers who fought the Vietnam War look, most of them fought just as hard as the men did in World War II."

"Then why didn't they win the war?"

"Because our government wouldn't let them win the war. And

the media undermined everything they tried to do over there. If the combat action in World War II would have been broadcast on television the way Vietnam was, or if the papers and magazines would have printed graphic photos the way they did during Vietnam, the public would have turned against America's efforts in that war also. You can't win a war when the media is allowed free access to the battle field. War is too brutal."

"Maybe you have a point, Shane."

Hodge and Shane visited with Bessie for another hour and a half, and actually found her fascinating, though a couple times they had to get her back on track. They also managed to pick up several more names of kids from the late fifties and early sixties. They didn't know if any of the names would do them any good. Only time would tell.

That evening—

"Did you tell him about Shiela?" Marlene asked.

"No, I didn't," Shane said. "I was going to, but it never seemed to be the right time. Maybe that's good."

"I'm sure there was a reason why it worked out that way. And I'm sure you'll know when to do it. Did you meet any interesting people today?"

"Funny you should ask." He went on to tell her all about Bessie Rogers

At home at the church house in Goshen, late-afternoon, Sunday March 27th, upon returning from Riva's treatment center graduation in Multnomah—

"Riva, I've had a lot I've wanted to tell you when you finished with the program," Desiree said. "I've run into those two guys, Hodge and Shane a couple times when I've been out in the Lost Creek area."

"What were they doing out there? Are they looking for the barn and money too?"

Desiree explained the code-sequence system she had come up with, and that her two confrontations with Hodge and Shane confirmed to her that there really must have been some money, and probably still is. She also told Riva about their offer to split the take.

"Surely you aren't that naïve, Desiree," Riva said, "to believe those guys have any intention of splitting the money with you."

"No, I'm not."

"And that part about there being another man involved in the hunt for the money, a known murderer no less. What did you do to make them think you were dumb enough to swallow that line?"

"I didn't do anything. And I sure as hell didn't swallow that line. They want the money for themselves, and they'll go to plenty of lengths to ensure they get it."

"You think they'd hurt us?"

"No. They aren't the kind. I actually kind of have a crush on that Hodge guy, and I think he's attracted to me too. He makes such an effort to come across as this powerful, self-confident, male chauvinist hunk. He hardly lets his buddy get a word in edge-wise. Who knows, maybe when all this is over, I'll call him up and ask him to buy me dinner."

"With the money they find before us?"

"I'm not giving up that money," Desiree said. "In fact, tomorrow you and I are going back up the creek to check out a few more of the addresses on my list, and probably talk to a few folks up that way."

"I'm up for that, Sis."

That evening visiting with Cambell Ritchey in Cam's living room—

"Cam," Kent said, "when I was over here the other night, I had wanted to talk to you about something that happened when we were kids."

"What's that?" Cam asked.

"I mentioned to you that Tommy Coleman's little brother and

one of his buddy's from Dexter had come to my place a while back. They're actually working on writing a history book of the people of Lost Creek Valley."

"What's that have to do with me?"

"Did a couple of young teenage boys come to your house at all in the last month?"

"No. Kids know better than to mess with me."

"I guess they do."

"No one ever comes in here, except you once in a while, and maybe my brothers and a couple cousins. Why don't you quit beating around the bush and say what's on your mind?"

"Okay. Part of the history of this valley has something to do with that little girl that was murdered in the bean field in 1960. I'm sure you remember that."

"No one could forget something like that. I was picking out there when it happened."

"I didn't know that," Kent said. "You would have been around eleven then, wouldn't you, if you graduated with Ed?"

"That's right. It was the summer between fifth and sixth grade. Ellen Brock was a couple years younger than me."

"Apparently there's been some new information in the case."

Cam suddenly sat up straight in the rocking chair, went from dead-pan to serious, and said, "That case was closed over forty years ago. There's new information?"

"Actually, Cam, the case was never closed. Homicides always remain open until the killer is caught. The case was suspended in 1975."

"How do you know so much about it?"

"*I don't know* so much about it. I just remember reading about it in the papers."

"Is that where you found out the case has been re-opened?"

"No. And I never said the case had been re-opened. I don't know whether it has or not."

Getting irritated, Cam said, "Then get to the point. What is this new information? And what does it have to do with me? Why are you talking to me about it?"

"I just thought that since you were about Ellen's age, you would be interested to know what's going on."

"*What is* going on? First you tell me about Tommy's little brother gathering information for his history book. Then you tell me this stuff about Ellen Brock."

"Okay, Cam. Do you think Ellen Brock's killer is still alive and living in the Lost Creek Valley?"

"I don't know what you're up to, Kent. But the last thing I need right now is to put anymore of that kind of stuff in my head. It's all I can do with the My Lai nightmare."

"I'm sorry. I guess I wasn't thinking."

"What happened to Ellen Brock was a terrible thing. But when you've been through Vietnam and all that went on over there, the Ellen Brock thing doesn't mean so much anymore. One little girl.

"You know how many dead little girls I saw in Vietnam? Not just at My Lai, but in other places. There were so many dead kids over there you wouldn't believe it. If it wasn't what our guys did at My Lai, you should have seen what the Viet Cong (VC) did in some villages. And then the Arvin (ARVN- Army of the Republic of South Vietnam) killed plenty too, whichever ones they suspected were sympathetic to the VC and NVA (North Vietnamese Army). The whole thing was a blood bath. And for what?"

"I'm sorry for bringing it up, Cam. I wouldn't have if Bessie Rogers hadn't told me that you or one of your relatives might know more about it?"

"Why would that old busy-body say something like that? She's one of the many people in the valley that always acted like I had the plague if they ran into me at the Lost Creek Store. I don't care what she or the rest of them think or say."

"I didn't mean to get you wound up."

"It's not your fault, Kent. You were just being a friend. I don't blame you. It's those other nosy gossips that bother me. Ellen Brock is gone, just like all those other kids. No one is bringing her or them back, and it's not going to do anyone any good to bring up something like that from fifty years ago."

"I'm sorry, Cam. I won't bring it up again."

"Well tell your little buddies to leave it alone also. If they want to lay out the facts as they've been known for years, in their book, then fine. But if they want to try to stir up some tabloid crap, they're asking for problems."

"I understand. I better get going. Can I come by again sometime?"

"As long as you don't bring up My Lai or Ellen Brock."

"It's a deal."

18

The Chicken Barn

At the last house on Lost Creek Road, the next day, Monday, March 29th—

"Knock harder," Riva said, "There's got to be someone home with these vehicles out here."

Desiree knocked more persistently. Then said softly, "I don't know Riva, maybe we should leave. This place is kind of creepy."

"But it was on your list, and it has an old barn. Here let me knock."

Riva pounded her fist on the door several times. They waited fifteen seconds, and still no one came to the door.

"Let's go, Sis. They're either not home or they're busy."

"Maybe whoever lives here is out at the barn. We could go out there."

"No," Desiree said. "Let's just come back another time."

As they walked away from the house, a gray-haired woman in her sixties peered out from behind the shades of a window to the left of the front door.

On the way out the driveway in Desiree's car, Riva said, "Including this place, that makes seven of fourteen you've marked so far that have an old barn. When are we actually going to start looking around in the barns?"

"We need to talk to each of the people first to find out how long they've lived in those places, and whether they know if someone matching Sam's description ever lived there."

"What if he hid the money in someone else's barn? What if the correctly coded address where Sam put the money wasn't even his barn?"

"This is hard enough already without that being the case," Desiree said. "Let's don't make it anymore complicated yet, okay?"

They stopped at three more of the six other houses that had barns and managed to talk to someone at each place. They eliminated one because the owner had owned and lived in the house since 1962, which meant that Sam couldn't have lived there as an adult. Desiree and Riva both believed Sam had to have come into the money later in his life, probably through an inheritance.

At one of the other houses, they learned Hodge and Shane had already interviewed the owners, but never asked about Sam. They had simply asked some leading questions about local farmers and the kids that worked for them. Desiree was puzzled by that. They were obviously using a different tactic than she and Riva were.

As they pulled onto Lost Creek Road after visiting their last house, Desiree spotted Hodge's truck a quarter mile away, headed up the creek. She sighed in relief that they hadn't seen her.

Headed in the opposite direction from Desiree and Riva—

"Maybe Desiree has actually taken our advice to lay off," Shane said, "since we haven't seen her out here in several days."

"I don't buy that for a minute," Hodge said. "I wish I knew if she's been talking to anyone, and if so, what she's been asking."

"Did you ever do the background check on her and Riva?"

"Actually I completed it yesterday. I couldn't find either a Desiree Lebron or a Riva Lebron listed anywhere. Of course we don't even know that Riva goes by the last name Lebron. She's probably changed her name as much as she's changed prescribers."

"You mean suppliers, don't you?"

"You know what I meant. I found hundreds of Lebron's but no Desiree's or anything similar. Lebron could be her married name, but she would have turned up under vital statistics for marriage licenses or something. I think they're both using aliases."

"That doesn't surprise us, though, does it?"

"Hardly."

"Are you going to confront her about using the false name?"

"What good would it do?"

As they reached the Eagle's Rest Bridge, Shane said, "Why don't you pull in across the bridge here and park, Hodge. I've been meaning to talk to you about something."

"What'd I do now? It's not another problem with my politics I hope."

"Nothing like that. It's just something I need to tell you."

Hodge drove over the bridge and parked in the wide spot on the right.

"With you having me park and all, I've suddenly got this nervous feeling in my stomach, like I'm about to get some of the worst news of my life. It's about Shiela, isn't it?"

"Yes, buddy. I'm afraid it is," he said, playing one of Hodge's games. "Why don't we go over on the bridge?"

They walked back to the concrete bridge and peered over the edge into a nice long pool that used to always have a nice trout in it when Shane fished this stretch of the creek as a teenager.

"Marlene had a conversation by phone with Shiela several days ago. She said I should be careful how I broke the news to you.

"She made her decision that she can't take me back?"

"Yes. She made the decision that she's going to rent out the house in Portland and move back down here to Lane County."

"What?"

"She said if you guys are ever going to be able to take the next step toward reconciliation, she needed to move here."

"You wouldn't kid me about that, would you, Shane? She's moving here because she wants to get back together?"

"I wouldn't kid you about that, old buddy. God's obviously been working on her heart. She didn't say she was definitely going to reconcile, just that if that was possibly going to happen in the future, she needed to live down here."

Hodge grabbed Shane and hugged him tight, crying. "I don't deserve this, Shane. I don't deserve for God to give me another chance with the most wonderful woman on the planet. Not after what I did to her."

"Whether you deserve it or not, He's giving you another chance. Remember, in ourselves, none of us deserves anything good. Our righteousness is as filthy rags, and it's only by God's grace through the blood of Jesus that we are worth anything. Don't blow this chance. You won't get another one if you do."

"I won't blow it, buddy. I promise. I need you now more than ever."

"We both need each other, Hodge."

Later, while getting ready for bed, Marlene asked, "Did you get around to telling him today, honey?"

"Yes, I finally did," Shane said. "It couldn't have happened at a better place. He hugged me and cried. I know he'll be the man he once was to her. I know it's all going to work out."

"I'm so happy for both of them, Shane. And for you and me getting our old best friends back together. Now I'm going to reward you."

"How's that?"

"You can take me all night long."

"Oh baby."

The next morning, Tuesday—

The man parked his truck back in the willow thicket half a mile above Bessie Roger's place and quickly made his way downhill through the young Douglas fir forest. When he reached the edge of the clearing only fifty yards from Bessie's chicken barn, he stopped and waited.

The long and wide, two-story chicken barn, had once housed several hundred laying hens at any given time. Now there was a scant twenty or so kept in the lower level of the twenty foot long section of the barn closest to the house, two hundred feet away. Between them they consistently produced a dozen eggs a day.

On a typical day, Bessie went to the barn around nine to feed the chickens, and then returned by noon to pickup the eggs. It was now 8:45 a.m.

The man was nervous, as he leaned up against a tree and peered at the barn. He hadn't killed anyone in years, though he still lived each day with the guilt of what he had done. He had washed the blood from his hands years ago, but was never able to wash it from his memory. He had never planned to kill, he told himself. He just got caught up in the frenzy of the moment.

Bessie opened the back door, grabbed the coffee can full of feed from its place on the back porch, and walked toward the chicken barn. When she disappeared inside the barn, the man made his move, hustling up to the side of the barn. He immediately crouched down and moved along below the screened windows until he reached the door facing the house. He slipped in undetected, and shut the door behind him, as Bessie was bent down facing away from him, spreading some feed for the hens. They were too pre-occupied with pecking at the corn and grain to notice him.

"Bessie," he said.

She screamed and jolted upright, while spilling the remaining feed onto the floor, which was covered by several inches of dried chicken manure mixed with down and feathers of varying sizes and colors. She turned and faced him. He was a towering man six-two or three, wearing a brown jacket and blue jeans. His head was covered with an old-man mask, with long stringy gray hair.

"Who are you?" she said.

"Kent Simons said you've been stirring up trouble with your big mouth again."

"What do you mean?"

"Buck Coleman's boy and his buddy. You've been talking to them, and Kent."

He was obviously trying to disguise his voice, but it still sounded vaguely familiar to her. She probed her memory trying to place it.

"Yes, I have talked with them. They're doing a history on the people of Lost Creek Valley. How has my talking to them about that caused problems?"

"Because you're saying some damaging things about some of the locals."

"I've never meant any harm in anything I've ever said. How have I damaged you?"

"You're like every other gossip. Always wanting to pass on the latest, and throwing in your opinions and whatever else you can to make it more interesting. You've gone too far this time—"

"Wha... What's that supposed to mean?" she said.

"Ellen Brock. You've connected her to the wrong people."

"I don't understand."

"Talking about who the local kids were at the time she was killed. Is it ringing a bell now?"

She licked her lips, her mouth was dry. "*You* picked beans there when she died?"

"Believe it or not, Bessie, not everyone has to tell everything they know. Some people know how to keep their mouths shut, unlike you and the other busy-bodies in the valley."

Her hands began to tremble. "I'm sorry if something I said upset you, or if someone took it the wrong way."

"Gossip is like taking a down pillow up to the top of the Empire State Building, cutting it open on one end, and shaking it. The feathers fall out into the wind and drift any which direction. Many of them end up miles away. And you know what the worst part is? Once they're out there, no one can ever gather them all back up and put them back in the pillow sheet. You've been doing that with your mouth forever. Everyone always knew that if they wanted to find out what was happening with anyone in the valley, all they needed to do was talk to Bessie Rogers."

"I'm sorry. I never looked at any of it that way. I was just talking to my friends."

"Well you talked to the wrong people this time, Bessie."

With his *right* hand, he pulled a nine-millimeter semi-automatic pistol from his coat pocket, and pointed it at her chest.

She dropped to her knees begging, "Please, mister. Please have mercy on me. I never meant to harm you or anyone else. I'll go back to Buck Coleman's son and the others and tell them they misunderstood me. Please."

As she stared up at the black barrel, he pulled the hammer back. Click.

"God forgive me. I never meant any harm. Please forgive me, mister."

He stepped up closer and raised the barrel, pointing it at the center of her forehead from ten inches away.

She looked down, as drops of sweat beaded up on her forehead. She couldn't bear to see the flash, though she would never recognize it. She would already be dead.

"No. Please don't shoot me. I promise I'll keep my mouth shut about all of this. You don't have to shoot me."

Five seconds passed. Then fifteen. She dared to look up. The barrel was still right there, inches from her head, and shaking. Maybe he's just bluffing, she thought. Please just be bluffing. Why haven't you done it already if you're going to do it? Do you actually have a conscience? Please God, let him have a conscience.

Half a minute passed, though it seemed like much longer to Bessie. "You're not going to do it are you?" she said. "You don't have to do it. You don't want my blood on your hands."

"Why shouldn't I do it? It's never bothered you all these years to spread your poison around. And now you've stirred up rumors about Ellen Brock's murder."

She suddenly thought she recognized the voice.

"Cambell Ritchey? It's you, isn't it?"

No answer.

"I never thought you killed the Brock girl. You were too young. I've never said you did it. Where did you get that?"

"You know how rumors are. You of all people know. Do you have any last words, Bessie?"

"Please, Cambell. Don't go through with this."

"I'm sorry, Bessie. I don't have any choice."

She looked up just as he squeezed the trigger.

The hammer fell. Click.

"I forgot to chamber a round."

She cried, "Please. I'll sign my place over to you. I'll never tell anyone you were here."

As she watched, he grabbed the slide with his left hand, pulled it back, and then released it, while depressing the slide latch with his right thumb. The slide slammed into the forward position. To Bessie it sounded like a guillotine blade hitting the bottom of its tracks.

She tried to speak, but no words came. He lowered his arm slowly, pointing the gun at the floor in front of her. She saw the hammer was pulled back, ready to fire.

He raised the gun back up, and held the barrel an inch from her head.

She prayed silently.

He pulled the trigger.

Click.

"It misfired," he said.

She cried violently.

Twenty seconds passed.

"Just get it over with," she finally managed to say,

He worked the action again.

Her entire body shook, tears poured freely down her cheeks, like the gossip had always flowed freely from her mouth.

Suddenly she collapsed to the floor on her face, and lay still.

He felt her right wrist for a pulse.

Nothing.

He palpated her neck next to the windpipe.

Nothing there either.

Just then, he heard someone yelling near the house, "Bessie... Mrs. Rogers." He quickly removed the empty magazine from the pistol handle, and loaded a full one. He worked the slide, feeding a live round into the chamber. He cracked the door behind him open just enough to look out. Two men were walking alongside the house, coming toward the back.

"Her car's parked out front. She's got to be around somewhere," Shane said. He looked at his watch, then at the chicken barn. "Maybe she's feeding the chickens."

The man in the barn hurried through the door at the back of the first section of the chicken barn, as the chickens made a big commotion. He sprinted twenty feet to the next door and opened it. He ran through each of the remaining six sections and out the back door, then stayed against the building until he got to the edge to see his relationship to the house and the two men. They were not in sight.

He sprinted across the short opening into the oaks that adjoined the fir forest and escaped up the slope.

Hodge and Shane looked at the back porch to see if she might be sitting there. When she wasn't, they walked directly toward the chicken barn, where they could here the chickens cackling.

Shane opened the barn door and stepped in, with Hodge right on his heels.

"She's down," Shane said. "Bessie, are you alright?"

Shane quickly approached her, bent down and felt for a carotid pulse.

Nothing.

Hodge felt for a pulse. "She's still warm. Let's turn her over." They turned her on her back, observed the perspiration and noticed that the color was gone from her face. Hodge touched it. "She's already beginning to cool off," he said, looking at Shane. "It's too late, buddy. If she was younger, I'd give CPR. But it was just her time. She's lived a full life."

Shane felt numb as he stared at her dead face, her eyes still open. It seemed he was gaining a knack for turning up dead bodies lately.

19

Unwelcome Women

At Cambell Ritchey's front door that evening—

"Cam, Bessie Rogers is dead," Kent Simons said.

"She's dead?"

"Yes. Shane Coleman stopped by a while ago and told me they found her dead in her chicken pen this morning. It was either a cardiac arrest or a stroke."

"That's too bad," Cam said. "That's a huge piece of Lost Creek history gone with her. I think she's lived up there since she was a girl."

"Yes, she has. Her grandma and grandpa Rogers settled on that very place in the 1880s. According to my dad, the Bristows are the only other family that has lived in the Pleasant Hill-Dexter-Lost Creek area longer than hers."

"Did Shane Coleman get all the history he was hoping for from her?"

"No, actually he didn't. That's why they went there to see her again."

"I guess there is one small consolation to her dying: the airways should be a little clearer. At least for awhile."

"I'm sure some other old lady will pick up the slack," Kent said. "They always do."

The next day, Wednesday, March 31st, at the last house on Lost Creek Road—

"This is the last one on my list, Shane," Hodge said. "We know one thing, this couldn't have been the place where Sam lived during his teens. It's too far away from any neighbors."

"I agree. There's no way he got up in the middle of the night and hiked in the dark to this barn," Shane said. "If Sam had anything to do with this place it would have been later."

They walked up to the front door and knocked, but got no answer.

"The boys didn't have a completed survey from this house. Either the people didn't want to be interviewed, or felt nothing they could say would benefit us."

"I'd like to know which."

They knocked again, and still no one answered.

They left.

The same gray-haired lady who watched Desiree and her sister two days earlier watched Hodge and Shane walk away from the house.

On the phone, same day, with Kent Simons—

"Kent," Shane said, "Hodge and I have been talking it over, and we're beginning to wonder why Bessie Rogers threw Cambell Ritchey's name out there like she did. And she mentioned something about his cousin being the old postmaster at Dexter. We'd love to have a chat with Ritchey if you could arrange it."

"I would, but I stopped by his place the other day for a chat, and he made it clear he didn't want anything to do with Hodge's Lost Creek history book," Kent said. "He said he thought highly of

Tommy, but that he can't help you guys."

"Can you at least give me his phone number and address?"

"He doesn't have a phone. And as far as his address, sure I can give you that, but the place is thoroughly surrounded with No Trespassing signs. And he doesn't make exceptions except for me, his brothers and a couple cousins. People have gotten hurt trying to go on his property. He's still fighting the Vietnam War in his head. I wouldn't risk it if I were you."

"He's in that bad a shape? The boys marked on the Census map that they had visited his house."

"If you were getting paid $2.50 a piece for each filled-out survey form, and nothing for the places where you didn't get one filled out, would you risk going to the house of a screwed up Vietnam combat vet who had previously booby trapped other kids?"

"I see your point. Can you at least go back yourself and try to pick up some information about Ritchey's cousin, the postmaster?"

"You didn't mention him before today," Kent said. "What did you hear from Bessie about him?"

"Nothing really, other than that at first she thought he was a teen in the late-fifties, then decided she had her years mixed up. That's one of the reasons we went over to talk to her yesterday, to see if she had come up with anything else on him or any other local kids from those years."

"I see," Kent said. "I can tell you that the one cousin worked as postmaster at the Dexter Post Office from the late seventies into the early nineties. His name was Scott Welker."

"Do you know if he's still in the area, and how old he is?"

"He's got to be pushing seventy, but I don't know if he's still around or not. I haven't heard anything about him in years. He used to live somewhere up at the end of the creek, but I couldn't tell you where. That was well after I moved away from the area. I know he was a mail carrier in some other county before he took over as postmaster here," he said. "Bessie said he grew up in the Lost Creek area?"

"That's what I understood."

"It would have been before my time. I don't remember him. You know how it is when you're young, you don't know all the older kids."

"I know. Could you see if you can get Ritchey to meet with us."

"Shane, that's a dead end, leave it alone."

At the Coleman's, over dinner, that evening—

"Honey, I talked to Shiela today," Marlene Coleman said. "She asked if she could stay at our place over the weekend while she looked for a place to rent."

"Did you tell her I told Hodge?" Shane said.

"Yes, after we had talked awhile."

"How did she react?"

"She didn't give anything away, and I couldn't read her. I think inside, she's still hurting pretty bad, and doesn't want to get her hopes up. When you've been crushed like she has, I can understand her caution."

"Me too. Did you tell her we'd love to have her here?"

"Of course I did. I'm thinking if she's up for it, maybe we could go out on a double date—like the old days."

"Wouldn't that be a blast?"

"Absolutely."

The next day, Thursday, April 1st, mid-afternoon—

As Desiree and Riva walked up hill from their car toward the walkway to the last house on Lost Creek, Desiree said, "I sure hope someone is here this time. I definitely don't want to come back up here."

They knocked on the front door and waited. Same scenario as their previous visit, they knocked harder and more persistently.

Finally an old man about six-foot-three opened the door, stepped out on the porch as if to intimidate the women with his size, and said in a deep voice, "What is it with you people? Can't you read the no trespassing, no solicitors signs?"

"We aren't soliciting anything," Desiree said.

"But you're trespassing, just like you did three days ago."

"So *you were* home."

"Between you and those other two guys, my place has become grand central. What do want?"

"We're trying to find my uncle," Desiree said, flashing a bit of charm at him with her eyes. "He's supposed to be living out this way somewhere."

"I don't know anything about who else lives up the creek these days, so you just as well leave before I get anymore irritated."

"My uncle is about your age. He's bounced around a lot, used some different names over the years. I think he got to doing that when he was traveling with the circus."

"I wouldn't know him—"

"His name is Sam Hostick." As soon as she said Sam's name, she sensed a quick hint of recognition in the old man's eyes.

"I don't know any Sam Hostick."

"He grew up out here on Lost Creek. He was close to your age. He may have gone by another name when he was a kid. Did you grow up out here?"

"Look ladies, I've answered all the questions I'm going to answer. You can leave now, or I'll personally throw you off the place."

"You knew Sam, didn't you?" Desiree said. I saw it in your eyes when I said his name. You knew him."

He immediately grabbed each of them by an arm and led them down the walkway, until they jerked free and ran for their car.

"Don't ever come back here!" he shouted.

Driving away down the man's driveway, Desiree said, "Did you see it, in his eyes?"

"Yes," Riva answered. "He definitely reacted when you said

Sam Hostick. Not much, but enough."

"Why do you think he's so unwilling to talk to us?"

"Who knows. At least we confirmed that one person that's still living out here knew Sam."

"Maybe Sam Hostick *is* his real name."

"Maybe we should go back right now, and tell him that Sam died homeless under a bridge."

"What if he knows a lot more about Sam?' Desiree said. "Maybe he already knows Sam is dead, and therefore knows we were lying about him."

"How would he know Sam is dead? No one knows Sam is dead. No one could have figured out it was Sam from that little notice in the paper."

"I did."

"But chances are that guy never even reads the paper, living up here, probably by himself. And even if he did put two and two together—which the odds against that are astronomical—our being Sam's nieces and looking for him isn't a big deal. He could easily assume we hadn't learned of Sam's death."

Thursday evening, at the Coleman's, while clearing the table—

After putting the leftover green salad away in the refrigerator, Marlene said, "Shane, I was thinking if everything goes okay Friday evening with Hodge and Shiela, maybe we could invite Rawly and Kindra out for pizza and bowling with the four of us Saturday evening."

"As much as you wanted to slow *me* down on this thing with Hodge and Shiela, it sounds like you've really got your motors running now," Shane said.

"I guess you're right. I'm just real excited about Shiela moving down here. I already ran the idea by her, and she seemed open to it. She said having the kids there would probably make things a lot more relaxed."

"I don't know about it helping things be more relaxed. Maybe if you warn Rawly ahead of time to keep his girlfriend off her political agendas."

"And I'll be sure to warn my husband too."

Shane put the plates he was holding into the sink and then snuggled up close to Marlene's back, wrapped his arms around her waist and across her belly, and kissed the side of her neck. "How was I ever lucky enough to get a beautiful woman like you, Baby? Whenever I see you I get weak in the knees."

"You do, huh? What do you want me to do about that?"

"I can think of *one* thing right off the bat."

She tipped her head back, as he continued kissing her neck, and said, "I want you right now, honey." She then turned around, gently grabbed his hand and led him out of the kitchen, down the hall, and into their bedroom."

Friday afternoon at Cambell Ritchey's house—

"Why can't we just skip this place, Sis?" Riva said, as they drove up the quarter-mile-long driveway. "I've never seen so many No Trespassing signs in my life. I have a bad feeling about this place."

"Relax, Riva. Look how old that shack of a house looks. I don't even see any power lines out here. Whoever lives here has probably been here forever and might be able to help us."

"But there's no barn. The address isn't even on your code list."

"Give it a break, Riva. If you want to stay in the car, then fine. But I'm at least going to try to talk to the people here."

Desiree parked the car on the right side of the driveway across from the house.

"Someone's out back," Riva said, pointing behind the house toward a small shed.

"Let's go. If we catch them outside, they can't act like they're not home."

They both got out of the car and walked briskly in the direction of the shack, where a long-haired guy with a large build was bent down with his back to them. As they got to within thirty feet of him, they could see he was pounding something into the ground next to the building with a short-handled sledge-hammer.

"Mister?"

He startled and faced them in a semi-crouched position with the sledge-hammer held at the ready.

They froze.

When he saw it was just a couple of women, he stood up and stared at them without saying anything. They noticed his scarred face and unkempt appearance and suddenly wished they were anywhere else.

Seconds passed, then finally, Riva said, "We're with the 2010 Census Bureau—"

"Then get off my land. Can't you read. 'No Trespassing.'"

"Actually we aren't with the Census," Desiree said. "My sister has an odd sense of humor."

"Then what do you want?"

"We were just hoping to be able to ask you a few questions."

"I don't have any time for your questions."

They both looked over at what he had been pounding on, and couldn't make heads or tails out of the two metal rods in the ground or the other pieces of wire and metal laying on the ground there. "We didn't mean to interrupt your project. What are you doing there anyway?"

He gave them a dirty look, then glanced behind him at his work.

"It doesn't concern you—yet."

They didn't know what to make of that, but knew they better leave well enough alone.

Desiree suspected he was a combat veteran because of the bad scars on his face and neck, and asked in her most compassionate voice, "Are you a veteran?"

"Yes," he said.

Judging his age, she said, "Vietnam?"

"I don't want to talk about it. You ladies need to leave."

"We're looking for my deceased husband's old place. He grew

up out here."

"Well he didn't live here. If he was your husband why don't you already know where he lived?"

"We never got out here. How long have you lived in the Lost Creek Valley?"

"Long enough. I don't have time for anymore of your questions. But *I will* give you a piece of advice, and then you can both leave quickly if you know what's good for you. The next time you go talking to a stranger up here, *you better* have your stories straight."

"Thanks for your time, Mister," Desiree said. "Sorry we bothered you."

They turned and walked briskly back to their car and left.

Driving away, Desiree said, "He sure wasn't the least bit friendly."

"You're not kidding. I tried to warn you about these backcountry people," Riva said. "What do you think he meant about keeping our stories straight? Do you think it was because I started off by saying we were with the Census, then you switching up to try to salvage something?"

"Sis, you couldn't have come up with a dumber line than us being with the Census. The last thing a guy like that wants is to be counted or interviewed by the Census people. As far as what he said about keeping our stories straight, I don't know what he meant. I can't believe that guy ever talks to anyone else up here."

"Didn't you think his response to your question about his project was weird?"

"The guy gave me the creeps. I don't think he was all there upstairs."

"Me either, and I'm sure never going back to confirm it."

20

Bowling

After the women left, Cam finished rigging the booby trap at the front of the shed, and then inventoried the makeshift materials he would used to set up the series of mines on his place. It had been over ten years since he'd had any active mines or booby traps. But Hodge Gilbert and Shane Coleman's history book project had stirred up too many people, and he had to ensure people got the message that Cambell Ritchey's was one place you stayed away from.

No one ever found out about the bum that wandered onto Cam's place in 1976 and blew a leg off on one of Cam's home-made mines—one that operated like a "Bouncing Betty, but with less bang to it." He had the mine setup between the outhouse and another building where he kept many of his tools and equipment.

At around 9:30 one August night, there was an explosion, followed immediately by persistent bone-chilling screaming. Cam hurried out to see what the commotion was and found a bum bleeding profusely from the stump of what was left of this upper left leg. When he shined his flashlight around, he immediately spotted one of his chainsaws laying a few feet away from the injured man. Then he saw the leg hanging from the barbed-wire fence ten feet away. He knew the guy was in the process of stealing the saw, so he had no problem with what he did next.

He quickly grabbed a square-tip shovel and beat the bum to death with it, hoping none of his distant neighbors had heard the screaming. As far as Cam was concerned the guy had it coming. In fact, Cam reasoned, he had kept the guy from stealing anybody else's property, or doing something worse. After wrapping a garbage sack around the dead man's pulverized head and securing it at the neck, and doing the same with his leg stump, to avoid leaving a blood trail, Cam carried the man's body into a heavily wooded canyon, half a mile behind his place, on the BLM land that bordered the back of his property. There he dug a hole several feet deep and buried him in it. He then piled various logs and other woody materials and brush over the grave.

When Cam got back to the house, he immediately dug a hole behind one of his out buildings and buried the bum's severed leg which he had taken off the fence earlier. He then used his wheelbarrow to haul old, darkened, sawdust from a pile on his place to the area where the man's blood saturated the ground, and spread the sawdust all over to cover up the blood. It was one time when he wished he had running water on his place, so he could have used a hose to wash the blood away. After spreading the sawdust, he hauled a bunch of old lumber over and made a stack over the top of the sawdust. He then took a damp towel around and wiped away any blood he found on the outhouse wall and on the fence where the leg had hung.

For weeks afterwards, Cam worried that someone might have heard the man screaming and reported it to the police. But nobody ever showed up to investigate it. After that experience, Cam used rock salt for the shrapnel in all his mines, and set them with very light charges. His goal was mainly to just scare people, and at the most, cause multiple superficial flesh wounds to the victims. He wasn't looking to go to jail.

After completing his inventory, Cam went inside and grabbed some of the dried venison from the deer he had poached and smoked up a few weeks earlier. He threw the meat into a pot of water, along with some potatoes, onions, celery, carrots and seasonings, then set the pot on his propane stove. After cracking the kitchen window open, he fired up the stove, then went back outside and piddled around with his mines, while his meal for the next couple days cooked.

After supper, he jumped in his pickup and drove up the creek to the last house on Lost Creek Road. He wanted to update his cousin on the latest development in the Sam Hostick saga.

The banging of balls on pins at the Emerald Bowling Lanes on Oakway Road in Eugene on Saturday evening was something the Coleman's and Gilberts hadn't experienced together in years. Before Hodge and Shiela had moved to Portland, the couples had bowled in a few leagues together. Back then either of the women led off, Shane rolled third, and carried a 167 average, while Hodge anchored the team with his 178 average.

After the move, the couples often went bowling whenever the Coleman's traveled to Portland—which was rare—or the Gilberts came to the Upper Willamette Valley.

Tonight the three men (Shane, Rawly and Hodge) were competing together against the women (Marlene, Kindra and Shiela), who they spotted with a team handicap of 110 per game. The first game had gone to the women and the second one to the men. Now they were in the 10th frame of the rubber match, the guys up by thirteen pins, with each team's cleanup bowler remaining.

Shiela, working on a strike behind her 115 pins through eight frames, stepped up to roll her purple twelve-pound ball. "Come on Shiela," Hodge said, "keep it going."

She found her spot, took four steps on the approach and released the ball. "You've got it nailed, Baby," Hodge yelled, as her ball rolled into the one-three pocket perfectly and all ten pins went down.

"Yes!" she shouted, clapping her hands, and turning to walk back to the ball tray to wait for her ball.

"Give us another one, Shiela," Marlene said. "These guys need some humble pie."

She picked up her ball, returned to her spot, and delivered another perfect ball. Strike!

As Shiela stepped up to roll her third and final ball of the tenth frame, Shane said, "Come on Shiela, put some real pressure on the old goat."

Shiela turned around and winked at Hodge, just like she used to do. Her gesture caused him to feel overwhelmed with love for her. God, I don't deserve that woman. Give her a strike.

She released another ball that was destined for the pocket. All the pins went down. Strike!

"You did it, baby! You really put the pressure on me."

"One-seventy-five, Shiela. Great game," Shane said.

Shiela high-fived Hodge, and said, "Top that, big guy," as he stepped past her to bowl his tenth frame.

"Don't you dare give it away now, old buddy," Shane said. "They have to earn this."

Hodge rolled his blue sixteen-pound ball perfectly into the one-three pocket and slammed all ten pins back.

"One more and they're toast," Rawly said.

"He'll never do it," Kindra said.

As Hodge's next ball approached the pins, he leaned to the right to try to steer it. It did no good. The ball hit high on the head pin and left a seven-ten split.

"You bet!" Kindra yelled, while all three men groaned.

When Hodge stepped over to his spot, Shane said, "Play for the tie, just take the seven out."

Hodge turned and said, "When have you ever known me to settle for a tie? I'm getting both of them."

As his deliberately slow-rolled ball approached wide left on the seven pin, it looked like he might just pull it off. But at the last second, the ball dropped into the gutter.

"We win!" Kindra shouted, jumping up and down.

When Hodge walked to the scorers' table, Shiela intercepted him with a huge hug and kiss. "I don't care who won, Hodge. You looked just as sexy on your approach as you always did."

They held each other for half a minute, as Hodge said, "I love you, Baby. I've missed you so much. Great game." He knew everything was going to be alright now.

Shane held Marlene tight in bed that night as they reflected on the last two evenings.

"God has answered our prayers, honey," Marlene said. "And He did it faster than I ever imagined He would."

"You're not kidding," Shane answered. "Hodge is one very lucky man. And Shiela is one very forgiving woman."

"He's lucky to have a friend like you."

"And I'm blessed to have a wife like you, that didn't give up on them. And who has never given up on me."

They kissed tenderly as they continued holding each other.

"You did very well with the kids tonight too. I was so proud of you."

"I've got a sensible side to me, sweetie, no matter how it seems sometimes."

"That's one of the hundred and one reasons I married you."

Wednesday morning, April 6th, Lost Creek—

As they sat in Shane's truck, parked on an old log landing several hundred feet above and nearly a mile west of a couple of old farms north of the Old Guistina Mill Road, Hodge looked through his binoculars, and said, "From everything we've learned so far, if I had to bet money on it, I would say those two farm houses with the barns down there were where alias Sam Hostick, and Ellen Brock's Killer lived the day she was murdered.

Shane looked at the farms through his own binoculars, and said, "If those are the right places, we have a problem since no one living in this valley now has the same last name as the people who lived on that adjoining farm in 1960—at least according to postal records? That means the killer no longer lives in the area. For all we know he could be dead."

"You don't believe that anymore than I do. You said yourself that Sam made it clear he had no intention of giving you the killer's name. If the guy was dead already, keeping his identity secret wouldn't have mattered so much to Sam."

"Maybe he was worried about the consequences to the killer's surviving relatives."

"I don't buy that as the reason. Your own dad told you the guy still lived locally. The killer's alive, somewhere," Hodge said. "And I believe he's living in this valley. It's possible he was a step-kid who went by a different last name."

"We could sure use Bessie Rogers right now to bounce some of this off. Of course how would we have got her to keep her mouth shut about the things we discussed with her?"

"No kidding. I'm betting someone in this community is breathing easier with her passing."

"Only if they thought she knew something that could finger them."

"Why don't we go over what we know so far," Shane suggested.

Hodge pulled out his spiral notebook, opened it to his list, and read,

—Sam Hostick was not Sam's real name.

—Sam lived next door to the killer.

—They were both sixteen when Ellen Brock was killed.

—The address 54916 is the house to the north down there. We

got that number by adding 6,4,2 to the last three digits of the tattooed address of 54374, the house with the burned barn where Desiree stopped.

—As far as we know, four of Cambell Ritchey's cousins grew up on Lost Creek or Rattlesnake Roads. But Kent Simons insists that Cambell Ritchey won't talk to us under any circumstances, so we can't learn anymore about his cousins from him. From what Kent has said Cambell doesn't even want Kent to bring up Ellen Brock's name around him anymore.

—We have the names of three other teenage boys that lived on Lost Creek, who would have been sixteen, give or take a year, at the time Ellen Brock was killed. But we know there were probably at least a half-dozen other boys around that age living on the creek then. We're just not able to determine any of their names.

—The names of the three boys we do know about are Wayne Pilpitt, Mark Joness, and Ken Marney. But none of them still live in the area, nor have we been able to track them down.

—No one who lived here when Cambell Ritchey's cousin was postmaster wants to talk about him because he apparently left the post office under unfavorable conditions. But no one will tell us what those conditions were.

—We know Scott Welker was postmaster from 1977 to 1994, and carried mail in another county before that. But we don't know where he lives, or if he's even still alive. We don't know how old he was in 1960, or where he lived then, other than Bessie said he grew up on Lost Creek. The only person—Bessie Rogers—who seemed to want to talk about him, or even confirmed he was Cambell Ritchey's cousin, is now dead.

"That's what we've got," Hodge said.

"What about what we know about Desiree and the money?" Shane said. "Do you have that summarized?"

"Sorry." Hodge turned the page and continued reading,

—Desiree Lebron claims to have lived with Sam Hostick for four years, beginning a little over eight years ago.

—She has as much as admitted Sam had tens of thousands of dollars hidden inside the walls of his old barn. Of course, like us, she has no idea when he hid it. And from what we can gather she doesn't know where he got the money, other than maybe through an inheritance.

—We, on the other hand, suspect Sam may have been paid off by his ex-friend, Ellen Brock's killer, so Sam would keep his mouth shut about what he knew.

—We believe there's a good chance Sam never spent any of the money because he may have considered it to be blood money.

—We suspect at some point the killer quit paying Sam, telling him if he turned the killer in that long after Ellen's death, Sam could be found guilty of accessory to murder, obstruction of justice, and a number of other charges.

—We warned Desiree of the potential danger to her and her sister, Riva, if they continued to pursue the money. The four of us agreed to split whatever money any of us found. We are also certain that if she finds the money apart from us, she won't give us a bloody dime of it.

—We really have no idea whether there actually ever was any money, whether there still is money, or what happened to the money. The only thing we have to go on regarding there being any money, and where it might be, is Desiree's explanation about the tattoos, and then our confirmation of the tattoos matching the address of the house with the burned barn where Desiree stopped when we were following her that first day.

—For all we know, Sam made up the whole thing about the money in the first place. For what reason, we can only speculate. Maybe to make Desiree believe he was living on the streets by choice, not because he was a loser like all the rest of the homeless people.

—The tattooed address had some special meaning for Sam. According to Desiree, he once lived there. But from what we've been able to determine, he never actually lived at the tattooed address—though until we know Sam's real name, we can't be certain of that. We believe he just used the tattooed address for the basis of the coded address where he actually lived.

—We don't know if Sam lived at the coded-address as a kid, or later, after he grew up. If he hid money in the barn of the coded-address, it would have been after he was an adult because the killer could never have been paying him off while the killer was a kid, still going to high school.

—So far, we have been unable to determine Sam's real name, but if he lived at the house at 54916 Lost Creek Road, his last name would have been either James, Shelley, Slushman, Tendick, Reed, Carter, or Bradshaw. All of those people lived there between 1951 and 2001, when Desiree met Sam living on the street. We ruled Bradshaw out because he currently owns the place and is very much alive and well, not to mention he is a giant of a man, whereas Sam had a small build.

—No one we've talked to has been able to give us an age or physical description of any men who lived at that address, other than for Mr. Reed and Mr. Carter. Sam could have been either of them, but they were both married. We have no idea about Sam's marital or familial history.

"That's pretty much it," Hodge said.

"Imagine if we could go to Bessie Rogers with all that," Shane said. "She would have been a goldmine."

"Or just a mine."

"We haven't talked much about Cambell Ritchey's cousin, the postmaster. Why are you so interested in him? Is it because Bessie mentioned him being a kid that lived in the Lost Creek area around the time Ellen Brock was killed? Don't you remember how she corrected herself, and said she was mixing up the time periods?"

"Yes, I know she said that. But she seemed confused," Hodge said. "That's one of the things I was hoping to get straightened out the day we went back to her place and found her dead. Of course, part of my interest is because postmasters know the names of everyone on their rolls. And sometimes they have learned some details that very few other people know. But I also haven't ruled him out as someone that might have known the killer, if in fact he was an older teenager in 1960. Or—stranger things have happened—he might have been the killer."

"You can't be serious about that."

"I'm not really. But I've learned to be careful about who I rule out as suspects."

"There's no way he could have looked people from his own community in the eyes all those years, including Ellen Brock's own family, if he had been the killer. Hodge, you're barking up the wrong tree even thinking that."

"Doesn't the fact that no one seems to want to talk about him tell you something is askew, Shane?"

"Sure it does. But plenty of government officials and profess-ionals in all fields have resigned under pressure from the public, their own superiors, or some other entity. Resigning prematurely because you've had one too many run-ins with certain individuals is a far cry from being guilty of murder."

"Then why don't people want to talk about him? Are they afraid of him for some reason? Maybe there were other people, besides your dad, who believed Ellen Brock's killer was someone from the area. And maybe some of those people believed it was Scott Welker, who later became the postmaster."

"If that was the case, some of them would surely have put all kinds of pressure on local law enforcement officials to bring him in and charge him a long time ago."

"Maybe some did in the beginning, but the law wasn't able to come up with the necessary evidence to charge him."

"I still say you're out in left field thinking he could have been involved."

"That fits with my left-wing politics then, doesn't it?"

21

The Deer

Hodge and Shane got out of the truck without closing the doors and walked over to the east edge of the landing. Just as they looked over, they spooked a blacktail doe and a fawn that were crossing the unit thirty yards below them. The deer bounded away into the big firs to their left.

"There aren't near as many deer out here as there were back when so much of the surrounding area was being clearcut," Shane said.

"How do you know that?" Hodge said.

"I've talked to a few of the hunters out here, and the ODFW (Oregon Department of Fish and Wildlife) surveys confirm that."

"I sure miss hunting, Shane. Maybe we can go deer hunting together next fall."

"I'm up for it."

As they were overlooking Lost Creek Road off in the distance, Shane raised his binoculars up suddenly and looked at something below.

"Is that Desiree's car pulling into that driveway?"

187

Hodge looked through his binoculars and said, "You darn right it is, and the druggie sister's with her."

"Ex-druggie, Hodge. You heard what Desiree said, she's completed a drug rehabilitation program."

"Once a druggie, always a druggie."

"They couldn't possibly be going in there to ask about Sam or look for the money, could they?"

"There's no other reason for it. Let's go." Hodge hustled toward Shane's pickup. "Come on, Shane, we've got to get down there."

They jumped in the truck, started the engine, slammed it into gear and spun out turning around on the landing. "It'll take us at least ten minutes to get there from here," Shane said.

"You can do it in less time than that. Get on it."

As they sped around the next corner with their wheels slipping on the road's loose gravel, suddenly the same doe and fawn they had scared off a few minutes earlier, jumped into the road in front of them. Shane stomped on the brakes, causing the truck to go sideways and slide over the right embankment and down a fifteen foot drop into a mound of soft dirt covered by grass.

"Darn those deer!" Shane said. "Are you okay?"

"I'm fine, but we're never going to get down there in time now."

Shane pulled out his cell phone and called Marlene.

"Marlene, Hodge and I have been in an accident—"

"An accident—a car accident? Where are you? Are you hurt?"

"We're okay. We're up in the hills above Lost Creek. A couple deer ran out right in front of us. I braked too hard and ended up in the ditch, down an embankment. (He wasn't about to tell her he was going way too fast in the first place.) The truck may have a dent or two on the right side, but it's fine other than that. I need you to get the number to a couple of the Dexter area tow trucks for me, so I can call and get pulled out of this ditch."

"Just a minute, honey. I've got to get the phone book. Are you sure you're okay?

"Yes. We're both fine."

"I'm turning pages now. What were you guys doing up in the hills?"

"I can't believe you're asking me that, Marlene."

"I'm sorry. I know how much you like to get up in the woods. I was just asking because of the accident. I'm sorry. Here are the numbers."

She read Shane the numbers, then hung up after he assured her that he'd be home toward evening, as previously planned. He made contact with someone at the first number. Help was on the way.

"I guess we get to eat crow on this one," Hodge said.

"While the girls down there get the money."

"Desiree and her sister won't try to recover the money in broad daylight. As a matter of fact, we really didn't need to rush to get down there. What could we have accomplished? I just got caught up in the emotions of seeing them drive in there."

"Now you tell me. Does that mean you'll help repair any dents?"

"Let's get out and see how bad it is."

They jumped out and looked the right side of the truck over.

"Only a slight dent behind the front wheel," Hodge said. "Marlene must pray a bunch for you. Or do you just live right?"

"Got to be the prayer," Shane said. "Hopefully I didn't screw up the front end."

They got on their hands and knees and examined the underside of the truck. "I don't think you did any damage," Hodge said.

"We'll find out for sure as soon as that guy gets us back up on the road."

At the farmhouse below, 54916 Lost Creek Road—

The huge man, six-six and about three hundred pounds, in his early sixties, answered the door and asked if he could help the women.

"We're looking for my uncle who lives out here on Lost Creek. I was told he was holding a large sum of money for me," Desiree said. "Part of an inheritance from a grandparent."

"What's your uncle's name?" the man said with a mid-western accent. "You don't have his address?"

"Your address is the one we were given. His name is Sam Hostick, at least that's what he went by in recent years."

"I'm definitely not him, unless I have some lost nieces that I was unaware of," he said. "And I'm sure not holding any large sums of money. You say he goes by Sam Hostick?"

"Yes," Desiree answered, feeling hopeful.

"I don't know any Sam Hostick."

"He might have gone by some other name, too," Riva said.

"Why would he have done that?" he said, with suspicion.

"He used to travel with the circus and changed his name from time to time. When he lived out here, it's possible he went by one of his circus names."

"I've heard some good lines in my life, ladies, but that's got to be right in there with the best ones."

Desiree glanced at Riva with a quick look that said, why couldn't you just let me do the talking, then said, "He really did travel with the circus, but that was when he was a young man. My sister sometimes likes to see what kind of a reaction she can get from people. She has an odd sense of humor."

"Well we country folk don't take to being toyed with."

"I didn't mean any offense, sir," Riva said, "really."

"Can you tell us who lived here before you?" Desiree asked.

"We bought the place in 1997 from a couple named Carter. I can't remember their first names. Couldn't say who owned it before them. We moved out here from the Midwest."

"Well, sorry to have bothered you, Mr.—

"Bradshaw."

"Thanks for the help Mr. Bradshaw."

As they drove out Bradshaw's driveway, Desiree said, "I don't know why, Sis, I just have a good feeling about this place. The address fits one of the sequencing codes I came up with, using a correction of 6,4,2 for the last three digits, and everything about it seems like the kind of place where Sam would have lived."

Taking a drag off her just-lit cigarette, and blowing out a puff of smoke, Riva said, "I appreciate your enthusiasm, Desiree, but if Sam ever lived here, why would he have ever left? The place is beautiful."

"I have no idea. There's a lot about Sam I don't understand. One thing I do know is that you and I are coming back here to look around in that barn."

Riva blew another puff of smoke into the car forcing Desiree to roll the front windows halfway down with her remote switches.

"Could you lighten up on the cigarettes while you're in the car?"

"Sorry," Riva answered. "I'm not sure I want to come back here. What if we get caught? Old man Bradshaw looks like he could wield a powerful pitchfork."

"We won't get caught. Did you see or hear any dogs?"

"No, but maybe they were in the house or away from the property."

"Maybe," Desiree said. "But maybe we'll get lucky and they won't have any dogs. If they were in the house, chances are they keep them in at night too."

Desiree turned north out of Bradshaw's driveway onto Lost Creek Road, and headed back to the Goshen church house to get some rest before coming back that evening to scout the place.

"It's funny we haven't run into your friends out here lately," Riva said. "Do you think they're still working it?"

"Of course they're still working it. I'm thinking maybe it would be a good idea to call Hodge and compare notes, kind of make sure they aren't as close to finding the money as we are."

"Maybe they've already been to Bradshaw's and retrieved the money," Riva suggested.

"They would have called us by now if they had."

"Why would they call you? If I were them I wouldn't. I'd keep all the money for myself."

"They're smarter than that. What I figure they'll do is say there was only a fraction of the money we believed there had to be, and give us half of that."

"You're probably right, and we'd have no way to prove otherwise. I think you better call them."

Desiree had Riva pull Hodge's PI card from her wallet and dial his cell number, before passing the phone to her.

Hodge's phone rang just as the tow truck driver arrived.

"Hodge here."

"Hodge, this is Desiree Lebron. Do you have a minute to talk?"

"Can I call you back in twenty or thirty minutes? We're kind of tied up right now."

"I'll call you in thirty minutes," Desiree said, knowing her name and number were blocked from coming up on his caller ID.

"Okay," Hodge said, then hung up.

Half an hour later, Hodge's phone rang again—still unknown name, unknown number.

"This is Hodge."

"Yes, Hodge, Desiree again."

"Good to hear from you, Desiree. Has there been a new development?"

"Not with us, how about with you guys?"

"Oh yeah. We're picking up some great stories. The Lost Creek Valley people lived through some interesting times."

"Have you learned anymore about Sam, like what his real name is, or where he might have hid the money?"

"We haven't got much of anything on Sam. We've checked out a number of places that we thought might have been his old place, but so far have come up empty. It would sure be a lot easier if we knew his real name."

"My thoughts exactly," Desiree said. "We'll chat again, Hodge.

I've got to run."

"Talk to you later."

"It sounded like she was on a fishing expedition, judging by your responses," Shane said.

"Would you expect anything else from her, Hodge said. "And she still hasn't given me her phone number."

"She obviously wants to be the one in control."

"Maybe that's the real reason Sam left her. A guy from his generation doesn't take so well to strong-willed women like her."

"Who really knows what happened between her and Sam, or if they really ever were lovers living together. I've never been sure we could believe a word she says."

"Me either. But I do believe Sam mentioned the money to her," Hodge said. "She's shown her hand on that, between her reaction to things I've said, and the fact she's obviously looking for something. I'm sure her drug-free sister already has plans for using her share of the money for evangelizing the street people with the value of abstaining from drugs."

"Just say no," Shane said. They both chuckled.

22

Bradshaw's Horse Barn

That night, 11 pm, three hours after dark, the Bradshaw Farm—

Desiree and Riva, approaching from the east, snuck along the three-rail, wooden fence that ran east and west along the north side of the ten acre horse pasture on the south side of the Bradshaw place. Several horses whinnied as they took off on a dead run to their left, spooked by the women's presence. The women hoped no one noticed.

As the women made their way toward the horse and hay barn, they stopped even with the Bradshaw's house to look and listen. So far, so good. No dogs, no people, no lights on. Probably typical farmers, early to bed, early to rise.

They entered the barn through an open horse stall, stayed low until they got to the inner stall door, then listened. Nothing. Desiree shined her flashlight around inside the barn.

"This concrete floor had to have been put in here within the last twenty years or so," Desiree said softly. "I sure hope *if this is the barn*, the money wasn't actually hidden under the old plank floor that this concrete undoubtedly replaced."

She continued to scan the inside of the barn with her flashlight. On the east end to her right, there was a green, medium-sized John Deere tractor, with a six by ten foot trailer beside it. She noted a couple of wheelbarrows and several bales of straw, off to the right of the tractor. Along the opposite wall from her were various large farm tools, rakes, shovels, leatherworks, and three fifty-five gallon drums, undoubtedly full of grain or miscellaneous supplies.

They opened the stall door and walked into the main barn. To their left were three more stalls on the near side, a tack room directly across from the nearest stall and beyond that a big stack of hay.

"Where would we even begin to look for money in here?" Riva said.

Just then the barn light came on; both women screamed and jumped back toward the stall door. "You won't *begin* to look for money in here anywhere, circus ladies."

They looked to the right where the voice came from, and immediately big, bad Bradshaw stepped from the shadows into the open, carrying a pitchfork in his right hand."

They considered running, but knew he'd probably immediately call the police and maybe catch them at their car, parked across Lost Creek Road on a short dead-end road a hundred yards south of Bradshaw's driveway. For all they knew he or the police already had Desiree's car boxed in there anyway.

Bradshaw walked slowly, deliberately toward them, breathing heavy—like a gorilla in the rut—the pitchfork in his right, baseball-glove-sized hand. The women looked at each other, thought about taking their chances anywhere other than here, but neither could take the first step. They were frozen in fear.

When Bradshaw got to within six feet he stopped, his six-foot-six-inch, humongous frame towering over their slender, five-foot-three and four-inch bodies. He seemed twice as large to them here in the barn as he had outside earlier in the day.

"Maybe you should try working a little of your circus-clown-uncle's magic and see if you can disappear right before my eyes," he said. They thought they saw steam coming from each nostril as he spoke. He stood there, holding the pitchfork with it's four long metal tines facing up, seemingly eager for action.

"I don't want to hear anymore of your stories, ladies. I'll give you one chance to come clean with me." He didn't say what would happen if they didn't, but as their eyes went back and forth between his face and the fork's tines, they had some ideas. And none of them were good.

Riva looked at Desiree, with a pleading look that said, well...

"The guy we were asking about earlier today isn't really our uncle," Desiree said. "But you already had that figured out, didn't you?" He didn't answer. He just stood there with a mean, serious look on his face that said, how's it feel to be standing neck deep in your own do-do?

"The guy we were asking about, Sam Hostick, was my lover and roommate for almost five years, until a few years ago when he left because of health problems. He was old enough to be my father, but I loved him from the day we met. And he loved me." She started crying. Bradshaw figured the tears were just more of her deception.

She went on to tell Bradshaw about Sam growing up on Lost Creek, him dying homeless on the river, her seeing the notice in the Register-Guard and going to the county morgue to claim Sam's body, having him buried, and then all about the hidden money and, finally, the armpit tattoos. When she got to the part about the tattoos, Bradshaw burst out laughing.

"Now I've heard it all," he said. "I suppose he had his nipples pierced too." The women didn't answer. "I'll give you this much, ladies, I could get wealthy off the two of you and your story-telling abilities on any street corner in America. And I wouldn't even have to join the circus like your uncle did. Ha!"

After twenty seconds of belly-laughing, Bradshaw said, "And now you want me to believe that the numbers tattooed under Sam's arms match the address of my place here?"

"That's right," Desiree answered, giving a quick stern look at Riva as a warning to keep her mouth shut and go along with her.

"Here all these thirteen years, my wife and I have lived on a farm that was once owned by a filthy-rich homeless guy who loved the place so much that he tattooed the address in his armpits, and used the walls of the barn for his personal bank. Ha."

Suddenly he stopped laughing and said, "I don't think anyone could make up a story like that and really believe anyone would buy it."

Desiree's face instantly lit up with new hope. "So you believe me?"

"Yes I believe your story. But I seriously doubt there's any money. Why would this Sam, or whoever he really was, die homeless under a bridge on the outskirts of Springfield when he had a pot of gold in some barn on Lost Creek?"

"Oh he had money alright," Desiree said. "My Sam was as honest as the sun is bright."

"Where did he supposedly get all this money?"

"He never told me. I assumed it was from an inheritance or something like that. Will you at least let us look for the money in your barn?"

"Actually I'm not going to handle it that way," Bradshaw said.

"Then *how are* you going to handle it?"

"You want me to just let you tear up my barn looking for money that most likely doesn't even exist, and when you discover there isn't any money, you can say, "Wham, bam, thank you ma'am, and be on your merry little way to try to figure out where else Sam's money might be. Maybe you'll ask to tear out the walls of my house next."

"We would be more than happy to split the money with you when we find it," Riva finally spoke up."

"That's right," Desiree said, "that would only be fair, it being hidden in your barn and all."

Again Bradshaw laughed.

"Maybe I'll just call the police right now and have the two of you hauled off to jail for trespassing. I'd love to hear you tell them your story down at the jail. And then I can find the money and keep it for myself. But I might end up homeless under some bridge too."

"But you seem like a nice guy, a fair guy."

"That's right," Riva chimed in, "We both felt it earlier today." Desiree gave her another one of her looks.

"You *felt* it?" Bradshaw said.

"My sister meant we had good vibes about you earlier," Desiree said.

"I'll be honest with you ladies. I'm going to let you go on your way tonight if you promise me three things."

"No problem."

"First, you won't tell anyone else about your visit here tonight and our little chat. Second, you will give me your telephone number and not come back until I've had a chance to search for the money. And third, we will in fact split the money right down the middle. You ladies get half, and I get half. I figure that I probably never would have learned about the money if you hadn't told me, so therefore you are entitled to half. Does that sound fair?"

"More than fair," Riva said, as both women giggled like a couple of school girls.

"Good, now give me your phone number," Bradshaw said.

"Do you have something to write with out here?"

"I'll get a pen and paper from the tack room." He walked to the room, retrieved the pen and paper and wrote down the number Desiree gave him.

"I'm just curious, Mr. Bradshaw," Desiree said. "How do you intend to search for the money? Are you going to tear each board off the walls?"

"I'll probably do a thorough search for any boards that look like they were put on in such a way to easily be removed. If I don't find the money that way, I'll take a one inch drill and drill a few holes, at different heights, in between each stud on the wall, then look inside with a flashlight for the money."

"Those sound like some good ways to do it, Mr. Bradshaw. We hadn't thought that far ahead yet," Desiree said. "Oh, I just happened to think of one other little detail that you should know concerning the money."

"What's that?"

"There are at least two other parties looking for it. In fact you may have already met one of the parties, two guys named Hodge Gilbert and Shane Coleman. They're supposedly writing a history of the people of Lost Creek Valley, and said they just happened to hear that some guy name Sam Hostick had hidden a lot of money in his old barn out here somewhere."

"You just now remembered to tell me that *little* detail?" he said. "I'm curious, are there any other little details?"

"Yes. Actually there's one more. The other person looking for the money is dangerous and will go to any measure to get the money, including murder."

"How do you know all this?"

"Hodge Gilbert told us," Desiree said. "He said the other guy has already murdered one person."

"I filled out Gilbert and Colemans' survey and talked with them briefly when they stopped by here a week or so ago. So they aren't really writing a history book, but are using that as a cover for trying to find the money?"

"We're not really sure if they're writing a book or not. But we know they are definitely looking for Sam's money, so you have to watch out for them."

"Do they know about the tattoo, and that *this* is where Sam once lived?"

"Not that we're aware of. Obviously, the sooner you can find the money the better."

"I gather that."

The next morning, April 8th, Hodge and Shane on Hwy 58, driving to Lost Creek—

Hodge's cell phone rang at 9:20. He answered, "Hodge,"

"Hodge, this is Desiree, she said with urgency in her voice. "Will you definitely split the money? Not lie about how much you find, and then give us a much smaller cut?"

"Of course. Do you mind if I put this on speaker phone so Shane can hear?"

"No, go ahead." She waited a few seconds, then said, "I wasn't totally candid with you on the phone yesterday."

"How's that?"

"Yesterday morning Riva and I actually stopped at a farm that I'm convinced is where Sam lived when he hid the money. We talked to the land owner; his name was Bradshaw."

"Which place was it?"

"The address is 54916. It's the next to last driveway on the right before you get to the Old Guistina Mill Road."

"Why are you giving me this information now instead of yesterday?"

"I've been thinking about what you said: that it's best to let you and Shane handle things—safer for us."

"That's right."

"I guess you could say, Riva and I have felt more and more afraid the deeper we've got into this search. Some of the people we've talked to gave us some scary vibes."

"Yeah?"

"We want to take a back seat for now and let you guys run the whole show."

"That's fine with us."

"You promise you'll give us our fair share when you find the money?"

"Of course," Hodge said, "You've got nothing to worry about."

"Keep in touch."

"I'll need your phone number."

"Oh yeah. It's 541-746-1887."

"Got it. Talk to you soon."

A minute later, Shane said, "Doesn't it strike you odd that Desiree is suddenly shying away from things?"

"I've seen it before with women when things seem to be getting too heavy for them," Hodge answered. "Can you blame her? She's probably been thinking about the murderer we warned her about, then when she felt she was getting close to the money, got scared. Remember, *I did tell her* the money wouldn't do her any good if she wasn't around to enjoy it."

"Yes you did. I suppose you're right about her just getting cold feet when she felt she was really close. Do you think we're really that close to the money?"

"I don't know about close to the money, but I do believe we have found Sam's old house. Hearing Desiree come to the same conclusion apart from us, and after talking with Bradshaw, could be a good sign for us."

"I'll trust your judgment, Hodge."

"What do you say you and I do a little night-time reconnaissance tonight at the Bradshaw place? Maybe we'll get better vibes than Desiree got there."

"Hodge, I've been meaning to ask you, at what point do you think we ought to start packing pistols?"

"I wouldn't worry about it just yet. When we get close to Ellen Brock's killer we'll definitely want to pack."

"How about we call it a day, go home and get some rest this afternoon? You can pick me up sometime after dark." Shane said.

"I'll be at your place at 10 pm."

23

Ambushed

Hodge parked his SUV in the same out of the way pull off where Desiree had parked her car the night before, though he didn't know it. As he and Shane made their way in the dark, with their mini-maglites adjusted to dim, along the three-rail wooden fence on the north side of Bradshaws' horse pasture, they had no idea that Desiree and Riva had traveled that exact path the night before. The sawdust that Bradshaw had recently spread with his tractor along the inside of the fence ensured the women had left no tracks. Had Hodge and Shane observed the women's tracks, they might have figured something was amiss.

When the two men reached the horse barn, Hodge led the way in through the stall next to the one the women had used. After stopping and listening for several seconds, Hodge adjusted his mini-maglite to full power and did a quick scan of the inside of the barn.

"Let's stay together," Hodge said. We'll start down here along the right wall and search for any boards that look like they may not be permanent. I'll take the lower half of the walls, and you take the top half. That will help us focus easier."

Hodge led the way past the last stall on his right and began inspecting the inner wall of the barn. Shane moved along a few feet behind him as they gradually covered the twenty feet to the corner of the barn. From there they began examining the ten-foot high wall boards on the east side of the barn, got to the open doorway to the sawdust storage room and moved past it in the dark.

As Shane came across the opening, suddenly a huge figure burst from the darkness, tackled him to the floor, and started wailing on his head with his fists, as he struggled to try to get out from under the man's weight. Hodge inadvertently dropped his flashlight in his haste to jump on top of the man. He attempted to pull one of the man's arms behind his back, but it was no use; he was too big. It had to be Bradshaw.

Shane groaned as he covered his head with both arms, at the same time trying to elevate his hips to bounce the heavy man off him. Hodge began pounding on the sides of the giant's head as he wrapped his legs around his mid-section. All of them huffed and grunted as they struggled in the dark.

Hodge's blows to the giant's head seemed to have no effect, as he yelled, "You big bastard!"

Finally the big man stood up and heaved his right elbow into Hodge's chest. The impact knocked Hodge backward several feet and forced a huge burst of air from his lungs. For several seconds, he felt like he was going to pass out from the pain and sudden loss of oxygen from his diaphragm. He staggered for ten seconds trying to catch a breath. Finally it came. He sucked in some fresh air, took another big breath, and charged the man's waist in the darkness. At the same time, Shane managed to turn to face his attacker and charged him as well. Bradshaw wrapped his huge arms around Shane's belly and elevated his legs several feet off the ground, while Shane groaned from the strength of his grip around his middle.

Bradshaw held Shane in the air effortlessly, oblivious to Hodge's attempts to take him to the floor. The giant swung Shane around trying to knock Hodge off him, but was unsuccessful. He tried again, but did no better. Finally, he let Shane back down, released his grip around his belly and began slamming his huge fists into Shane's sides.

Shane groaned from the pain and gasped for air; he knew he was losing it fast. He let go of the giant, quickly backed away from him, taking a blow to the left side of his head in the process. He knew if he passed out now, they were both dead. There was no way Hodge could beat Bradshaw by himself.

He wished he had ignored Hodge's words that morning when he said there was no need to bring a pistol yet. He wanted one desperately now. But even at that, in the complete darkness, he couldn't have shot at Bradshaw anyway because he might hit Hodge. And how would it look to the law that he shot and killed Bradshaw in his own barn while he and Hodge were trespassing there in the middle of the night?

He inhaled a couple lung-fulls of oxygen, moved to the right and charged into the outside of Bradshaw's left knee. Somehow, between Shane and Hodge they got him to the floor and began wailing on his head and body. Nothing they did to him seemed to faze him, as he continued to breath hard and grunt, working to get back up.

Soon Bradshaw got his knees under him and, using his massive arms, rose up to the kneeling position, as both continued their fruitless onslaught. Once to his knees, Bradshaw raised his torso and grabbed hold of Shane around the midsection again and began squeezing as hard as he could while Hodge pounded away on his head and upper body. Hodge accidentally hit Shane in the face in the darkness and bloodied his nose. Shane tried to tell Hodge he hit the wrong guy, but all of his oxygen was gone; he couldn't speak. His head began spinning; he thought his ribs would break any second.

Just then Hodge yelled at Bradshaw, "Let go of him now you big bastard, or I'll shoot you." Hodge drove the barrel of the Smith and Wesson 4003 that he had pulled from the back of his jeans, firmly into Bradshaw's neck below the left side of his jaw.

Bradshaw continued to squeeze, thinking about making a quick grab for the gun. Shane couldn't believe Hodge actually had a gun and wondered if he was using something else to bluff Bradshaw. But Bradshaw held tight preventing Shane from taking in the oxygen his body was starving for. Shane grew dizzier by the second.

"Let go of him now, Bradshaw. I mean it!"

He held for a few more seconds, then suddenly eased his grasp. Shane sucked in hard and coughed several times, then backed away from Bradshaw. He took several more breaths and felt his strength returning.

Hodge said, "Now get down on your belly, Bradshaw."

Bradshaw didn't move. "This is my barn!"

"Get down on your belly now!"

Bradshaw complied.

"Where's the light switch in this damn barn?" Hodge asked, breathing hard and fast.

"There's one just to the left of the opening I came through."

Shane probed for the wall in the dark, found it, then felt for the opening to the storage room. He found it and slipped his hand around until he contacted a switch. The lights at the near end of the barn came on.

Ahead of Hodge and Bradshaw was the John Deere tractor with the trailer beside it.

In the light, Hodge and Shane looked at each other to assess the damage. Hodge noticed Shane's bloody nose immediately, and said, "Your nose is bleeding, Shane."

Shane pulled his shirt up to his nose and held it there to stop the bleeding. He had a big welt on the left side of his face and a large knot behind his left ear. He thought he might have some cracked ribs. During the fight he hadn't noticed just how beat up he was. Now his whole upper body ached.

Hodge felt his own face for any cuts, but found none. Then he tasted blood; the inside of his mouth was cut. His chest hurt like the dickens from the elbow Bradshaw gave him, and he had a scrape on his left forearm that was bleeding. Other than that he wasn't hurt too bad.

While Bradshaw continued to lie motionless on his belly, with Hodge continuing to point his S and W at his torso, Hodge said, "You were laying for us, weren't you?"

"I didn't know if you'd come tonight or not, but knew it would be soon."

"It was the girls that stopped by here yesterday morning, that tipped you off, wasn't it?"

"Yes."

"I sure would've liked to have heard that conversation," Shane said.

"Me too," Hodge added.

"You guys are trespassing, and now you're holding me hostage. If my wife heard any of this and called the cops, you guys are going to be in deep crap."

"Maybe, maybe not," Hodge said. But he knew they would sure force his hand.

"I don't understand. Aren't you guys here to look for Sam Hostick's money?"

"What do you know about Sam?" Shane asked.

"I only know that name because those women came here yesterday morning asking about their Uncle Sam Hostick. They said he was holding a large sum of inheritance money for them, and that he was supposed to be living here."

"Trust me, he isn't their uncle," Hodge said. "In fact he isn't anybody's uncle. And if he ever was, he's not anymore. He's dead."

"I learned all that last night."

"Last night?" Shane asked.

"The girls were here last night, and I ambushed them."

"I talked to Desiree on the phone this morning, and she didn't sound beat up," Hodge said. "She didn't say anything about coming here last night."

"Can I sit up?" Bradshaw asked. "I'm sixty-three years old, and don't do so well laying face down on a hard surface like this."

"You can sit up against that tractor tire." Hodge motioned toward the right rear tire with his gun.

Bradshaw slowly got to his hands and knees, then crawled the ten feet to the tractor tire and sat with his back up against it.

"I didn't ambush the girls like I did you guys."

"That's nice to know," Shane said. "For an old guy, you are one big, tough, mean, son of a gun."

"No old guy about it," Hodge said. "Just plain big, tough, mean son of a gun."

"I used to wrestle and play football for the Oklahoma Sooners, 1964-68."

"I bet you played water boy," Shane said.

"And wrestled feather weight,'" Hodge added. They all chuckled. Shane didn't dare laugh as sore as his ribs were.

"I played nose guard at Oklahoma, where I got the nickname Monster Bradshaw, then played several years in the NFL as defensive tackle for a couple different teams. Never started regularly there, but saw quite a bit of action."

"I guess we picked the wrong barn to sneak into tonight," Shane said, looking at the bloody shirt he gripped in his left hand, while gently massaging his bruised chest and stomach with the right. "If Hodge hadn't pulled the pistol when he did, I'm sure you would have broken every rib in my body, then probably killed the both of us. Hodge is an ex-police officer with the Multnomah Sheriff's Department. Now he's a private investigator."

"Who are you working for?" Bradshaw asked. "There's a lot more to this case than the girls told me, isn't there? And you're not really writing a history of the people of Lost Creek Valley, are you?"

Hodge put his pistol back in it's holder on the back of his belt, then said, "Actually we're working for ourselves. And *I am* writing a history, at least if this case works out like I hope it does."

"What does this Sam Hostick, or whatever his name is, who

supposedly lived here in the past, have to do with your case? Did he really hide a lot of money in this or some other barn?"

"Go ahead, Shane, you fill him in on everything," Hodge said. "It all started out as your baby anyway."

"Two months ago, I was running my fur trapping line on the McKenzie River near Springfield when…" Shane went on to explain to Bradshaw the basic details about Sam, Ellen Brock, Desiree, the money and the likelihood that the killer is still alive in the Lost Creek Valley somewhere and they intend to find him.

When Shane finished, Bradshaw explained more of what he and the girls had talked about.

"So the girls are only in it for the money, know nothing about the girl killed in the bean field, have no idea why you guys are really up here, and probably don't believe their lives could be in serious danger," Bradshaw said.

"That's about the gist of it," Hodge said. "Other than they obviously deliberately set us up with you. That's why Desiree called me this morning. She knew whether it was tonight or some other night, you would confront us, probably get the law to pick us up for criminal trespass at the minimum, and possibly even breaking, entering, burglary and vandalism among other things. Her competition for the money would have been out of the picture."

"She probably figured I would pull a shotgun or something on you, and never considered the possibility that I'd handle it like I did, and one or more of us would end up dead."

"Maybe that's exactly what she figured might happen," Hodge said. "You said you and the girls agreed to split the money in half. Maybe she didn't want to share the money with you anymore than she wanted to share it with us."

"I'm liking and trusting Desiree and her sister less and less," Shane said. "And I'm beginning to understand why Sam probably didn't want anymore to do with her."

"Me too," Hodge said. "She's turning out to be a manipulative little witch."

"Are you guys going to tell her about our run-in tonight?" Bradshaw asked.

"How about if we don't?" Hodge suggested. "Let's neither of us contact her. Let her get impatient and try to contact one or the other of us."

"I'm not up for looking for the money tonight," Bradshaw said, "but do you guys want to come back in a few days after we've all had a chance to heal a little?"

"That sounds good to me," Shane said. "I'm sure I won't be much good for several days."

"Waiting is fine with me," Hodge said. "But to be perfectly honest, I don't expect to find any money here, and maybe not anywhere."

"But the girls seemed pretty sure it was here," Bradshaw said, a bit disappointed.

"If this turns out to be the house and barn where Sam Hostick grew up, I seriously doubt the money would be here. But it's possible some other clue to Ellen Brock's murder could be."

"I don't understand," Shane said. "You've said there's no way the killer would have kept Ellen's shirt. What other clues or evidence could be here?"

"Probably none. But we'll know that when we have a chance to search the barn."

The men talked a little longer, and then Monster Bradshaw drove Hodge and Shane out the long driveway and up Lost Creek Road to Hodge's SUV.

When Shane walked into the master bedroom at home, Marlene sensed something was wrong with him at once. She hadn't been able to sleep and had been praying for his safety.

She immediately turned on the lamp on her side of the bed, and observed his swollen face.

"Honey, what happened to you? You look like a truck ran over you."

"A monster truck," he said. "We ran into Monster Bradshaw and he beat the tar out of us."

"Oh, honey." She wanted to take him in her arms, but saw the blood on his shirt and that he was obviously favoring his upper body, and instead said, "Sit down here on the bed. I'll get some ice packs and wet a couple towels."

He carefully sat down on his side of the bed. He wouldn't be taking a shower tonight.

When she got back to the bedroom, she gave him three Advil tablets and a cup of water to drink them down, and then went to work nursing him. She helped him get his jacket and shirt off.

"Oh," he groaned, "could you go a bit lighter on those ribs."

"How did this happen? You told me you guys were just going to check out a barn."

"You really don't want to know how this happened, sweetie. It was a misunderstanding between me, Hodge and a guy they call 'Monster Bradshaw.' As you can see, we found out the hard way why they nicknamed him Monster." He wasn't about to tell her how close she came to becoming a widow. Or that when she went down to the county morgue to identify him, she would have thought they mistook a fence post for her husband.

"How bad was Hodge hurt?"

"Not as bad as me. He's got a pretty sore chest. He managed to stay behind Monster most the time. But not all is lost, Monster's our buddy now, and he's going to help us on the Sam Hostick-Ellen Brock case."

"You men sure have a strange way of making new friends— fighting with them first."

"That's why we always called Hodge, 'junk-yard dog.' He never walked away from a chance to fight."

"Next time, tell him to do it when you're not around, okay?"

24

Double Crossed?

Two days later, mid-afternoon, Saturday, April 10th, Lost Creek Road—

Desiree Lebron and her sister, Riva, had grown impatient with both Mr. Bradshaw and Hodge Gilbert for not returning any of Desiree's phone calls.

Consequently, Desiree and Riva decided to drive up Lost Creek and see if they could find out what was going on. As they were about to go past Cambell Ritchey's driveway, Cam was waiting to pull his old, green, Chevy pickup out onto Lost Creek Road. When Desiree recognized the waiting truck as the one parked at his place a week earlier, she suddenly hit the brakes. "That's the Vietnam vet we talked to last week. Maybe he'll talk to us today, since he's obviously not in the middle of a project on his place."

She pulled off at the head of his driveway and stopped directly in front of him, blocking his path.

"What are you doing, Desiree?" Riva said. "He made it perfectly clear that he didn't want to talk to us. I thought you were convinced Sam's money was in that Bradshaw guy's barn."

"I'm not convinced of anything. I just want to try to talk to this guy one more time."

Desiree shoved the transmission into park, then got out of her car and walked part way around it to get to Ritchey's truck.

About that time, Ritchey looked at Riva inside the passenger's side of the car, and realized who was blocking his way. He immediately jumped out and yelled at Desiree as she walked toward him, "Lady, if you don't want serious trouble, you need to get right back in your car and get the hell out of here!"

Desiree quickly did an about face, ran back around her car, got in, burned rubber and threw gravel on Ritchey's truck getting away.

They then drove on up the creek until they reached Delvin Bradshaw's driveway, where they made the right hand turn and drove into his place. When they pulled up at the backside of the house, where they could see the horse barn and other out buildings, Desiree said, "For being such a beautiful Saturday, there doesn't seem to be any activity around here. Maybe he's working in the barn."

"Why don't we go to the house first," Riva suggested.

They did, and no one answered the door. The women then walked to the barn and went inside, but found no one there or anywhere else around the place. The horses were grazing out in the middle of the pasture they had snuck through a few nights earlier. From what they could determine, all the vehicles that were present on their previous daytime visit were still there: a newer-model, red Ford pickup, an older green Ford one-ton flatbed truck and a couple of newer cars.

They knocked on the front door of the house a final time, with no luck, then left.

"I don't understand why Bradshaw hasn't returned any of my phone calls," Desiree said. "And now they're not even home when we stop by."

Just before Desiree turned her car left onto Lost Creek Road, she dialed Hodge's number on her cell phone. He *still* didn't answer.

"This is too frustrating."

Riva said, "Maybe there was an accident or—"

"Or what?"

"Some kind of serious confrontation and everyone is in the hospital or worse... I didn't see any blood in the barn, but maybe it happened somewhere else. Of course, we weren't looking for blood when we were in the barn or anywhere else on the property. You should have thought about that when you set Hodge and Shane up like you did, knowing Bradshaw would be waiting for them."

"I figured he would just confront them with a shotgun or something and get the police to take them away."

"Maybe you figured wrong and they were all hauled away in an ambulance or hearse."

"Well Bradshaw's wife should have at least answered the phone or been there today—"

"Unless she's at the hospital or a funeral service. We better go to the library and look in the Register-Guard for the past couple days to see if we can learn anything about them."

"Maybe Bradshaw double-crossed us and is actually in cahoots with Hodge and Shane. Maybe they're all out at some fancy restaurant enjoying an expensive dinner with our money."

"It did seem too easy, didn't it," Riva said, "the way he agreed to split the money with us. Why should he have agreed to give us any of the money? We were trespassing on his property, and had already lied to him several times."

"I've got a bad feeling about all of this right now," Desiree said. "I don't believe there was an accident or a confrontation. I bet old man Bradshaw got on the phone first thing the next morning and conspired with them."

"I bet that's exactly what happened, Sis. We've been screwed."

They continued driving north on Lost Creek Road, headed down the creek.

When they reached Eagle's Rest Bridge and came out of the hair pin corner there, all at once, Desiree stomped down on the gas pedal. The little Pontiac went from twenty-five to sixty in no time at all.

"Slow down, Sis. Why are you going so fast?" Riva yelled.

The Pontiac hit eighty as they were nearing the last couple hundred yards of the straight stretch in front of the old Johnson house on their right.

"I'm so angry!" Desiree said, her hands clutching the steering wheel with a death grip.

"Slow down now, or we'll never make the corner."

Desiree braked hard, but not too hard, just as they passed the last house on the right and reached the short section of road bordered by small fir groves on either side.

Just before they went into the sharp left-hand corner, with their speed still too fast, about fifty, but coming down quickly, a long-haired man wearing a ball cap that shaded his face, jumped up out of the left ditch holding a shotgun. He took three quick steps into the left lane, and pointed the barrel directly into the windshield of Desiree's car that was almost to him, in the other lane.

"That man has a gun, Sis! He's pointing it *at us!*" Riva yelled. "Do something!"

Desiree rammed the brake pedal, and turned the steering wheel hard to the right. Too hard. The car jagged right, and then Desiree overcorrected, pulling hard to the left. The car veered back to the left, then the passenger side tires caught on the pavement. The car immediately rolled over multiple times to its right, down the highway. There was a terrible crashing noise of metal on pavement, and glass breaking, spreading all over the highway. The car rolled over the gravel embankment on the right side of the turn, kicking up a huge dust cloud, then came to a stop in an upright position in Lost Creek. The creek's cold water flowed against the back of the car and down the right side, almost to the top of the passenger-side tires, and began seeping through the doors.

There was moaning and groaning inside the Pontiac, but no

movement.

The man, carrying the shotgun, ran down the embankment as the dust cloud began to settle, and made his way quickly down the bedrock bank to the car. He peered in and saw both women with their faces cut up and bleeding. There was blood all over the front of them, neither of them was moving, though they continued to groan.

Then Desiree, whose head was resting on the jagged glass of the door, opened her eyes and saw the man next to the car, holding the shotgun, staring at her through the broken driver's window.

"Help," she managed to whisper.

The man heard gurgling in her chest as she coughed weakly a couple times, then closed her eyes. He waited several seconds for her to open her eyes again, but she didn't. Nor did she cough anymore. He felt her neck for a pulse, but there was nothing. She was dead.

He looked over at Riva and observed her chest rising and falling sporadically. He considered shooting her to finish her off, but decided against it. They would know it was a homicide. Police and detectives would flood the Lost Creek Valley looking for the perpetrator. No way he wanted that.

Riva's breathing became more labored and shallow. She was near death. The man quickly ran away from the car on the bedrock along the creek's south bank, then disappeared in the stand of fir seventy-five yards from the Pontiac.

Kent Simons and his dad, Doc, were in their backyard several hundred yards from the crash. Kent was trying to get the lawn mower started. They suddenly heard a horrendous scraping and crunching of metal out on Lost Creek Road.

"Did you hear that, Dad?" Kent asked, as they both stood up and looked toward the road. But their view was blocked by the house.

"It sounded like a car wreck," Doc said.

Kent hustled to the back fence, swung himself over it, then took off jogging to the east, down his driveway, in the direction the sound had come from. When he got to Lost Creek Road, he observed a dust cloud settling at the north edge of the road, three hundred yards away. He immediately broke into a sprint, anxious about what he might find when he reached the cloud.

In a minute he was at the edge of the road where the Pontiac went over. Breathing hard, he looked around, and noticed a couple people walking quickly toward him down the road from the south. Standing on the gravel shoulder of the road, he searched for the car, but couldn't see it. He quickly hiked down the embankment, reached the top of the stream bank, and peered over. There in the water below him was a blue older model Pontiac. He could see someone inside the car on the driver's side, which was toward him. He immediately pulled his cell phone from its holder on his belt and dialed 911 to report the accident, and talked with the dispatcher as he descended the last twenty feet to reach the car.

"There are two women in the front seat, both covered in blood," he reported. He felt the driver's neck for a pulse, but found none. "The driver is dead, but the passenger is still alive, though she's really struggling to breathe."

"Miss. Miss, can you hear me?" Kent said. No answer. "The passenger appears to be unconscious. The whole car is badly crushed. I'm sure they'll need the Jaws of Life to extricate the passenger. They better hurry; the creek water is several inches deep inside the car already."

Other people arrived at the top of the creek bank momentarily and were talking and pointing toward the car and back toward the road from where it had rolled.

The Dexter fire department arrived within ten minutes, followed shortly by a state trooper and a sheriff deputy. Fifteen minutes later an ambulance arrived. Riva was still alive, though barely, when they took her away in the ambulance twenty-five minutes after the fire department arrived and used the Jaws of Life to get access to her.

When one of the medics retrieved Desiree and Rivas' drivers' licenses from their purses, they discovered that they both had multiple ID's. He read the various names aloud. Kent was shocked to learn the women were Desiree Lebron and her sister. He immediately called Shane on his cell phone.

Marlene answered, and told Kent that Shane was lying down. When she asked Kent if she could take a message, Shane overheard Kent's name, and said, "Marlene, it's okay. If it's Kent, I'll talk to him. I'll take it on the phone in here. He picked up the cordless phone, whose ringer had been turned off earlier by Marlene, so Shane could get some much-needed sleep.

"Hi Kent. What's going on?"

"Shane, you'll never believe what just happened."

"What?"

"There was a roll-over car accident a quarter mile up the road from my place. Two women were in the car, one of them was killed and the other one will probably die before they get her to the hospital. It was Desiree Lebron and her sister, Riva."

"You're kidding me."

"No, I'm not."

"Which one was killed?"

"Desiree."

"Oh no. Here Hodge and I have been warning her that she could end up killed by Ellen Brock's killer, and she dies in a car accident instead."

"I thought you never told her about Ellen Brock."

"We didn't, we told her the dangerous person was someone looking for Sam's money. I can't believe she's dead. I'm just numb from this."

"Tell me about it. I won't be able to get the scene out of my mind for a long time—maybe never."

"Thanks for calling, Kent. I'm going to call Hodge and tell him. I'll talk to you later."

Shane explained what had happened to Marlene, who was sitting on the bed. She immediately went to praying, asking for God's grace and mercy on Desiree, and for Riva's recovery.

When she finished her prayer, Shane called Hodge and told him what happened.

That evening, over the phone—

"Delvin (Monster Bradshaw), this is Hodge Gilbert. I've got some very bad news for you. The two women from your place the other day, Desiree and Riva, were involved in a car accident a few miles below your place on Lost Creek Road."

"They were in that accident today?"

"Yes. Desiree was dead at the scene. Riva is in critical care at McKenzie Willamette (Hospital in Springfield).

"That's tragic. I don't know what to say," Delvin Bradshaw said. "Do you know what caused the accident?"

"No. I'm hearing that speed may have been a factor, but they're still investigating it."

"Has Riva been able to talk?"

"No. Apparently she's been unconscious since it happened. She's really banged up, broken ribs, a punctured lung, concussion, broken bones in one of her shoulders, and numerous gashes, cuts, and bruises on her face, arms and torso. It was a rollover crash. The best estimate says their car rolled over at least four times. Both women were wearing lap belts."

"My gosh, she's lucky to be alive," Bradshaw said. "I wonder if my not returning Desiree's phone calls had anything to do with why they were out this way in the first place."

"I wouldn't put anymore meaning on it than you have to," Hodge said. "Even if they were up there to try to talk to you, you're not to blame for their accident."

"I know that, but I can't help but feel a little responsible."

"That's understandable, but you weren't driving the car. None of it is your fault."

"Thanks. How are you guys doing with your wounds?"

"My chest and head are pretty sore, but I'm doing better than

Shane. He's a hurting unit. You really worked him over."

"I guess I did, didn't I," Bradshaw conceded. "Maybe I should have hung a sign outside the barn that said something like, 'Don't cross this line unless you are desperate to get your butt kicked.'"

"Well you sure kicked ours," Hodge said. "I'll get back to you early next week to figure out a time to come over to search your barn. *Actually*, I'm comfortable with you doing the search without us being there, if you want to."

"I'm going to take it easy for another couple days myself. You guys got some good blows in on me. I'm not in my twenties anymore."

"That makes me feel a little more like a man, knowing we did a little damage."

"I guess some of us kids never grow up, do we, Hodge?"

"No we don't, Monster. I'll be in touch."

25

Accident Follow Up

At McKenzie-Willamette Hospital, Springfield, April 13th, three days after the accident, eighteen hours after Riva awakened from unconsciousness—

The pretty, young, red-headed nurse said, "You can see her now," to Hodge, who was waiting outside Room 113, in the Critical Care Unit. "You'll have to keep it brief; we're making an exception just letting you go in there." The nurse had already informed Hodge that Riva had been told about her sister, Desiree's death.

"Thanks," Hodge said to the nurse, "I'll only be a few minutes."

With a solemn look on his face, Hodge walked into the dimly lit room and up to the right side of Riva's bed, near her stomach, gently touched her left hand and said softly, "How are you doing, Riva?"

"Not so good," she answered so weakly that Hodge had to strain to understand her.

He stood silent for ten seconds, then said, "I'm deeply sorry about Desiree—"

"I know; I am too. I already miss her terribly." As she lay

motionless on the bed—most of her body covered by a white sheet and several white blankets, in a horizontal position with her torso raised a few inches and her head resting on a pillow—her eyes got wet and leaked a few tears down the sides of her face, past her ear lobes. With her arms immobilized, she was unable to wipe them. Her neck and right shoulder were in a brace. She had various tubes and hoses hooked up to her arms and hands, and an oxygen tube going into each nostril. Her face was badly bruised and swollen. Much of it was covered with bandages. An IV bag, dripped fluid slowly into a hose that ran down to a needle taped to her left forearm. A monitor at the top of the IV pole, with numerous gauges and dim lights, beeped a soft steady pulse.

"The hospital official that called me said you asked me to come in. She said you told her you had no family, and I was the closest thing to family you had, now that your sister is gone."

"Yes."

"I'm so sorry for what's happened to you. And I take it as a great compliment that you called me in and said those kind words to the hospital staff."

"It's okay," she said, barely above a whisper. She looked at him for several seconds, neither of them speaking, then she said, "There was a man in the road."

"A man in the road?"

"Yes. He caused the accident."

"The man walked into the path of your car?"

"No. He came out of the ditch and stood in the opposite lane as we approached. He had a long gun. It looked like a shotgun."

"The man in the road had a gun in his hand?"

"Yes," she coughed a couple times. "Could you give me an ice cube?"

Hodge used the spoon that was in the ice container next to the bed to feed her a single cylindrical-shaped ice cube. She sucked on it for nearly a minute until it was gone. The nurse stuck her head through the open, wide doorway and asked, "How is she doing?"

"She's doing okay," Hodge answered.

The nurse left.

"The man pointed the gun directly at the windshield. Desiree turned the steering wheel hard to the right and almost lost control of the car, but then she overcorrected back to the left, causing us to roll."

"Have you talked to the police yet?"

"Yes."

"Did you tell them about the man?"

"No. When the police woman was in here, I was pretty confused. She asked about the accident, if I remembered what happened, what caused it."

"And you didn't mention the guy with the gun?"

"No. I'm not up to answering a bunch of follow up questions for the police right now. And now that I've had a chance to think a little about it, I'm not so sure I *should* tell the police about him."

"Why is that?"

"Because I think it is the man you warned Desiree about—the other guy who is looking for the money."

"Why do you think that?"

"Just after the car came to a stop in the creek, he came to the window right next to Desiree's head. He was holding the gun. I was semi-conscious, but I saw him approach the car out of the corner of my eye, then closed my eyes and prayed silently for him not to shoot us."

"You're sure the guy with the gun came down to the car and looked in?"

"Yes. I could hear him breathing pretty hard. I think he must have run down off the highway. When Desiree said, 'Help,' he didn't say anything. He just stood there breathing hard. Then I passed out. When I woke up, I was here. That was last night. They said I had been unconscious for two days. Do you think I should tell the police?"

"I can't tell you what to say to the police," Hodge said. "But I *will* tell you this. If the police learn about the man with the gun it will open up a can of worms with them and the press, not to mention the huge investigation they'll do. And if they find out that there might be money in that barn or another, they'll figure Sam had to have stolen it from someone. Then everything we've been working on will go down the drain. We won't ever have a say about anything that goes on with Sam's money or anything else again. I'm sure you've had a run-in or two with the police over the years. You know how it can be."

"Yes, I do," she said. "For now, I'm not going to mention the man. I'll just tell them, Desiree was going too fast and lost control. She *was* going too fast."

"Did you get a good look at the man? Good enough to be able to identify him if you saw him again?"

"No. He was wearing a hat and his face was shaded when he was on the road. It all happened so fast. And when he walked up to the car... like I said, it was out of the corner of my eye, and I immediately closed my eyes. But I did notice he had long hair."

"That's great," Hodge said. "Do you remember how big he was?"

"He seemed pretty big at the time, but maybe that was partly because of how scared I was, and how fast everything happened."

"That's understandable. I'm going to let you alone so you can get some rest now, but I will check back every day if you want me to."

"Please do. Thanks for coming today."

Hodge rubbed her forearm once, and then left.

In the hospital parking lot a few minutes later, Hodge on the phone with Kent Simons—

"Kent, I just came from Riva's hospital room. She said the accident was caused when a long-haired man with a shotgun suddenly came up out of the ditch and pointed the gun at their windshield. Desiree turned the car away from him, then overcorrected, causing the car to roll."

"A man pointed his gun at them?" Kent said. "I didn't see anyone around when I got over there; he could have ducked back into the woodlots on either side of the road. No one would have even looked for him, because nobody thought it was anything but an accident. I had to run from the back of my place to the corner where their car went over; that's about four hundred yards. Do you have any ideas on who it might have been?"

"It had to be someone the women have talked to, or someone connected to someone they've talked to in their quest to find Sam's old place, or the money. We all know they used the Sam-was-their-uncle line several times. I never believed anyone would try to kill them, or intimidate them over Sam's money."

"But if someone figured out who Sam really was," Kent said, "and decided that you and the girls were actually out in the valley to look into Sam's connection to Ellen Brock, then taking the women out of the investigation through intimidation or murder is a very real possibility."

"That's why we warned the girls to let us handle things—not only for their own protection, but to keep the case from being spoiled."

Kent was beginning to think maybe he was the weak link that had talked about the wrong things to the wrong people, but he wasn't about to mention that to Hodge. Not yet anyway. He would try to figure things out himself first.

"And since the girls didn't heed your warning, one of them is dead, the other one is in serious condition, and you and Shane got your butts kicked," Kent said. "Makes a guy wonder how much worse it's going to get before it's over."

"The butt kicking wasn't related to what happened to the girls. But if this is any indication, it could get plenty worse, Kent. If you want to drop out of the case *anytime*, I wouldn't blame you."

"I'm in it for the long haul, Hodge—especially now."

"I'm going to call Shane up now and tell him what I've learned. I wanted to call you first to see if you could go out to the woodlots and look for boot prints."

"That's exactly what I'm going to do. If I find some, do you want me to call you?"

"Absolutely. I'll bring what I need to take some plaster impressions."

As soon as he got off the phone with Hodge, Kent walked from his house over to the area surrounding the car accident. Fortunately for him, it hadn't rained since the accident. Even if he found prints, they really wouldn't be able to tie them to the accident because of the elapsed time since then. If they had known to look for the man immediately following the accident, the prints definitely could have been helpful.

Thanks to the damp April ground, Kent, did in fact find several boot prints from the same set of boots in two different areas. He found four complete tracks and several partials in the woodlot on the west side of Lost Creek Road around the corner from his house, on the side where the man came up out of the ditch. The other prints, which were partials, were upstream seventy yards from where the car ended up, right where the dirt bank met the bedrock along the creek.

He knew right where he was headed next, though he wondered why an experienced woodsman and combat vet wouldn't have been more careful about leaving any tracks.

Kent parked his car at the end of Cambell Ritchey's driveway, and walked in. He was hoping to catch him outside, where he could possibly see some of his fresh boot tracks.

Luck was with him. Cam was doing something near one of the sheds behind his house. Kent had to be careful that Cam didn't catch him studying his tracks. When he got to within thirty feet, Cam—who was standing with a shovel in his hand—noticed him, turned, and said, "Kent, what brings you back so soon?"

"Hey, Cam, what are you working on?" Kent said as he closed to within five feet and glanced around for tracks. He immediately spotted a few fresh tracks from Cam's boots in some mud at the front of the shed. He was relieved to find they didn't match the ones at the scene. He knew it was possible Cam had worn a different set of boots, but the prints he spotted at the shed were at least a few sizes smaller than those near the accident scene.

"I had a family of raccoons move in under this shed the last week. I'm trying to figure out whether to trap them, or just let them be."

"Raccoons? If it was me and they weren't bothering anything, I'd probably leave them alone."

"I've thought about catching them so I could smoke them up. They make excellent jerky."

"Yes, they do," Kent agreed. "I shot a few with my bow years ago. Spot-lighted them. You almost never see a 'coon during the day. I think they're one of the most nocturnal animals I've ever seen."

"I think you're right about that," Cam said. "I heard there was a car accident down near your place a few days ago. Anyone hurt?"

Kent knew he had to be very careful how he talked about the accident. The last thing he wanted to do was alienate Cam. His suspicion that Cam could have been the man in the road had already proven unfounded. Yet something told him, Cam was somehow connected. He just wasn't sure how.

"I was home when it happened. My dad and I were in the backyard and heard a terrible crash. I ran over as fast as I could. When I got there, I found two women in a Pontiac that was sitting upright partially in Lost Creek. The driver was dead, and the other one was in very bad shape."

"That's a shame."

"It was the same two women that have been talking to a lot of different people on the creek here about an older man that they're supposedly related too." Kent noticed some recognition on Cam's face, so he asked, "In the last month or so did those women happen to come to your place?"

"Yes, a couple weeks ago they did, but they only stayed a few minutes. I made it clear that I couldn't help them, and that they could leave immediately and not come back."

"And you never saw them after that?"

"No. They never came back to my place. Did the other woman live?"

Kent studied Cam's face to see if there was any deception on it, but it had returned to its normal deadpan expression. "Yes," he said, "but she's still in critical care."

"Is she conscious, or in a coma? Do *they think* she's going to live?"

Cam's interest surprised Kent. "She's conscious."

"Has she been able to say what caused the accident?"

"She said her sister was going too fast coming into the corner."

"And now she's dead. That's too bad. Hopefully the other one will make a full recovery."

"Let's hope so."

Something about Cam's interest and questions didn't add up for Kent. But maybe he was just looking for something that wasn't there.

"I don't know if you remember that Tommy Coleman's dad, Buck, used to be the postal carrier out here." Cam said.

"Yeah, now that you mention, I remember that."

"Shane Coleman said that one of your cousins, Scott Welker, used to be the postmaster. You never mentioned that to me before, that he was related to you I mean."

"Why would I have?" Cam said, obviously irritated. "Why are you bringing that up now, of all times? Where did Shane Coleman hear that anyway?"

"I guess Bessie Rogers told him and Hodge Gilbert when they were talking to her about the history of Lost Creek Valley."

"I should have guessed. That's one old lady I can't say I miss."

"It's true then, that Welker is your cousin?"

"Yes."

"Whatever happened to him after he retired? Does he still live out here somewhere, or did he move away? Word has it that he was forced out of the postmaster position."

"Look Kent, I appreciate our friendship. But I *don't* appreciate you wanting to discuss my family heritage or any of my relatives. I don't ask about your family, relatives, or anyone else's family."

"No you don't. You don't ask about much of anything, and that's perfectly okay with me. It's just that there's been a rumor started lately around the valley that your cousin the postmaster picked in the bean field at the same time Ellen Brock was murdered. Is that true?"

"We're done here Kent. I told you I didn't want to talk about that girl again…" Then realizing what Kent had just asked, Cam got angry and said, "What are you getting at anyway?"

"I'm not getting at anything. I'm just trying to clear up some details that have come up in Shane Coleman's research for the history book they're working on."

"What are you, Coleman's lackey?"

"No, I'm not anyone's lackey? But they want the history book to be as accurate as possible, and they know that I'm your friend. They saw your no trespassing signs and respected them. That's more than you can say for some people, including those two women."

"Maybe it is, but I've got nothing to add to their history book. It sounds like it's just going to be a gossip book anyway."

"The murder of Ellen Brock *was part* of the history of the Lost Creek Valley, and they are devoting a section of their book to it. They just want to get the details correct, and thought maybe if your cousin actually worked in the field when she was killed, he might be able to clarify some of the details."

"Next time I hear from him, whenever that is, I'll pass that along."

"I'd appreciate that. I better leave you to yourself now. I'll talk to you later."

"Not as long as you're Coleman's lackey."

After leaving Cam's, Kent called Hodge and told him about the boot prints he'd found near the accident scene. Hodge wasted no time getting over to Kent's. From there they walked to the sites where Kent observed the boot prints. Hodge snapped some photos of the tracks, then took some plaster impressions. He said if it came down to it later, he could show that evidence to law enforcement officers.

But the fact the prints weren't found until three days after the accident would make them suspect at best. And the law would no doubt call into question Riva's account of there being a man in the road in the first place, considering her history of drug abuse. For all the law would know, Riva made that story up so the auto insurance company couldn't renege on paying her medical bills, saying they didn't cover for wreckless driving.

26

Hodge's Revelation

In bed at the Coleman's later that evening—

"That was Rawly on the phone," Marlene said, "He's had a bad evening."

"Why is that?" Shane asked.

"He broke it off with Kindra."

"You're joking, right?"

"No. He even cried a little. He said she continued to bad-mouth your trapping. He finally realized he could never be in a permanent relationship with an animal-rights woman. That he didn't need any woman's love that bad."

"I can't believe he finally came around."

"I told you he would. I think it's a shame she couldn't change her thinking. I really liked her."

"Look, sweetie, that whole liberal crowd never changes its way of thinking. Facts and common-sense mean nothing to those people. They get on some agenda and there's no reasoning with them. They don't care that God created animals for man, not the other way around."

"I hope Rawly finds a more conservative girlfriend next time."

The next morning, Wednesday, April 14th, in Monster Bradshaw's Barn—

"Nice to see you guys again," Bradshaw said. After he finished putting some grain in the feeder at the last stall. He bent down to take a close look at Shane's face. "Those are some nice shiners, brother."

"They don't look as bad as my ribs still feel," Shane said, gently rubbing the ribs. They all laughed.

"I got some more information on Monday and Tuesday that you guys need to know about," Hodge said. "I'm sorry I haven't talked to you about it before now, Shane. But with you laid up, I figured I wouldn't bother you anymore than I already did, and by waiting I wouldn't have to go over it again when we met with Monster. Let's sit down."

They all walked to the straw bales near the first stall and each sat down on one.

"I have confirmed that Sam Hostick actually lived here on this farm when he was a kid."

"So we were right," Shane said. "Where did you get that information? Was he a stepchild?"

"I'll get to that in a minute, Shane." Hodge then pulled out his little spiral notebook, opened it and began relating details. "Sam Hostick was actually born *Randall Samuel James*. His family, the James, bought this farm in 1951 and lived here until 1963, at which time they sold the place to the Shelleys."

Between his ribs still hurting, and the excitement he felt over what Hodge had just said, and anticipated he was about to say, Shane couldn't sit still. He got up and stood in front of the bale he had been sitting on, then said, "So that means you've figured out who the neighbor was too, right, Hodge. We're that close to the killer. Or do you know that too? Geez, Hodge I always knew you were a good cop and investigator, but this tops it all."

"Hold on, buddy. We have some of the puzzle put together, but we're not home yet."

"Let's have the rest of it," Shane said, rocking slowly side to side, shifting his wait from foot to foot.

"The James only had two kids, Randal Samuel and his younger brother. My two sources knew Sam only as Randy. They didn't know his middle name or initial. I got that off one of the internet genealogy sites. My sources knew Randy to be an easy-going kid, with a subtle sense of humor, who always seemed to want to get along with all the other kids. Apparently Sam's younger brother was killed in a car wreck the last year the family lived here, in 1963. The parents died in the late eighties, early nineties. So Sam had no immediate family still living."

"That's sad," Monster said.

"It sure is," Shane added. "He lost his best friend, in a big sense, when he was sixteen, and his baby brother three years later. Maybe his brother dying is part of what he was referring to when he said God judged him. Imagine if he lived with not only the guilt of keeping his mouth shut about Ellen Brock's murderer, but then believed he was the reason his little brother was killed. I'm not looking forward to telling Marlene about that. She's already felt real bad for Sam all along—dying out there with no one."

"Makes a guy thankful for what he has, doesn't it?" Hodge said.

"Sure does," Monster said.

"What else did you find out?" Shane asked.

"Sam actually *did live* at the house with the burned barn that had the same address as his tattoos. He owned the place and lived there alone from 1975 to 1981, under the name Randall James. I was able to figure that out after I finally had the James' name. According to Escrow records, he put five thousand down and carried the remaining thirty-eight grand on a thirty year mortgage. But then he sold the place in 1981. He came back there years later and rented a room for six months from the folks that lived there at the time. I'm not clear on the exact time period but it was in the late eighties, supposedly about the time his dad died."

"That's amazing," Shane said. "If that's true, is it possible the money really did burn with the barn? Or have you found out anymore about the money?"

"No. I haven't learned anymore about it. If we're lucky, the money will be in this barn, though now I highly doubt it. There's no reason why it would be. If I had to bet on anything, it would be that Sam was honest with Desiree about where he hid the money, at least where it was hidden at one time. But we may never know how much money there was, where he got it, whether it was still in the barn when he told Desiree about it, or if it was still there later when the barn burned."

"Tell us about Sam's neighbor," Shane said.

"I'm still working on that. But I do know that *the Beasleys* definitely lived right across the pasture to the south of here from 1954 to 1965. I haven't learned much more about them other than that Mr. Beasley was supposedly quite a drinker and took it out on the wife and kids. As yet I don't know how many kids they had or anything else about them."

"I bet Bessie Rogers could have helped us with that, now that we've got things narrowed down."

"I have no doubt," Hodge said, "or at least she would have broken her phone finding out." They all laughed.

"The past several days, as I've been recovering, I've been thinking a lot about Bessie," Shane said, "or rather the timing of her death. They never did an autopsy on her, did they?"

"No," Hodge said. "I talked to her daughter and son-in-law several days after she died. Why, what's going on in that amateur-sleuth mind of yours, Shane?"

"What if she didn't just die of cardiac arrest like they told us? What if she was poisoned, or something else?"

"Go on."

"She was ninety-two years old. Sure she very well could have just died from natural causes, *and probably did*. But what if she didn't? What if the same guy who pointed the shotgun at Desiree and Riva was somehow involved in Bessie's death? Think about it. Desiree and Riva obviously talked to the wrong person about something and someone wanted to shut them up. What if that same person wanted to shut Bessie up?"

"This is good," Monster said. "Could you get the authorities to exhume Bessie's body and do an autopsy?"

"There are some huge problems with that," Hodge said. "Just to get them the least bit curious, we would have to tell a fair amount of what we know. Then if they bought any of that, I guarantee you the next thing they would do is put everybody involved—from Doc and Kent Simons, to Riva, you guys, me, Marlene and anyone else they think may have withheld evidence—on the hot seat. Of course that could lead to one or all of us being charged for withholding evidence in not only a known unsolved homicide case, but potentially two or three. It could get very complicated for all of us. And it would ruin any chance of Ellen Brock's killer being brought to justice, because he would flee the area the first time he got wind that the law was involved.

"Then throw in the lack of cooperation from Bessie's living relatives, and their skepticism about our motives for making the claims we were making. Some would undoubtedly say we were fabricating the whole thing to juice up our history book. There's no limit to the problems. And with her being ninety-two, well past the time when most people die of natural causes, well ... you see what I'm getting at."

"I'm almost sorry I mentioned that," Monster said. "Makes me feel kind of foolish."

"No need to feel foolish, Monster. You and Shane aren't ex-cops or private investigators. You had no way of knowing all of that."

"At least I know you aren't going to make me dig her up like we did Sam," Shane said.

"Don't be so sure of that, Shane," Hodge said. "I didn't say *we couldn't* or wouldn't dig her up on our own..."

"Don't give me that crap, Hodge. I'm never digging up another human corpse. Not for you or anyone else."

Hodge closed his notebook and put it back in his pocket. "What do you say we get to work looking for that money?"

"Let's do it," Shane said. "At least this time we can turn on all the lights and open up all the windows and doors to get as much light on the subject as we can."

"No more sneaking around in the dark like a couple of criminals," Monster said.

"Or getting jumped by ex-Oklahoma Sooner ghosts," Hodge said.

After two hours of searching, broken up by a coffee break in the tack room, Hodge said, "I guess I was right. The money was never hidden in here. Not one board looked like it was ever removed."

"Maybe it was hidden in the old plank floor," Monster suggested. "This concrete floor was put in here a few years before I bought the place."

"If it was," Hodge said, "I hope whoever tore the old floor out and found the money, at least gave the farmer a good break on the concrete job."

"Chances are it was the farmer himself and his family and friends that did the whole job," Monster said. "Farmers are pretty much do-it-yourself guys."

"You would know," Shane said. "Sounds a lot like fur trappers."

"Well Monster, sorry you didn't end up a tycoon over this. If and when the time comes for us to get up close and personal with Ellen Brock's killer, would you be game to join us?"

"I wouldn't miss it. Just give me a call."

"We'll do," Hodge said, as the three of them walked out of the barn.

Driving down Lost Creek Road a few minutes later—

"That's kind of a let down, isn't it, Hodge," Shane said.

"Yes," Hodge answered, "but it never added up for me that Sam would have hidden the money in a barn he didn't live in as an adult. And I was pretty certain by ten days ago that Monster's place and the adjoining farm had to be where Sam grew up. I'm convinced now that he hid the money in the barn of the tattooed address."

"So do you think there was ever anything to your code-sequencing theory?"

"Not now I don't. I think it's just a coincidence that the place where he grew up fit into one of my sequence codes. There would have been no reason for him to code Monster's place. Sometimes you go with a theory in your investigation and it proves altogether wrong. If Sam hid any money, it had to have been at the address he showed Desiree."

"What do you say we stop by there now, just for a look see."

"Couldn't do any harm. We'll talk to the owner and see if he or she minds if we come back later and search through the rubble. We won't mention the money, just that we're curious because we both played in that barn when we were young teenagers, and thought we might possibly find some keepsake from back then. Who knows, maybe we'll find some money that never burned."

We'll have to get some good light-weight rain gear and gloves to keep from getting soot all over us. And we'll need a couple of steel rakes, and some shovels, too. By the way, you never did say who your sources were for the information you gave us. I kind of figured maybe you didn't want Monster to know who they were."

"You figured right. Nothing against Monster, but my sources were willing to speak to me off the record, with the understanding the only other person who would know who they were was you. One of them was a woman whose maiden name was Pensalen. She grew up on Lost Creek, and was a friend of Sam's younger brother. She still lives on her parent's original place, but her husband bought the place from her parents when they moved to Arizona back in the eighties. The other source was one of our old classmates, Josh

Standifer."

"He didn't help us much when we talked to him earlier," Shane said.

"Remember we didn't have much to go on the first time we talked to him. We never brought up Ellen Brock or Sam Hostick or any of that stuff."

"That's right. Did you tell him much about our investigation?"

"No. He was an honest enough guy when we were kids, but I was never close to him back then. How about you?"

"No. He was always a little different. At least I thought so."

"It turns out his oldest sister graduated from Pleasant Hill in 1962, the same year as Randy James, alias Sam Hostick. He didn't know that much about Randy himself, but just remembered his sister had said on a few occasions that Mr. Beasley, Randy's neighbor, was an alcoholic. Josh couldn't remember anything else about them."

"Are you going to try to talk to his sister?"

"Yes. He was going to get back to me in a day or two after he had a chance to tell her I'm working on the history book, and he had asked her if she would talk to me. She lives on the east coast somewhere."

"Did you ask Josh if he knew anything about the Ellen Brock case?"

"No. As little as he knew about Sam's neighbor, I knew there wouldn't be any point."

"You're probably right. And why arouse unnecessary interest. Do you plan to bring it up to the sister?"

"I'll play it by ear. If she starts volunteering information in response to my light probes, I'll certainly jump on it."

That evening Shane filled Marlene in on the latest developments. Then she told him Shiela had found a place to rent in Springfield and would be moving down over the weekend, and that it looked like she already had a renter for her place in Portland. Shane volunteered himself, Rawly and Hodge to help unload things on this end.

27

The Burned Barn

The next morning Hodge joined the Coleman's for a breakfast of country omelets and hash browns, over which he learned he had been drafted to help unload Shiela's furniture and other stuff when she arrived in the early afternoon on Saturday. He couldn't wipe the smile off his face no matter how hard he tried; nor could Shane. But something they encountered later in the morning would.

As Hodge and Shane went to work pulling charred pieces of board off the pile of rubble at 54374 Lost Creek Road, Shane looked up at the sky that was becoming darker by the minute, and said, "I sure hope the rain holds off. It's already bad enough dealing with this debris. It'll take a week to get all the black washed off as it is."

After an hour, the men had a few large piles of burned remains stacked off to the sides, including little pieces of leather attached to old bridle bits or rings, saddle buckles, metal buckets, shovel and pitchfork metal heads, and all the things one would expect to find in a horse barn. Then they uncovered the skeleton of a horse.

"What a shame." Hodge said. "This horse must have been locked in its stall when the barn burned."

They pulled a few more pieces of burned wood from atop the skeleton then stood there looking at it. "Ashes to ashes, dust to dust," Shane said. "A person's dreams, riches and life can go up in smoke in just a few minutes."

"Life can be fragile, that's for sure."

Suddenly changing the subject, Shane said, "Remember how funny Cindy Helber's little sister always was whenever we came over."

"I wonder what ever happened to her after they moved away," Hodge said. "Even though she was four years younger than us, I always had a crush on her. Did she ever stop giggling?"

"She was a perfect contrast to Cindy, who was so much more serious. But man was Cindy cute."

They continued raking debris away, until finally Shane said, "It's obvious we're not going to find any money in this mess, Hodge. No paper could have survived this fire. What do you say we call it a day?"

"Let's work a little longer; the clouds have held back their water this long. Maybe there's a reason."

"You're not getting religious on me, are you, old buddy?" Shane chuckled.

"Not me. But we've dug things out this far, why not go for a little longer?"

A few minutes later, they saw a flash of lighting from up over Mt. Zion, two miles away to the southeast, then ten seconds later heard the thunder. "It's going to get wet in a hurry any minute now," Shane said.

"When it starts raining we'll quit, and say we gave it our best effort."

They each pulled a few more boards off, then Shane hooked something interesting on the tines of his steel rake. He raised the rake up and noticed the tines held what looked like a bracelet.

"Look here, Hodge. I think I found me an old bracelet."

Hodge immediately stepped over beside Shane and said, "What do you think the chances are that was one of the Helber girl's?"

"From thirty-seven years ago? No way. They moved away from the valley before we graduated. It was probably some girl's that lived here after them."

Shane took the chain bracelet, attached to a soot-covered metal piece, off the rake tine with his gloved left hand.

"See if it says anything on it," Hodge said.

Just then lightning flashed to the east again, followed a few seconds later by thunder. Then it started raining—*Hard*.

As the two of them stood huddled together in the downpour, Shane turned the bracelet over so the top was exposed to the rain. Several drops hit the metal plate and sprayed black, sooty-water into their faces. He wiped the metal with his right thumb and looked close. He shook his head.

"What is it, Shane?"

"It can't be..." Shane choked up. He raised the metal toward Hodge's face.

Hodge focused his eyes, and read, "E.B.— Daddy's Angel."

They stood silently for several seconds, neither able to speak, or even knowing what to say. Then Hodge said, "I knew something inside me told me to keep searching. But never in a thousand years would I have believed we'd find something like this."

"And the way the rain held off until that exact moment. It was almost as if God was waiting for us to find this, and then poured out his heart once again over the sadness of Ellen's death."

"There is a God!" Hodge cried. "I don't care what anyone says, there is a *Mighty* God!"

"And she's with him right now," Shane added, tears streaming down his face, just as they were Hodge's.

"Turn it over, buddy," Hodge said. "Sometimes bracelets are inscribed on both sides."

Shane immediately turned the metal over, and rubbed it several times with his thumb. He read,

"Ellen, whether you are near or far away, you are always dear to our hearts. Love Dad and Mom."

At that moment, as fathers of their own daughters, both of them felt some of the pain Ellen Brock's dad and mom must have felt fifty years earlier when they lost their little angel. Now a part of her was found and they weren't around to find out. Probably a good thing.

They stood there in the pouring rain for several minutes, both wondering why Ellen Brock's bracelet would have been in Randy Samuel James', alias Sam Hostick's, barn. Then Hodge reached his gloved hand out, palm side up, and Shane placed the bracelet on it. They each grabbed a couple of tools, stepped away from the blackened mess, and walked to Shane's truck. There they placed the tools in the bed, and Shane retrieved a plastic grocery sack from the tool box inside the bed, which he handed to Hodge. After Hodge placed the bracelet in the bag, both men quickly peeled off their blackened rain suits, and gloves, and laid them under the tool box across the front of the bed. They both hastily got in the truck's cab.

Shane started the truck's engine to let it warm up, but neither man was ready to leave. As the windshield wipers swept back and forth across the windshield, both of them stared at the old barn's blackened remains in the field in front of them.

Finally Shane said, "The bracelet raises a lot of questions, doesn't it?"

"No kidding," Hodge answered, wiping his forehead off with a hand towel. "Like *was Sam* actually the killer?"

"I don't believe that for a minute."

"Then why didn't he tell you about the bracelet?"

"Maybe he would have if he hadn't died first."

"I told you from the start how common it is for criminals to come only *just so clean*."

"But you agreed with me that Sam had nothing to gain or lose by not telling me the whole truth on his death bed."

"What if you were wrong? What if we were both wrong?" Hodge said, obviously irritated. "What if Sam *was* the killer and we have been on a wild goose chase? That means we got Desiree killed, and maybe even Bessie Rogers, and got our butts kicked for nothing."

"Desiree's death isn't our fault. Neither is Bessie's. In fact if Sam was the killer, that would mean Bessie died a natural death. And what about the man with the gun in the road? Riva said he even came to the car afterward and didn't help?"

"What about him?"

"Hodge, you're letting your emotions take over again, and your anger over Ellen's death, and how it must have been for her parents. Stop for a minute and think. No one was going to kill, or threaten to kill, Desiree and Riva over their inquiries about Sam holding inheritance money for them. Someone had a lot more at stake than any money. It's the only explanation. And if someone actually did kill Bessie, or literally scared her to death, it wasn't because she was just a big gossip. It would have been because someone stood to lose an awful lot if she didn't shut up. You never met Sam, or talked with him. He was genuine. I know I'm not a perfect judge of character, but Sam was telling the truth that he was the killer's friend. He was *not* the killer."

"Then how do you explain Ellen Brock's bracelet being in the barn at the address tattooed in his armpits?"

"He must have found Ellen's shirt *and* the bracelet, but only returned the shirt. He then kept the bracelet just in case he decided to turn his friend in later. Think about it. What would have been easier for the killer to misplace? The bracelet. And what would have been easier for Sam to find? The shirt. Since Sam returned the shirt, the killer would have figured he never found it. And if the bracelet was in the hay as well, the killer would have figured Sam couldn't have found the bracelet and not found the shirt. Sam would have taken the shirt when he took the bracelet. The killer might have thought some animal must have carried the bracelet away—perhaps a cat, a raccoon, a squirrel, or even a rat. Since bracelets are shiny, and have a lot of dried, salty sweat on them, they can be attractive to animals.

"Imagine the anxiety the killer would have felt over misplacing the bracelet—the incriminating evidence. He couldn't just go to Sam and ask about it because he would have been admitting his involvement in her disappearance. And since Sam didn't take the shirt, the killer would have been pretty sure he didn't find *it or* the bracelet."

"And you think Sam took the bracelet with him when he moved away after growing up?"

"Yes."

"And I thought I was a good detective," Hodge said. "You always have had a very analytical mind, Shane. I know that helped you to be the successful trapper you've always been. I used to watch how you studied the animal sign, interpreted it, thought situations over, and then used that information to outsmart the animals you trapped and hunted. I was always amazed by how you did that."

"Thanks for the compliment, Hodge. So you're seeing my point. Do you still think Sam was the killer?"

"I still think that's a possibility. Only a foolish cop would rule that out after finding the bracelet. But I think we better go talk to Riva to see if anyone she and Desiree talked to gave any indication that they knew who Sam was."

"Let's go get cleaned up and go to the hospital," Shane said. "When do you expect to talk to Josh Standifer's sister to get more information on Sam's old neighbor?"

"I'll call Josh tonight to see if she's willing to talk to me."

Room 163, McKenzie Willamette Hospital, 3:10 pm, the same day—

"Riva, it's great to see you've been moved out of critical care and been upgraded," Hodge said. "You're looking a little better."

"I still feel like I stepped in front of a train, but thanks," she said, her voice noticeably stronger than before. "Shane I'm glad you came. I'm sorry if I or Desiree were rude to you before."

"You've got nothing to be sorry about, Riva," Shane said. "I'm very sorry about your sister."

"I know."

"Riva, we've got a lot to talk to you about, but we aren't going to do it until you're doing much better," Hodge said. "We don't want to wear you out. But we do want to ask you just a few questions."

"You're so kind, Hodge. Thanks for being here for me. You'll never know how much it means."

"It's the least I can do." He gently squeezed her fingers. "When you and your sister were trying to get a lead on Sam's money, did anyone you talked to admit to knowing Sam, or someone who matched his age and description?"

"No," she answered. Hodge looked across the bed at Shane, with a disappointed look. Shane returned the same.

"Did anyone give you any hints that they might have known Sam, but didn't want you to know they knew him, or that they were obviously uncomfortable talking about him?"

"Yes, actually a couple guys did."

Shane gave Hodge the hint of a grin, which communicated, *now* we're getting somewhere.

"Where did those two men live, and how did they react to your inquiries about Sam or your uncle?"

"The one old guy that lived at the last house on Lost Creek Road had long hair and looked like he could have been one of the original hippies. There were no trespassing signs all around his place. Both Desiree and I felt he knew who Sam was—even though he denied it—because he gave it away with his eyes. And then when we told him *we knew* that *he knew* who Sam was, he grabbed each of us by an arm and forcibly led us away from his house. We broke away and ran to the car."

Hodge and Shane looked at each other with raised eyebrows.

"No one answered the door the first time, a few days earlier. But the second time we were there, he did." she said. "He told us you guys had come by too."

"No one answered the door for us," Hodge said. "If he told you he saw us, he must have been watching us, but just didn't answer. What about the other guy?"

"He was a screwed up Vietnam vet, a weirdo. He lived back off the road in the woods on the right, just up the creek from Eagle's Rest Bridge. Talk about a lot of no trespassing signs. And he was just plain rude right from the start. Kicked us off his property and warned us never to come back."

"Could either of those guys have been the man with the gun?"

"Actually, I don't know why I didn't make the connection before," she said, raising her voice and opening her eyes wider, "Maybe my memory was clouded from the head trauma. About half an hour before our accident, Desiree pulled her car right in front of the Vietnam vet's pickup just as he was about to pull out of his driveway. Then she got out and walked around to talk to him. When he recognized us, he got out of his car and told Desiree, in no uncertain terms, to get out of the way if she knew what was good for her. So we left in a hurry."

"But you weren't sure if he was the one with the gun a little later?" Hodge asked, rubbing his beard.

"I wish I was. Maybe it will become clearer with a little more time."

"Well you've been a big help, anyway, Riva. We're going to go check on some of this now. Thanks for the information. I'll be back sometime tomorrow to visit you."

As they walked down the hall, away from Riva's room, Hodge said, "She was obviously talking about Cambell Ritchey, when she described the place just up from Eagles Rest Bridge. It just seems odd to me that if Ritchey was the one in the road less than a half hour after he ran her and Desiree off from his driveway, she can't remember that. She seems to be remembering all the other details pretty well. I doubt it was him."

"Maybe it was the guy at the end of the creek," Shane said.

"According to tax records, the place is owned by a woman. But maybe he lives with her. I wonder if it's possible that guy is the retired postmaster."

"She said he had long hair and looked like a hippie. That doesn't sound like an ex-postmaster."

"And you thought I was narrow-minded when it came to the street people."

28

Kent Comes Clean

From Shane's pickup, in the hospital parking lot, Hodge used his cell phone to call Kent Simons.

"Kent, Shane and I have a bunch of new information to talk to you about. But we want to talk in person. Can we meet you in the morning?"

On one hand, Kent was excited that there was new information. Yet, the way Hodge said they wanted to meet him in person suddenly made Kent ill at ease. Had they somehow figured out that he hadn't been candid with them on everything he knew, and in fact, had been free-lancing the case on his own.

"Yeah, I can meet with you," Kent said hesitantly. "Did you guys want to come on over to my place?"

"That sounds good," Hodge said. "How about eleven? I have to talk to a woman on the east coast before that."

Marlene wasn't home earlier when Shane stopped to clean up before going to the hospital, but she was there when he got back.

"Marlene, when we were digging around in the burned rubble at

Sam's old house, I found something that shocked both Hodge and me."

"You found the money buried in a fireproof container, so we get to go on a cruise?"

"No. I found a bracelet that belonged to Ellen Brock."

"No way!"

"I'm not kidding."

"So Sam was the killer all this time?"

"That might seem like the obvious conclusion, but I don't believe that." Shane went on to tell Marlene what the inscriptions said on the Bracelet, and explained all the circumstances and theories that he and Hodge had discussed earlier. When he was done talking, Marlene was convinced—as he was—that Sam wouldn't have given a half-confession if he actually was the killer, and that him not saying anything about the bracelet before he died was probably because he didn't want to stir up trouble for anyone.

The next morning, April 16th, 7:30 Pacific Daylight Savings, 10:30 East Coast DLS time—

"Brenda, this is Hodge Gilbert, calling regarding Randy James."

"Hi Hodge."

"It's very nice of you to talk to me," he said. "Is it as beautiful on the East Coast this morning as it is out here in the West?"

"It's definitely a nice day. What can I help you with?" she asked.

"I don't know how much Josh told you, but I'm working on a history book about the people of Lost Creek Valley. I was fortunate enough to run across your brother in the process. I'm gathering as much background as I can on certain people and events and then sift through it to get the cream that will be factual, yet very enjoyable to read."

"That sounds like a worthwhile project. Did you grow up out there yourself?"

"Yes, in Dexter actually. I graduated from Pleasant Hill in '75."

"I see."

"As I'm sure Josh told you, I need more information on Randy James, who graduated from Pleasant Hill in your class. I've managed to get a hold of the Pleasant Hill High School 1960 year book and I'm actually looking at your class's individual photos right now."

"Yes?"

"I'll just get right to the point," he said. "Did you know the neighbors directly to the south of Randy James?"

"Yes. The Beasley's lived there." Hodge already knew that from looking up the county records, but wanted to hear it from her.

"Is it true the father was an abusive drinker? And were there any kids the same age as you and Randy?"

"You got right to the point, didn't you," she said. "Yes, Mr. Beasley was a heavy drinker and sometimes abused his family. And yes, they had a boy the same age as Randy and I."

As he stared at one particular boy in the sophomore class of the 1960 yearbook pages in front of him, Hodge said, "I don't see any Beasley's in your class's photos—"

"The boy's last name *was not* Beasley." Hodge smiled. Spit it out already, lady. "He was Mr. Beasley's step-son. His mom was married to Beasley. The boy's name was Scott Welker."

Hodge shook his head, he was over-run with emotions.

After several seconds of silence, Brenda said, "Are you there?" not sure if her cell connection had been lost.

"Yes, I'm here. You said the neighbor boy's name was Scott Welker?" he said, careful not to give away the excitement he felt.

"Yes. He came back to the area in the mid-seventies to be the postmaster. That was just before my husband and I moved our family from Lane County to the East Coast."

Hodge was numb. Shane's dad had been right. It *was* a local teenager who still lived in the area, at least as late as the early nineties. That is if all he had now learned was fact. But he had to be careful not to jump the gun despite having that feeling every cop or private investigator gets when they know they finally have most the dots connected in a case.

"Thanks, Brenda. I knew Scott Welker had been the postmaster, and grew up somewhere in the area. But until now, I had no idea exactly where he lived when he was a kid. A sad piece of history that I've run across again and again is the tragic death of Ellen Brock in 1960. Did you know her?"

"No, but I sure heard plenty about her later. I was sixteen and she was only nine when all that happened. From everything I heard, she didn't live up Lost Creek. It was so sad. I've thought about her occasionally over the years. Once in a while when I happen to watch a movie involving the abduction of a young girl, I'll think about it. But that's the sort of thing one tries to forget, if that's possible."

"I understand," he said. "Well, your piece of information about Scott Welker living next to the James will be a big help. No one seems to want to talk about Welker. Do you have any idea why?"

"No. Like I said, I left the area in the late seventies. I haven't kept up on anything out there since then. And I've only made it to one of my class reunions."

"I've appreciated you taking the time to talk to me, Brenda. You were definitely helpful."

On the way out to Kent Simons place, Hodge filled Shane in on the Scott Welker connection, then said. "It's all coming together. We'll have to be especially careful how we handle things from now on. If one word slips, the whole case will blow up in our faces."

Shortly before noon, the three men sat on Kent's front porch discussing the case. Doc wasn't home because his oldest son, Ed, took him to his place outside of Roseburg for a few days.

Hodge updated Kent on everything he knew, including the latest information about Scott Welker. Kent was amazed at the new revelation, but seemed a little upset over it. When Hodge was done explaining everything, Kent said, "I have to make a confession to you guys. I haven't told you everything I've said to Cambell Ritchey."

Hodge and Shane looked at each other like— you better not have said the wrong things.

"Remember the day I told you guys that I ran into Bessie Rogers at the Lost Creek Store, and got an earful. I was actually the one that got the conversation in high gear by mentioning that when you guys interviewed my dad and me for the history project, you brought up the Ellen Brock case. I said nothing more, and never told her I was in on things with you. She volunteered that if you guys could ever talk with Cambell Ritchey or one of his cousins, they would probably be a big help with some of the details. I had no idea what she could be talking about, so I figured I would see what I could get out of Cam myself, then pass whatever I learned on to you. At that point I had no idea that the ex-postmaster was one of Cam's cousins.

"The day before Bessie died, I went to Cam's and told him there was some new information in the Ellen Brock case. I asked if he believed her killer was still alive and living in the valley." Hodge's face instantly flushed red; his hands started shaking. Shane saw it and was afraid he would pounce on Kent any moment, but couldn't blame him if he did. Neither of them could believe Kent could be so stupid. "I told Cam that Bessie told you guys that he or one of his cousins might know more about the case." Hodge was breathing faster.

"Then one of the times I went back to talk to him after Bessie died, I asked why he had never mentioned the connection between himself and Scott Welker before. When I told him there was a rumor going around the valley that his cousin, Scott Welker, picked in the same bean field as Ellen Brock at the time she was killed, he got very upset with me and told me not to come back as long as I was Shane Coleman's lackey."

At that, Hodge sprang out of his chair and grabbed Kent by the throat with his left hand, raised him up from his chair, and cocked his right fist back to punch him in the face.

"What the hell do you think you were doing, Simons? You screwed up our whole case right there!"

Shane felt the same way, but jumped up and grabbed Hodge's fist before he could unload it. "Settle down, Hodge! Beating Kent up isn't going to change anything now."

"I'm sorry, Hodge," Kent gasped, his face red from fear and lack of oxygen. "I just wanted to get to the bottom of things... to get more information for you guys. I didn't think things through. I'm sorry."

"You got Desiree killed, and probably Bessie too. What the hell were you thinking? You weren't thinking!"

Hodge's arms were shaking, saliva was running down his chin. It was all Shane could do to hold him back.

"Hodge, relax. What's done is done. Let it go."

After fifteen seconds, Hodge released his grip, then walked heavily around on the far end of the porch, breathing hard and fast.

"You imbecile, Simons. I can't believe you wanted to bring this guy in on this case, Shane."

"So he went about things the wrong way, Hodge. His intentions were good."

"Intentions get people killed, and they did."

"You can't blame Kent for anybody's death. Desiree isn't dead because of anything Kent did. You know that as well as I do. Her own mouth and her own driving got her where she is. Stop blaming Kent."

"I'm sorry, Hodge," Kent said. "I'm sorry Shane. I never meant to harm the investigation or get anyone hurt. I just thought that since Cam and I were friends, I could use that to our advantage. I screwed up."

"Here all along you've been talking to the cousin of one of the most likely suspects in the case, the suspect who has now been confirmed to be the killer," Hodge said. "And you made sure to keep him up-to-date on the progress of our investigation."

"I didn't do that, Hodge. There's actually very little Cam knows.

You've got to remember, the girls talked to him too."

"He's right, Hodge," Shane said. "Don't be so hard on him. I thought we weren't going to come to premature conclusions. You're already convinced that Scott Welker is the killer. He probably is, but we aren't certain of that. We don't even know if he's still in the area, or even still alive. Kent admitted he didn't get any information on Welker's status or whereabouts from Cam. We need to think this through."

Finally, Hodge settled down and apologized to Kent for reacting the way he did. He conceded that Kent was just trying to help and that it wasn't his fault that anyone got killed—though he still believed Kent was a big reason for it.

Kent agreed to stay away from Cam until the case was settled, but still wanted to go with the men whenever they did confront Welker. Hodge admitted they might need all the manpower they could get when the time came, which he anticipated would be soon. He also said the time had come when he had to bring at least one of his ex-classmate police officers in on the case, off the record. He needed a way to get access to the official police record on Ellen Brock. Hodge and Shane decided Martin Steen, who was a captain with the Oregon State Police out of Springfield, would be his contact. Little did any of them know that Steen was good friends with Scott Welker when Steen lived in Dexter during the first dozen years of Welker's postmaster duty there.

29

OSP Captain Steen

Over the weekend Shiela Gilbert got moved in to her rental place in Springfield. Then on Sunday evening she, Hodge, Shane and Marlene enjoyed a wonderful steak dinner together at the Outback Restaurant in Springfield. Hodge and Shane also visited Riva at the hospital over the weekend.

First thing Monday morning, April 19th, Hodge called the Springfield Oregon State Police office.

"Could I talk to Captain Steen?"

"Hold one, may I ask who's calling?"

"Tell him it's his old classmate and fellow cop Hodge Gilbert."

A minute later, Steen came on the line. "Steen here."

"Martin. It's your old friend Hodge Gilbert.

"Hodge. Good to hear your voice," Steen said. "They told me it was my fellow cop friend. I thought you got out of law enforcement and went into private investigating."

"I did, but I knew I would get more attention introducing myself that way."

"I see."

"I've got some information on a very old local homicide case and would like to meet with you to talk it over."

"What old case are you talking about?"

"Do you remember the Ellen Brock murder in 1960?"

"Yes I remember. What information could you have in that case? It was suspended long before either of us became cops."

"I think I'm getting close to closing the case."

"You're kidding."

"What I don't have is the official police records. I'd like to take a look at everything they learned during the original investigation. Is there any chance you could meet me when you get off your shift this afternoon and bring the file?"

"Hodge, I'm eager to learn what you have, but I can't give you the file, if I can even find it."

"I'm not asking you to turn it over, just let me look through it. I need to confirm certain details."

"Okay," Captain Steen said. "But let's keep this under the hat for right now."

"That's exactly what I want to do. If I'm as close to figuring this thing out as I believe I am, the last thing I want to do is tip off the killer."

"You know who the killer is?"

"Not yet, but were real close," Hodge lied, knowing enough to not trust anybody else, including any police officers, with the final pieces of his puzzle. "I should tell you that our old classmate Shane Coleman is the one who picked up the information that got the ball rolling. If it's okay with you, I'd like him to join us this afternoon. We've been working the case together."

"Shane Coleman? He was always a rugged outdoorsman. I ran into him a couple times over the years, back when I was working game enforcement. Does he still trap?"

"Actually he was trapping when he got the information on this case."

"I can't wait to hear about it."

"Can you come over to my place after you get off your shift this afternoon? I'll pick up some Chinese food. I think you can appreciate why I don't want to meet in a public place."

"That sounds good. What's your address?"

Hodge gave the address, and they hung up.

Over dinner at 5 pm, at Hodge's, the three men renewed their old friendship. Hodge and Shane explained a fair amount of what they had learned in the case, though they didn't tell about finding the bracelet or that Scott Welker, the ex-postmaster of Dexter, was the prime suspect. Nor did they mention Welker or Cambell Ritchey's names. Hodge had thoroughly briefed Shane on where to draw the line, and to let Hodge do most the talking.

Finally, Captain Steen said, "This whole confession thing sounds genuine, and the way you've tracked down various locations and people, and pursued your information is very good." Hodge and Shane could hear a *but* coming, and given the limited amount of information they gave Steen, they could understand why. "But I think you're further from solving this case than you think, Hodge. And the story the drug addict gave, about the man with the gun in the road, sounds shaky."

"You sound like you're giving us the standard law enforcement brush off, Martin."

"I'm sorry if it sounds that way. I just need solid evidence. You've told me this story about a disabled Vietnam vet possibly being involved in the deaths of two women, whose deaths were already determined to be from natural causes and an accident. You gave me a very interesting theory concerning Sam's pay off money. But the only person who ever said Sam actually had a large sum of money is now dead. You know nothing about that woman's background other than what she and her sister told you. She had several different ID's in her purse when she died, so we don't even know who she really was. Do you see the problem?"

"Yes," Hodge said, "I do. But you and I both know that you, and every other police officer, have delved deeper into cases that had much less circumstantial evidence."

"But they weren't fifty-year-old cases."

Hodge suddenly reached in his shirt pocket and pulled out a sandwich baggie containing something and tossed it on the table in front of Steen. "How about this, Martin? Does this mean anything to you? Be careful not to touch it with your fingers, we don't want you to leave any fingerprints."

Steen grabbed the baggie and held the bracelet through the plastic, while opening the bag up to read the inscription. "E.B.— Daddy's Angel." His eyes got big, as he glanced up at Hodge, then Shane. He then turned the metal plate over and read the back, "Ellen, whether you are near or far away, you are always dear to our hearts. Love Dad and Mom."

"Where did you get this?" Steen asked, skeptically, scrutinizing the chain and plate to determine whether they were fake.

"I found it in the burned rubble at Sam's old place," Shane said.

"Why would it have been at Sam's?"

"It was in the burned barn. He had obviously kept it hidden there, probably along with the money."

"There's nothing obvious to me about this. You said Sam took Ellen Brock's shirt, not the bracelet."

"I didn't tell you about the bracelet yet because it's the best evidence we have," Hodge said.

"And you wanted to reel me in with weaker evidence before you sprung the clincher. The only thing this bracelet proves is that at some point around the time Ellen Brock went missing, she had played in that barn. Or the other option is that Sam was the killer, and *he took* the bracelet. Neither of those options supports your case.

Captain Steen set the bagged bracelet down on the table, then quickly shuffled through several pages in the police report. He skimmed a page with his hand, stopping a third of the way down. It says here,

'She may have been wearing a silver bracelet inscribed, "E.B. Daddy's Angel." The parents have said that she often wore that bracelet, and that they have been unable to locate it. But neither of her parents or anyone who was questioned in the bean field remembered whether she was wearing it the day she disappeared. The parents said, "She sometimes placed the bracelet in one of her pant pockets when she wasn't wearing it."'

"The bracelet *proves* she *had it* with her the day she disappeared," Hodge insisted. "And that the killer took it from her, along with the shirt that also said, 'Daddy's Angel,' on it."

"That's circumstantial," Steen said, "and it definitely doesn't prove who took it. If anything, it would make Sam look guilty. But *I will say this*, now that you've shown me the bracelet, I may consider re-opening this case myself. If I do I will requisition this from you, and any other evidence you haven't revealed to me."

Hodge instantly shoved his chair back, stood up and slammed his hand down on the table. "Don't you dare pull that, Steen! I didn't bring you here so you could steal the case from us. And without Shane's testimony of what Sam said on that river bank, you haven't got anything. You know that."

Steen backed off, and said, "Look Hodge, I wouldn't take your case from you. At the very minimum, I would let you continue to be a primary player. You do have some good theories—no matter how unsubstantiated they are—that could be just the way things happened. The problem is getting any district attorney (DA) to bring charges based on what you have. It's just not going to happen. Any DNA or fingerprints that might have been on the bracelet would have degenerated over time, and certainly been completely destroyed in the fire. So there would be no way to tie the bracelet to the killer if it wasn't Sam. Sam's own testimony doesn't even support a large part of your theory. You see the problem?"

"When you lay it out like that," Hodge said, "yes, I see the problem. But just because there's not enough evidence to take the killer into a court of law, doesn't mean he should continue to get away with what he did to Ellen, to her family, and—in fact—to the entire community."

"What are you suggesting, Hodge, that you and Shane are going to put together a vigilante force and deal with him yourselves in whatever way you deem appropriate? You're treading on dangerous ground if you do anything like that."

"What if we get a confession from the killer?"

"And how do you plan to get that, by shoving bamboo shoots up under his nails, or holding a knife to his scrotum?"

"I don't know, but if the law got a legitimate confession from him after reading his rights, what would you say about that?"

"A legal confession—in which your suspect confesses to killing the girl and acknowledges taking the shirt and bracelet from her body—plus the recovered bracelet, would be about as good as it gets. The DA would have no problem taking the murder case to court. But then you might get a sympathetic juror or several that say, he was just a kid when it happened and has lived an exemplary life in the fifty years since, if that's the case, so they vote *not guilty*. Of course, depending on the circumstances the killer confesses to, the DA might only go for a low level manslaughter conviction. Then everyone would have been drug through the mud in order for the man to probably just get probation. Is it worth the heartache to Ellen Brock's surviving relatives, or even to the killer's family?"

"That's what I questioned from the outset," Shane said, "whether I should just leave the whole thing alone. But now that it's coming together, I don't feel that way anymore—especially after holding that bracelet in my hand in pouring down rain."

"You want blood on your hands too, Shane?"

"For a police captain, your attitude about this surprises me, Martin," Shane said. "I would think you'd want justice if for no other reason than Ellen deserves it. She never had a say in any of it.

Her life was ripped from her in a few moments. She never got to be fifty-three years old, sitting around a table with two of her childhood friends, talking about where all the years went. Do you know she would be fifty-nine right now if that beast hadn't done what he did?"

"I'm just looking at things from a practical legal perspective."

"Then try looking at them from a father's perspective—*HER father's perspective.*"

"You said yourself he and the mother died years ago."

"Don't you have a daughter?"

"Yes."

"If this was your daughter we were talking about, what would you want done to her killer?"

"That makes it harder."

"We have to do what's right," Hodge said, "not what some DA thinks he can accomplish in a courtroom."

"It's a lot to consider," Captain Steen said. "You guys see what else you can come up with, and keep me informed. When I think you have enough to take it to the next level, I might run it by the Lane County Sheriff to get a second opinion. I'll warn you right now that any coerced testimony will be thrown out in a heartbeat. And I guarantee you, the only other way the killer would admit to killing the Brock girl is if he suddenly found God. Don't do anything stupid that could get someone killed."

"Don't you mean someone *else* killed, Captain Steen?" Hodge said. "Now I'd like the bracelet back."

"Right." Steen handed Hodge the baggie and said, "Good luck."

"Now can I go through the files before we break up here?"

"Oh yeah, I guess that's why you called the meeting in the first place."

30

An Old Friend

The next afternoon, after getting off his shift, Captain Steen decided to take a drive up Lost Creek. He hadn't been up there in nearly a year, even though at one time he spent plenty of time there enforcing fish and game laws, among his general Oregon State Police duties. Although Hodge didn't name the Vietnam vet he was talking about, Steen knew only too well who he was referring too. He had been to Ritchey's place a couple times after receiving anonymous tips from neighbors that they had heard a single suspicious gunshot come from the woods back of Ritchey's.

Since Steen was a former marine—post Vietnam—he sympathized with Ritchey's plight. On one of his trips to Ritchey's, Steen had found an untagged, out-of-season deer hanging in one of Ritchey's sheds. Ritchey had just stood there in Trooper Steen's presence—the deer hanging between them—without denying his guilt, without saying anything. What could he say? After standing there, looking back and forth between the deer and Ritchey for a couple minutes with a scowl on his face, scratching his chin and shaking his head, Steen had finally just turned his back to the deer, walked back to his truck, and left without confiscating the deer, issuing a citation or even saying a word.

Steen never knew that Ritchey was Scott Welker's cousin.

As Captain Steen drove his Dodge pickup past the Eagles Rest Bridge, he considered pulling into Cambell Ritchey's place just for a little chat to see what he could learn. But he decided against it. Instead he cruised clear up past all the houses and drove to where the paved road crossed back over the creek to the west, then pulled up the dirt road to the left. He drove back into the steep canyon, parked and walked down to the creek, which was much smaller there, and leaned against an alder tree to see if he could see any trout rise in the pool in front of him. He watched the hole for fifteen minutes and didn't see a single trout rise. Not surprising for that time of year.

He then drove back down the creek, and on a whim decided to stop in to see his old friend Scott Welker at the last house on Lost Creek Road. He knew Welker had maintained a low profile since his semi-forced retirement from the Postal service under speculation that he had said the wrong things to several different teenage girls in the community. But Steen never took any of the accusations seriously. He knew Welker to be an honest and hardworking man. He also knew the woman Welker had moved in with twelve years earlier owned the place where he was now living.

When Scott Welker opened the door, Steen was surprised to see how white Welker's long hair had gotten since he had last talked to him over three years earlier. Welker had grown his hair and beard out after leaving the post office.

"It's been a long time, Martin," Welker said, wearing a big smile.

"Too long, you old duffer," Steen, who was in plain clothes, said. They shook hands, then Steen asked Welker if he would mind if they walked out behind the barn for a little chat. Welker wasn't sure he liked the sound of that with all the recent happenings, but consented. Steen led the way to a grove of oak trees.

"How's life treating you clear back up here in the woods?" Steen asked.

"It's been alright, except for a few unwelcome visitors in the past month or so."

"Yeah, what did they want?"

"I don't know what the *two men* who stopped wanted; I didn't answer the door. But when the women came back a second time, I figured the only way to keep them from coming back again was to talk to them, maybe shake them up a bit. You know how I like my privacy."

"Sure I do," Steen said. "I don't blame you. Some of my happiest times were growing up on the creek here. What did the women want? With all the no trespassing signs, it must have been pretty important for them to come back a second time."

"They said they were looking for their uncle. The funny thing is, when they said who he was, I knew who they were talking about. It was an old guy that used to live on lower Lost Creek. The name the women mentioned was just one of the names he went by over the years."

"What was his name, or the one the women used?"

"Sam Hostick."

"Sam?"

"You knew him too?"

"I didn't know him personally, but I heard a little about him." Steen said. "How did you know Sam, Scott?"

"Just through the post office. He stopped in there from time to time to mail parcels."

"Did you know he grew up on the creek here?"

"No," Welker answered, suddenly feeling a bit uneasy.

"I actually learned some interesting information about him yesterday through the two guys that I suspect were the same two who stopped by your place."

"Yeah, what's that?"

"Turns out one of the guys was running his trap line on the

McKenzie River a couple months ago when he ran into Sam living homeless under a bridge."

"Sam ended up being homeless? That's a tragedy."

"Not nearly as much as the one he told the trapper about." Suddenly Welker felt sick inside, his mouth got dry.

"What tragedy was that?" he said, licking his lips.

"Seems Sam was dying, and the trapper came along just in time to listen to him give a death-bed confession. He said that when he was sixteen his best friend, who was also his neighbor, had killed a nine-year-old girl in one of the local bean fields. I'm sure you remember hearing something one time or another about the Ellen Brock murder."

Welker, standing to Steen's right with both of them facing the same direction, eased his right hand up on the pistol hidden under his shirt on his right hip, and considered silently releasing the leather strap. He didn't know if Steen was baiting him, or if he even knew there was a connection between himself and Sam. But Welker knew if Steen gave any indication that he knew Welker was the neighbor friend that Sam was referring to, Welker would have to do something.

Doing his best to maintain his composure, Welker said, "Sam knew who the Brock girl's killer was?"

Welker had never told Steen that he himself grew up on Lost Creek. He told him he was from Coquille, near the Oregon coast, which was partially true because he lived there until he was eight, when his mom married Beasley and they bought the place on Lost Creek. Welker's dad continued to live in Coquille for years after he and Welker's mom divorced in 1951, and Scott Welker visited him regularly. Back when Steen lived in the Dexter-Lost Creek area, Welker was confident Steen would never try to learn his true background; he had no reason to. After all, they were friends, and Welker was the postmaster, a law-abiding, first-class citizen. Welker also knew that when Steen was a fish and game officer, few

people in the valley were comfortable talking to him—so none of
the longer-time residents who might have known that Welker grew
up on the creek would have mentioned that to Steen. Even so, right
now Welker wished he had never come back to the Dexter-Lost
Creek area.

"Yes," Steen answered.

"Did he give the name to the trapper before he died? Do the
police have any idea if the guy is still alive or where he lives?"

"No, Sam didn't give the name. Apparently he made it clear that
he wasn't confessing to get anyone in trouble or to stir up anything.
He just wanted to get free of the burden he said he had carried for
the last fifty years—the burden of knowing who killed the girl, but
not ever telling anyone who it was."

"That would have been a heck of a burden, no doubt about that,"
Welker said, breathing a little easier.

"The trapper that found Sam is one of the two men working on
the Lost Creek Valley history project. Both men grew up in Dexter
themselves, though they were grown and out of the area before you
took over as postmaster. You may not have met them."

"What are their names?"

"Hodge Gilbert and Shane Coleman," Steen said. "Coleman's
dad, Buck Coleman, was the mail carrier for this whole area from
the late forties into the early seventies."

"I don't recognize Hodge and Shane, but I met Buck," Welker
admitted. "When I first took over as postmaster a number of people
said they were disappointed he didn't get the postmaster position
when it came open in the late-sixties. He was highly thought of by
his mail patrons."

"I remember seeing him running the mail route from time to time
when I was a kid up here," Steen said. "My mom always put a loaf
of fruit cake out for him before Christmas."

"He earned it. The mail load doubled, tripled, and even quad-
rupled, in December. Tons of parcels too. We all dreaded that time

of year."

"As my long-time friend and the ex-postmaster, I know I can trust you with one of the most interesting details Hodge and Shane have come up with during this history project."

"I'm listening," Welker said, afraid of what he might learn.

Steen walked up to the base of an eighteen-inch-thick oak tree, bent down and picked up an oak leaf. He was now standing several feet away from Welker. He began slowly tearing the edge off of the leaf, while keeping Welker in his line of sight.

Welker's stomach was in knots. He sensed the gavel was about to fall. He couldn't tell for sure if Steen was packing under his long shirt, but guessed he was. He knew Steen, like most cops, rarely went anywhere without carrying a piece. Welker had even shot Steen's service issue .38 automatic on a couple occasions while they were up in the woods together years earlier. But Steen had other pistols besides the .38. Welker knew he couldn't be carrying one of his revolvers because the shirt wasn't pushed out far enough from his hip.

Welker had no way of knowing if Steen had probed into his background enough to know he once lived right next door to Sam Hostick, or rather Randy Samuel James. He felt that same fear he used to live with in the days, months and years immediately following the tragedy. That whoever he was around knew more about him and what he had done than they were saying. That any minute someone was going to say, "We gotcha! We know you killed the girl."

Welker had joined the army right out of high school to get away from the Lost Creek area. To get away from the memory of that horrible day. But the military didn't take away his memories. No place he went, and nothing he did, took those memories away—or the nightmares.

The nightmares began a few weeks after they found Ellen Brock's body. In the two years he lived at home after the tragedy, he often woke up his siblings or parents with his screaming or loud groaning while having the nightmares—while reliving that devastating experience. None of his family understood why he had the bad dreams. He never told them the truth about the content of the dreams. He didn't dare. He said that in the dreams he was always being chased by these men that were half monsters, often on horseback, but sometimes it would be out on a lake in their speedboats, or in a huge city.

His parents even took him to a doctor, who said the dreams could be caused by his sugar level. They should restrict his sugar intake late in the day. Gradually the dreams diminished.

After he got out of the army, he returned to Lost Creek briefly, then moved to the Oregon Coast, got married, had three kids, one daughter, and finally ended up in Roseburg, where he became a postal carrier. From there he got the Dexter postmaster position. His kids were in their late-thirties, early-forties now, and his wife died fifteen years ago from breast cancer. For the past twelve years, he had lived with Irene Macklin, a widow two years his senior, on her secluded place at the end of Lost Creek Road. He never told her or anyone else his horrible secret. Over the years Ellen Brock had become a distant memory which he had effectively suppressed, and he eventually convinced himself someone else actually killed her.

But in the last six weeks, since this so-called Lost Creek Valley history project began, he had heard plenty from his cousin Cambell Ritchey about Ellen Brock and the guy named Sam Hostick. And the nightmares had come back. Nothing like before, because now in the nightmares it was a teenage boy doing the girl and hiding her. It wasn't him anymore. He was just a fading old man who had lived a productive life as a servant to his community—though in the end, the community didn't appreciate him.

"When Gilbert and Coleman were digging through the rubble of the burned-down barn where Sam once lived, they found a silver bracelet," Steen said.

"A bracelet?"

"It was inscribed with Ellen Brock's name and had a love message from her parents."

Welker was numb.

The day his neighbor Randy James asked him if he knew something he wasn't telling about Ellen's death, he wondered why Randy had questioned him. He figured it was because Randy knew him so well he could read the guilt on his face—in fact, all over his body. Then that night, as he tossed and turned in bed, he decided that Randy must have found the shirt and bracelet. It was the only way he could have known anything.

When he got out of bed the next morning, he dressed hastily and went directly to the hayloft in the barn, uncovered the hay from the special hiding spot, and immediately found the shirt. He was okay. *Everything was okay.* Randy hadn't found the shirt or the bracelet. He covered the shirt back over with a bunch of hay without looking to see that the bracelet was still under it. But a few days later, when he made up his mind he had to destroy the evidence, he discovered the bracelet was missing.

He panicked. He dug through the hay like a maniac. It had to be there. But it wasn't. He sat on a bale of hay and considered the possibilities. Maybe Randy took the bracelet. Maybe that's how he knew. *No.* He would have taken the shirt too. Should he ask Randy about the bracelet? *No way.* If it wasn't Randy, his asking would only confirm Randy's suspicions. He finally decided a rat or some other small animal must have carried it off. He searched all over the barn. Pried boards off of walls where he thought a rat or other animal could have taken it.

For months he lived in constant fear that the bracelet would suddenly turn up. Fear that maybe one of his siblings or his parents would find it. Or one of his friends. He went to great pains to keep all his friends out of the barn for the next year so they couldn't inadvertently run across it. Every couple weeks, when his fears would overwhelm him, he would search the whole barn all over again.

Now, all these years later, the bracelet that *once was lost,* was now *found.*

"So what does finding the bracelet in Sam's old barn mean?" Welker asked. His hand trembled slightly as he fingered the holster strap under his shirt. Since he could see Steen's hands were no where near his hip, he was certain he could beat him to the draw if he decided to go for it.

"What *do you think* it means, Scott?" Steen said.

Welker wasn't sure if Steen was leading him, whether they had the entire case figured out and just wanted to see what kind of line Welker would give him or what. He didn't know if Sam had actually spilled his guts on the river, and Steen was just toying with him now. For all Welker knew the police and FBI had his place surrounded with agents hiding back in the brush and trees. At this very second, a sniper could have his scope trained directly on his head or heart just itching to squeeze his trigger if Welker started to remove his pistol from its holster. He would play it safe. He wasn't ready to die just yet.

"I don't know. If Sam made a confession while he was dying that his friend killed the little girl, why would *he have* her bracelet hidden in his barn after all these years?"

"That's puzzling to us too," Steen said, speaking as if he was one of the officers assigned to the case. He bent down and picked up another oak leaf to tear apart vein by vein.

"Maybe Sam was actually the killer himself," Welker suggested. "Maybe he made up the line about the friend. It makes no sense to me that he would carry that kind of secret around with him his entire life, unless he had a lot to lose by revealing it. If you ask me, that sounds like the most likely scenario, that *he* was the killer. The bracelet was found in his barn. That's pretty incriminating evidence, isn't it?"

"Very incriminating. You probably read the little notice in the Register Guard about Sam dying homeless. Well the woman that claimed his body is one of the ones that stopped by your house and numerous other houses in the valley, claiming Sam was her uncle or ex-lover or any number of other things, and that he was holding a large amount of money for her. She was killed in that car wreck on Lost Creek Road ten days ago. You probably read about that too. Turns out her sister, who lived through the accident, has been doing quite a bit of talking to certain people about a man with a gun standing in the road and causing their accident. Somehow it's all supposedly tied into this thing with Sam and the little girl that was killed in that bean field fifty years ago."

"How are they putting all that together?"

"I don't know exactly, but from what I hear they basically have the case solved. They're now convinced that Sam actually did murder the little girl, then tried to cover it up with the story about his friend and the money. The DA is on the verge of closing the case and making a press release. It could come later this week or early next week."

"I guess you can never really know a person," Welker said. "Who would have thought that a nice guy like Sam would have done something so horrible, then lived a life just like anyone else afterwards?"

"You're telling me," Steen said. "Well I better get on home. The wife's bound to have dinner ready soon. You *will* keep a lid on it, won't you, Scott? I mean just until the news comes out in the paper."

"Absolutely."

Steen tossed the oak leaf stem, and said, "It sure was nice seeing you again, Scott."

"Don't be such a stranger, Martin. Stop by anytime. I'll walk you to your truck."

31

Cousins

After dark, Scott Welker drove his pickup truck down the creek to Cousin Cambell Ritchey's place. Welker and Ritchey had talked several times in the past six weeks about the so-called Lost Creek Valley history project and also about the two women who were after Sam Hostick's money. Welker had never told Ritchey that he had any connection to Sam or Ellen Brock. He knew the time had come to do so.

"Cam, I've never told you the secret I've harbored for the last fifty years," Welker said, as he sat on the couch in Ritchey's shack. "But with all this crap that's been flying around lately about Ellen Brock, now's as good a time as any to tell you what I know."

Sitting in his rocking chair, next to the burning oil lamp, facing Welker, Cam didn't answer.

"I always suspected my neighbor, Randy Samuel James, alias Sam Hostick, in the Ellen Brock murder at Duncan's bean field in 1960, but never had any evidence to prove it. Today, an old friend from the Oregon State Police dropped by my place and filled me in on what has really been going on with this so-called Lost Creek

Valley history project. It has actually been a law enforcement investigation."

"Are you telling me this whole history project has actually been an undercover investigation into Ellen Brock's death, after all these years? And you had a good idea who killed her all along?"

"Yes. The police captain, Martin Steen, the same one that caught you with your pants down after you poached that one deer—"

"He came to your place today?" Cam interrupted.

"Yes. He told me all about everything. He said Sam Hostick gave a death-bed confession, on the bank of the McKenzie River, to Shane Coleman. Sam told Coleman that for the last fifty years, he knew his neighbor friend killed Ellen Brock. Who do you think he was referring to?"

"I don't have a clue. I didn't even know Sam wasn't his real name until you just told me."

"*I was* his neighbor, Cam. We lived next door to each other from grade-school through high school. He and I used to be best friends. Sam was referring to me. Do you believe he could turn around all these years later and blame me for the girl's death, knowing he did it?"

"With friends like that a guy doesn't need enemies, does he?"

"Captain Steen told me that last week Coleman and Gilbert were digging through Sam's old barn and found Ellen Brock's bracelet."

"They found Ellen's bracelet after all these years? Geez, if they found that in Sam's old barn, that alone should tell them Sam had to be lying when he confessed about his neighbor. Sam had to have been the killer himself."

"That's exactly what I told Steen."

"And they haven't put two and two together and come to that conclusion themselves?"

"Actually they have. At least that's what Steen told me. He said the district attorney would likely be making a press release in the next week or so, saying the Ellen Brock case has finally been solved."

"That's great then," Cam said, looking Welker in the face. "You look troubled. What's going on?"

"I'm not convinced Steen was being straight with me. He kept his eye on me the whole time. Not directly, just kind of indirectly, so I wouldn't notice."

"But you said the two of you have been friends since the seventies."

"We have. I just got the impression from the way he said things that he was checking me out. I don't even know if he or anyone else has figured out that I was Sam Hostick's neighbor friend back then. I seriously doubt they have. How would they? I never went by that drunk bastard of a stepfather, Beasley's, last name."

"So you've got nothing to worry about. Who's still around that would know any of that?"

"Cockroaches can hide in a corner for a long time, then suddenly come out and do their dirty work."

"Well I bet you're glad Bessie Rogers is dead right about now. If anyone in this valley could have been that cockroach, it would have been her," Cam said. "But seriously, what difference does it make even if they do learn you were the neighbor. The bracelet being found in Sam's barn points directly at him. If they question you, you can tell them you always suspected his involvement, but never had any proof. That would be the end of it."

"Are you really that naïve, Cam? Tell me you're not. Especially with what you witnessed in 'Nam. Government authorities can twist things around any way they want to. I'm telling you, they'll be coming after me soon, because of one dead man's lying confession."

"You're awfully paranoid, Scott."

"I just don't want to be falsely accused and arrested."

"So what are you going to do?"

"If Steen *was* feeling me out, if he was just a pawn in the DA's chess game, I could have some serious problems in the next few days or week. Either way, until I see some news in the Register

Guard about Ellen Brock, I have to hide. If they finger me, I have to be a step ahead of them. As much as I've always liked Martin Steen, I can't make the mistake of trusting him. I've seen cops play these kinds of games before. You have too. What I want to do, just to be safe, is to take advantage of the tunnel and bunker systems we built way back when."

"I haven't been down in mine in years," Cam said.

"We don't need your tunnels," Welker said. "I've been down shaping mine up for the last month, ever since I first suspected what those people were really up to. My tunnels and bunkers are ready to put into action."

"What's your plan?"

"I've already got all the food and water I would need for months down there. Plenty of flashlights, batteries, gunpowder, wire and everything we need for booby traps, if it ever comes to that. And I've got plenty of ammunition too."

"I don't want to be involved in any killing. I got my fill of that already. All the mines and booby traps here on my place are designed to injure—not kill."

"I don't want to kill anyone either, Cam. But I'm not going to let them just come and falsely arrest me. I'll die before I go to prison for something I didn't do. I've seen and heard far too many stories where innocent people were locked up and never could prove their innocence. They're still locked up, at least those that are even still alive. I won't be one of them."

"I don't blame you for not wanting to be arrested. And I have no problem hanging out with you until this passes. You've always been there for me. But the only way I would shoot anyone is if they fire on me first. I'll draw the line at that."

"That's all I'm asking, Cam. For you to be there with me," Welker said. "I need to get back now. They could come as early as daybreak. If you want to be sure to get into the house before they come, you better come some time tonight."

"I'll pull some things together and head that way before

midnight."

"After you get your stuff into the house, we'll have Irene follow us up the creek and leave both vehicles stashed in the brush."

"Did you tell her what's going on?"

"Only so much. She has hard feelings towards the government and anyone connected with it because of what happened with her husband. I guess I never got into any of that with you before, did I?"

"No."

"He was a disabled Korean War vet, quite a bit older than her. First the government screwed him over on some of his disability payments, and then when he got cancer, the VA kept giving him the runaround. By the time they actually treated him, the cancer had spread to his lymph nodes. He only lasted five months after that. She's still bitter toward them, fourteen years later. So the idea that the police, or anyone connected to the government, might come to her place to mess with me, is enough to get her blood boiling."

"Is she going into the tunnel with us?"

"No, she'll run interference for us. They wouldn't hurt her."

"Okay."

"I've got to roll. Get up there as soon as you can."

"I will."

Cam didn't know that Welker was manipulating him, and fully intended to draw him into a gun battle if it came to that.

At 8:15 the next morning, with the window shades all closed at Welker's place, Scott Welker peaked out through an upstairs window, and immediately spotted two plain-clothed men walking up his driveway. It was the same two—Hodge Gilbert and Shane Coleman—that had been there before. He hustled downstairs and said to his woman, Irene Macklin, and Cambell Ritchey, "They're here!"

"The police are here?" Cam asked.

"I don't know. But Gilbert and Coleman are walking up the driveway right now. Let's move! Down in the tunnel. Irene, you put the carpet back down and roll that cart back over it when we're in there."

Welker quickly led the way to the master bedroom, opened the walk-in closet and pulled the portable file cart out of the way. He then lifted the carpet back from the corner of the closet and opened the door to the underground tunnel. He kissed Irene, then he and Cam went below.

A minute later there was a rap on the front door. Irene waited for them to knock a second time and then opened the door.

Hodge and Shane, who were both armed with concealed pistols now, were surprised that anyone opened the door, especially since no one answered previously, and there was now only one vehicle in the driveway near the house. The Chevy pickup that was present on their visit here three weeks earlier was gone.

"Hi ma'am. Are you Irene Macklin?" Hodge asked.

"Yes I am," said the tall, skinny, old woman with long, stringy, gray hair.

"We stopped by here a few weeks ago, but no one was home, apparently. You may have talked to some other people in the valley and know that we are doing a history on the Lost Creek Valley."

"Yes. I heard about that," she said. "I wouldn't be any help to you. I've only lived here the last sixteen years. And I don't keep up on anything."

"I guess we'll leave you alone then."

"Have a nice day," she said, as they turned and walked away from the house.

When they were twenty feet from the house, taking their sweet time, Shane said softly, "Did you notice there are two different sets of boot prints on the ground off to your right there?"

"Yes," Hodge answered. "The larger tracks are a perfect match for the casts I took off the prints in the woods near Desiree and Riva's accident."

"I agree. Aren't you surprised that she answered the door this time?"

"Not necessarily. She's no doubt running a screen for the guy staying with her. And at this point, I'd bet that guy is Scott Welker."

"Me too."

After Gilbert and Coleman had been gone for fifteen minutes, Irene keyed Welker on the intercom system.

"They're gone," she said. "It's safe for you to come back up."

Five minutes later the three of them were sitting in the living room discussing the situation.

"It sure strikes me odd that they came in on such a low profile if they are connecting you to the case," Irene said.

"They were casing the place out," Cam said. "That's what undercover cops do all the time, come in under false pretenses."

"Maybe you guys are just being paranoid," she said. "They seem like just you're average Joes. Maybe they really are just working on the history project."

Cam glanced over at Welker, wondering if he was ever going to fill Irene in on what was really going on.

"You don't really believe that, do you, Irene?" Welker said. "If he was just working on the history project, why didn't he come alone? There's more to it than that. I don't know exactly what it's about, but both Cam and I have had enough run-ins with the government to know they're casing this place and us for some reason. We'll have to be on guard until we figure out what their so-called history project is really about. We'll have to watch the news, and you'll have to pick up the paper each day from the box, so we can keep up on anything that comes out in that."

"Are you expecting some news?" she asked.

"I'm not sure. We just need to keep our eyes and ears open."

32

Pursuit

Two days later, mid-afternoon—

"Cambell Ritchey hasn't been back to his house the last two days," Kent said when Hodge and Shane arrived at his place. "I checked a little while ago. The thread across the drive-way hasn't been touched."

"What's that tell us, Hodge?" Shane asked.

"Since neither Welker's truck or Ritchey's were at either place on Wednesday, and neither truck has been seen since, I'd say the two skunks have hidden them, and are holing up together someplace. And I'm betting it's at Irene Macklin's. They were probably in the house watching us when we were there talking to her."

"They picked Macklin's because they knew she could cover for them. And since we didn't identify ourselves as law officers, they know we couldn't possibly have a warrant to get into the house."

"If that's the case, this could go on forever then," Kent said, "unless you have a plan to bring things to a head, Hodge."

"I do. The first thing we'll do is drive around the woods above Macklin's place to see if we can find where they stashed the two trucks."

"What if you're wrong and Welker has skipped the country for good?" Kent said.

"He's got no reason to do that yet," Hodge said.

"But you said I completely spoiled the case."

"I was very upset. Even with what you said to Ritchey, Welker would know that if the law wasn't involved already, there isn't enough evidence to bring him in. In fact, he would know there's *no* solid evidence. How could there be? By now Welker probably figured out that Sam is dead, and therefore can never testify against him."

"If he knows they have nothing, why would he hide?" Kent asked.

"He and Ritchey are probably both tired of hearing anything about Sam or Ellen Brock. And we still don't know why Welker was forced out of the postal service. If he was wrongly accused of something, he's probably just as paranoid of the law and the government as Ritchey seems to be. Then when you add the guilt he's carried around all these years, he would be even more paranoid."

The men spent the rest of the day in Shane's truck, driving every grown over road they could find that went back into the brush for miles upstream above Irene Macklin's place. Finally, shortly before dark they located the two trucks three miles southeast of Macklin's, off an old logging spur, near the top of the divide between Lost Creek Valley and Lookout Point Reservoir.

"I smell a rat," Shane said, as he drove into some thick brush. "Or I should say a couple of skunks."

"That you do," Hodge said.

They immediately parked, got out and walked up to the two pickups—a faded green 1976 Chevy, and a brown 2001 Ford—and peered inside the cabs. "I guess this confirms your theory, once again, Hodge," Kent said.

"I get lucky sometimes."

As they walked back to Shane's truck, Hodge said, "Tomorrow we're going to try to close the deal."

"How do you intend to do that?" Kent asked.

"We'll get Monster Bradshaw and Bill Starnet with his two Doberman's and see if we can't roust the skunks from their den."

"I didn't know you had talked to Bill," Shane said. "How did you know he still lived in Trent?"

"A week ago, I got to thinking that at some point, some dogs might come in handy. So I stopped at Starnet's old place and found him working in his shed."

"You never quit surprising me, old buddy."

"Well, let's hope we can all still say that after tomorrow."

"Why do you say it like that, Hodge?" Kent asked. "Maybe you should get hold of Captain Steen and see if they want to get in on this."

"I warned you early on that things could get ugly, Kent. We have no more evidence now than we had Monday, and I still haven't identified Welker to him as our prime suspect. So there's no way he's going to do anything. It's not too late to bail out if that's what you want to do."

"There's no way I'm missing out on this. I want to watch Welker squeal as much as you guys do."

"Glad to hear it," Hodge said. "Shane, you better ask Marlene to say a few extra prayers for us tonight. On second thought, maybe you shouldn't. She wouldn't let you out the door in the morning."

The next morning, Saturday, April 24th, eight a.m.—

Each of the five men drove their vehicles into the woods across from Irene Macklin's place and parked. The previous evening, after Hodge and Shane dropped Kent off, Kent drove back up the creek, parked his truck discreetly, then walked the driveway into Cambell Ritchey's place, where he retrieved a dirty shirt from the back porch. The shirt would provide the scent Starnet's dogs would need to get started tracking Ritchey, if it came to that. Bill Starnet's dogs were trained to freeze, point and remain silent if they spotted suspicious movement or picked up the right scent. Starnet would keep them on leashes, both so the men wouldn't lose track of them, and for the dogs' safety.

As the five men stood around their rigs, shortly after daylight, drinking coffee and eating donuts, Hodge announced, "Late last night, I called Captain Steen to tell him we were sure Scott Welker was Sam's neighbor when Ellen Brock was killed. I also told him we had learned that Cambell Ritchey was Welker's cousin. I felt I needed to give Steen that information, so he would know I wanted to play it straight with the law from now on. I also figured in the worst-case scenario I wanted him to know."

"You told him we were moving in on Welker and Ritchey this morning?" Shane said.

"No, I didn't. I told him we hadn't worked any of that out yet. But I'm glad I called him, because it turns out he and Welker have been friends since the days when Steen worked game enforcement out here beginning in the early eighties."

"Martin Steen and Scott Welker are friends?"

"I'm afraid so. He said there's no way Welker was the killer; that I needed to recheck my facts and not push any further with Welker. He said he stopped by Welker's and chatted with him early Tuesday evening. Apparently Welker told him about the Lost Creek Valley history project. But then when I asked for the details about the extent of their conversation on the history project, Steen seemed to hedge. I got the impression he wasn't telling me everything. I only hope he didn't say anything about Sam or Ellen Brock. And he damn well better not have mentioned the bracelet."

"What if he did?" Kent asked.

"If he did," Shane said, "that would explain why Welker and Ritchey have kegged up together. I have a bad feeling they're laying for us."

"Maybe we better call it off, and just let the law handle it," Kent said.

"Darn it, Kent," Hodge said. "You're either in all the way *or* you're not. Which is it?"

Kent looked around at the other three men, hoping one of them would share his concern, but got no encouragement from them.

"You're the only man here who never had a daughter, Kent," Shane said. "You have three wonderful sons. But there's no way you can see things quite the way the four of us do. Welker killed another man's daughter. And he got away with it—until now."

"What are you planning to do to him, if and when you catch him?" Kent asked.

"We'll know what to do when the time comes," Hodge said. "I know we can't kill him, unless it happens in self-defense."

"I have no intentions of killing him, for any reason, Hodge," Shane said, "If that's your intention, you can deal me out right now."

"Nothing we could do to him under these circumstances is going to be looked at as self-defense," Kent said. "We're going onto the man's property—or at least his girl friend's property where he lives."

"Of course I don't intend to kill him. Once we have him in custody we'll call Steen."

"If Steen thought we had enough to bring him in, he would've taken the information to the sheriff, just like he said," Shane said. "And he sure as heck wouldn't have told you to recheck your facts and not push it with Welker.

"Look, you guys," Hodge said, "if we don't take him today, chances are he'll be gone for good before we or the law has another crack at him. The fact that he and Ritchey have their trucks parked up on the divide tells us Welker knows something is up, and he's getting ready to fly the coop."

"I have to agree with Hodge, on that," Monster Bradshaw said. "I'm afraid this will be our only chance. If Steen hasn't taken any action already, other than possibly blowing the case for us, it's doubtful he will. And since he and Welker are friends, he's liable to buy any story Welker gives him. We've got to get Welker to confess before it's too late."

"Okay, then," Shane said, "Let's do it."

"Here's my plan men, providing each of you agree with your role," Hodge said. "Monster, I want you to go to the front door and see if you can get anyone to open it. I'm figuring your presence should be quite intimidating. I've thought this through as if I was in Welker's shoes all these years. If I were him, no matter where I lived, I would have had an escape plan, just in case Sam finally broke and reported me. I would have built myself an underground tunnel system that I could access from inside my house or barn, or any of my other buildings, so I could escape if more than one police officer ever came to my place at the same time."

"You really think he would have gone to that much trouble?" Kent asked.

"Why not? He *is* an army veteran, same as his cousin, Ritchey, who did time in Vietnam where the enemy had a maze of tunnels."

"Maybe that's where they were when Irene Macklin answered the door the other day." Shane said.

"I'd bet on it," Hodge said. "Anyway, while Monster is drawing attention to the front door, the rest of us will spread out and work our way up the property keeping our eyes out for Welker or Ritchey going out ahead of us, and also watching for anything that looks like a tunnel entrance. When we get to the barn and outbuildings we'll search them carefully. I brought walkie-talkies for each of us. It's vital that we maintain communication throughout. If we can get Welker into the open, I know we younger men can catch up to him. Bill, you stay in between us with your dogs. Monster, after you've made your mark at the front door, you go left with Shane."

"What do you figure the chances are of them shooting at us, Hodge?" Kent asked.

"Putting myself in their shoes, I wouldn't take a shot except as a last resort to keep from being caught—especially if I was Ritchey and had nothing to gain, but everything to lose by shooting someone."

"I don't think he would look at it that way, Hodge," Kent said. "I don't think he considers his life worth much."

Ignoring, Kent's comment, Hodge asked, "Are you all armed with a pistol and plenty of ammo?"

They all answered affirmatively.

"Okay, let's go!"

"Someone is walking up the driveway, Scott," Ritchey said over his field radio, while looking out an upstairs window with his binoculars. "And I see movement in the brush off to the left of him. I think this is the real McCoy."

"Alright, get down here," Welker answered. "Irene, you know what to do. Whatever you do, do not open the front door."

The two men hurried down into the tunnel underneath the house and quickly moved up to the first bunker that gave them a view above ground. They had already prepared the charges in case anyone discovered the tunnels.

Monster moved away from the door, and said softly over his radio, "No answer at the door, I'll check out the main barn."

"Roger that," Hodge said.

"Any chance they'll let us go right by them, then make a get away out the bottom?" Kent asked.

"They wouldn't be foolish enough to try that, because they would assume we'd have backup waiting below," Hodge said. "I'm sure they had to have seen at least two or three of us moving in the brush. They have to assume the worst case scenario. And them both being ex-soldiers, you know they will—especially Ritchey with his combat experience."

Starnet's dogs hadn't picked up anything yet, as he and the others ascended the gradual slope above the house. As Kent searched one of the smaller barns, he came across something suspicious on the floor in a corner. He grabbed a nearby hay hook, jammed its point underneath the edge, and lifted. "Hodge, I think I've discovered a tunnel entrance. You want to come check it out? I'm in the last barn to the south."

"Be right there, Kent."

Hodge hustled over to the barn. When he reached Kent, he pointed the beam of his mini-maglite around down the narrow stairway descending into the ground. "We really have to watch out for booby traps." He observed a sophisticated tunnel built out of planks and various studs and boards. "I'm going below. You wait here."

Hodge pulled his 9 mm Smith and Wesson from its holster and fed a round into the chamber. He had no sooner got to the bottom of the stairs when he spotted something several feet ahead of him. He shined his light back and forth across the tunnel, just above the floor. "It's a wire, Kent—a very fine wire, running about four inches above the floor."

"It's got to be a booby trap," Kent warned.

"I'm coming back up. We'll trip the wire from up there. See if you can find something long and heavy, like a crowbar."

As Hodge reached the top of the steps, Kent handed him a shovel. Hodge took it, and directed Kent to stand behind him, as he stood off to the left side of the hatch. He then tossed the shovel so it would land horizontally on top of the wire.

Boom! Charges exploded from either side of the tunnel several feet ahead of the wire.

"That's interesting," Hodge said over his radio. "They set the charges so the person who tripped the wire would be too far back to get hit. And since the explosions came from the sides where they did, they wouldn't even affect someone just a few feet back in the tunnel."

"Maybe they're intended to warn and not actually hurt anyone," Shane suggested over his radio. "Maybe whoever set them did it that way deliberately. Maybe Cambell Ritchey set them because he doesn't want anymore blood on his hands."

"If that's the case, Ritchey may actually work to our advantage," Kent said. "He's bound to know I'm with you guys, since he referred to me as 'Coleman's lackey.' Maybe he really doesn't want to hurt me or anyone else."

"I wouldn't count on that," Hodge said. "Welker's his cousin. Blood is thick. If push comes to shove, he'll do what he has to in order to protect his cousin."

"Are you guys going to go into the tunnel to see if you can locate them?" Monster asked.

"No. Everything would be against us. And just because it's possible that Ritchey doesn't want to kill any of us. I'd bet Welker would have no qualms about it."

"I agree," Monster said. "I bet they're only using the tunnel to escape to their trucks."

"And if they can get to them, they'll undoubtedly drop over to highway 58 on the other side," Shane said.

"Well, let's spread out and move up the hill," Hodge said, "Bill, I want you to stay in the middle with your dogs."

"Roger that," Starnet answered.

About three hundred yards up the hill, Starnet's dogs froze. "The dogs have spotted something ahead of us on the hill."

Just then, several shots were fired from a semi-automatic rifle about sixty yards ahead in the firs. Kent cried out in pain, "I'm hit!" as he fell to the ground in the mixed canopy of oak and Douglas firs, between Hodge, sixty yards to his right, and Bill Starnet about the same distance away on the left. "I'm hit in the lower thigh."

"How bad is it?" Hodge asked, over the radio.

"It's not good."

Hodge quickly closed on Kent's position. "That gunfire sounded like an M16 in semi-mode, or possibly an AR15," Hodge said on the radio. When he reached Kent, he took his hunting knife out and cut Kent's jeans away enough to gain access to the wound. "It looks worse than it is, Kent. He didn't hit any major blood vessels or bone. One of the good things about the outside of the leg." He immediately pulled out half of a white bed-sheet from his back pack, and tore a third of it off. He folded the torn piece up, and then wrapped it around Kent's leg and tied it snug. "Keep some pressure on both sides."

"You came prepared for getting shot, huh?"

"I was a boy scout, what can I say?" Hodge chuckled. "Will you be alright if I leave you alone. We're too close to lose them now."

"Go get 'em. Just be careful."

"Shane and Monster, where are you guys at?" Hodge asked.

"Can you yell, Hodge?" Shane said. "They already know Kent's position so you won't be giving anything away."

Hodge yelled, "H-e-l-l-o!"

"I'm about seventy-five yards up hill to your northeast," Shane said on the radio. "I have Monster in sight fifty yards to my south."

"You okay, Monster?" Hodge said on the radio.

"I'm fine, a little slow going up this hill. I'm sure you understand."

"Bill, are you holding position?"

"I've moved up another sixty yards," Bill answered. "The dogs are still on point, so the skunks can't be far ahead."

"Be careful."

Another burst of semi-auto gunfire, and then another. "They're both shooting at us now, Hodge," Monster said. "That was from two different weapons."

"I concur," Hodge said.

Another burst and Monster yelled out in pain, then said over his radio. "I'm down. I've been hit in my lower right leg. It's busted up pretty bad, but I can get it wrapped myself. Keep going. Get those bastards."

Another single shot, and a dog yelped and dropped to the ground beside Starnet. Starnet got a look at the shooter, dressed in camos, as he took off between trees further up the hill. He didn't know which one it was. As he was bent down looking at how bad his male Doberman was hit, the female managed to slip his grip on the leash and burst up the hill in pursuit of the man that shot her mate.

"Dan's dead," Starnet said over the radio, obviously in tears. "Annie, just broke free of me. I hope they don't shoot her too."

Just then two shots rang out in quick succession, and Annie yelped several times. All of them heard her pitiful cry, then silence. They all knew. Starnet broke down bawling. He lost his two best friends. Then, suddenly, he tore up the hill with a vengeance. But Hodge and Shane were already well ahead of him.

Another hundred and fifty yards up the hill, Hodge quickly moved through a dense patch of young firs and then broke into some sparser timber. He spotted Welker about forty yards ahead, and approached him as quietly as he could. Ritchey was nowhere in sight. When Welker looked over his shoulder and saw Hodge, he quickly turned and sprayed a few shots. Fortunately, Hodge managed to duck in behind a two foot thick fir and wasn't hit. When Welker trotted away, Hodge, dashed after him. He caught him part way up a steep grass bank.

33

The Hard Truth

As Welker struggled to get up the bank, Hodge pounced on him. The two men rolled several feet down the slope together. In the process, Welker lost his AR15. He tried to get free, but Hodge clung to him tenaciously with his legs and arms wrapped around him. Finally, Hodge, lying with his chest on top of Welker's back, pulled out his pistol and rammed the barrel into Welker's throat. Welker groaned as both men breathed heavily.

"What did you think: that you could just kill a little girl and live happily ever after?" Hodge shouted.

"I didn't kill anyone! You've got the wrong man. Don't shoot me!" Welker said.

"You know damn well we all know you killed her. And then you paid Randy James off for years to keep him quiet."

"I don't know what you're talking about. You have the wrong man."

"Then why did you hide, and then run from us? And why were you shooting at us?"

"This is why."

Hodge shoved the barrel deeper into Welker's neck. "I should shoot you right now, you lying bastard! A father and mothers' little girl was taken from them, and you did it. Own up to it! You've lived your life like nothing was wrong, like you were just another law abiding citizen. But all the time you knew you took that little girl's life. For what?"

Just then Cam, who had run out ahead, came out of the brush from Hodge's side, and stuck the barrel of his AR15 into the side of Hodge's neck. "Drop your weapon, you son of a bitch!"

Hodge glanced to his left, where Cam stood, and considered making a lunge at his legs, but knew he'd probably get shot doing it.

"I said, "Drop it right now!"

At that instant, Shane, who caught up to them, stopped behind a tree, sixty feet away, and shouted, "Put your weapon down, Ritchey!—or I'll blow your head off!"

Ritchey turned his head slightly in Shane's direction and spotted the .357 revolver pointed his way. He weighed the odds of Shane being able to hit him in the head at that distance, remembered Welker had told him Shane was the trapper who Sam confessed to, and realized Shane could probably make good on his threat.

"Do it now, Ritchey! Put your weapon on the ground."

Ritchey held the AR15's barrel on Hodge for several more seconds, then finally engaged the safety and laid the carbine on the moss beside him.

"Now put both arms straight out to your sides and walk toward me until I tell you to stop," Shane said. All the while, Hodge continued to keep his pistol's barrel planted in Welker's throat, right beside his windpipe.

Ritchey took ten steps in Shane's direction.

"Stop!"

He stopped.

"Now lie down, face on the ground, and spread eagle."

He complied.

Just then, as Shane stepped out of the brush and took a few steps toward Ritchey, Bill Starnet burst from the brush behind him and charged past. He got to Ritchey, who was the only one wearing camos, and immediately pointed the barrel of his 9mm at Ritchey's head.

"You killed my dogs, you damn bastard! Now I'm going to kill you," Starnet said.

Shane quickly moved up beside him.

"You can't kill Ritchey over your dogs, Bill," Shane warned. "I know how much they meant to you. But you'll get first degree murder if you kill him."

"He's right, Bill," Hodge said, keeping the pressure on his gun.

Ritchey didn't speak or move.

"I'm not killing him just for my dogs," Starnet said. "I'm killing him for the dogs and for helping his murderous cousin. Unless his cousin wants to admit to what he did, he can kiss Ritchey's ass good bye."

"Don't do it, Bill! We've got one murderer here," Hodge said. "You don't have to be the second one."

"Talk now, you bastard, or your cousin's a dead man," Starnett insisted.

Welker squirmed a bit, but didn't speak.

Several seconds of tense silence passed.

"Well, Welker?"

Still nothing.

Suddenly a shot rang out from Starnet's gun. Ritchey's body jerked.

"Bill. No Bill. Why?" Hodge said, as Ritchey lay motionless, his face on the ground. Hodge felt sick inside knowing Ritchey was dead because of Hodge's vigilante force—because he insisted on handling things his way. And now his old friend Bill Starnett was going away for murder, all because of him.

No one spoke for several seconds. Shane stared at Ritchey's body.

"The next one goes right into the back of his head," Starnet finally said. "Now spill your guts, Welker, and save your cousin's life while you still can, you murderous, child-molesting bastard."

Hodge studied Ritchey's still body, looking for blood. But at that distance, and laying belly down on top of Welker, he couldn't tell if Ritchey was bleeding. He looked up at Shane's face, looking for an answer. Shane was just shaking his head, staring at Ritchey's body. "Did he shoot him, or not, Shane?" Hodge finally asked.

"Not yet," Starnet answered. "But I'll count to five, and if Welker hasn't started talking, Ritchey's a dead man.

One. Two.

Three. Four—"

"Don't do it! Welker said, "I'll talk,"

Ritchey raised his head slightly, then put it back down.

"I did it. I did kill the girl."

"What was her name?" Hodge demanded. "She had a name, damn it! What was her name?"

"Ellen Brock." Welker began crying. "Her name was Ellen Brock. She was nine years old, and I killed her."

Hodge looked at Shane and Bill. They both nodded, sullen looks on their faces.

Ritchey raised his head several inches off the ground and said, "You did that, Scott? You killed Ellen Brock?"

"Don't judge me, Cam. After what you did to those kids in Vietnam. Don't you *dare* judge me!"

Ritchey put his head back on the ground without speaking further. He had never admitted to Scott Welker, or anyone else, that he had a part in the My Lai Massacre in 1968. Not until he opened up to Kent Simons recently.

Several seconds of silence passed, then Shane said, "Cam, you can sit up if you want."

Cam immediately got to his hands and knees without speaking, turned and sat on his rear, placed his hands on his lap, and looked at Hodge and Welker. Hodge's barrel kept the pressure on Welker's neck. Starnet put his pistol back in its holder on his right hip, while

Shane let his gun hand hang down to his right side.

"Tell us about Ellen Brock," Hodge said. "We want to know why, and how, you killed her."

Welker had no way of knowing exactly what Sam had told Shane, nor that he and Hodge had read the official police reports.

"It was never like people thought," Welker said. It started out as an accident, then got out of hand."

"Bullshit!" Hodge said.

"Hodge, let the man talk," Shane said.

Again silence.

Hodge nudged Welker with the barrel.

"I skipped picking beans that day," Welker said. "I told my parents I was sick before they left to go to their jobs in Springfield. They were gone all day. A little before eleven, I decided to go for a drive, then ended up going to Duncan's neighbor's back property by way of a back road. I parked a quarter mile from the neighbor's, then hiked to the fence-line between the neighbor and Duncan's, in the backwoods."

"Why did you go there?" Hodge asked.

"I don't know exactly. I guess I thought I wanted to watch the older teenage pickers swimming at the river at lunch break, without them knowing I was there. I climbed up a big maple tree and sat on a huge limb watching the action at the river a couple hundred yards away. After awhile, the kids all headed back to the bean field. Pretty soon a little dog came walking past beneath me, from the direction of the bean field. A minute later, Ellen Brock came along. She must have been following the dog.

"All at once, she spotted me up in the tree and screamed. She started running back toward the bean field, but tripped and hit her face on something. I immediately hung from the big limb I was sitting on, dropped to the ground, then ran after her. She was screaming and crying, as she got back up and looked back at me, then took off running again through the ferns and brush. When she turned to look at me again, as I got closer, I saw that her nose was bleeding, and her face was scratched. I knew I couldn't just let her go back to the bean field like that and tell everyone I had scared her. I wasn't sure if she recognized me, but I couldn't take a chance. I knew she knew me because my little sister often hung around with her and some other girls at lunch time, and I always had to round up my sister to get her back to picking."

Suddenly, Captain Steen and two other state cops, wearing their OSP blues and wide-rimmed hats, walked out of the brush from behind Shane and Bill Starnet, where they had been listening to Welker's forced confession. All three had their .38s drawn.

"Put your gun down, Hodge," Captain Steen said. "What do you think you're doing? I warned you about handling things this way."

Then turning toward the troopers, Steen said, "Arrest him."

Shane wasn't sure who Steen was talking about. But it became clear momentarily.

As both troopers pushed Hodge onto his belly in the moss beside Welker, one of the troopers quickly relieved him of his pistol. With a knee on Hodge's butt, the troopers pulled his arms behind him and snapped a pair of handcuffs on his wrists.

"You're under arrest…," one of them said, then started to quote his rights.

"You're arresting me, Steen?" Hodge said. "You idiot! Welker's the killer. He's admitted it."

Cam suddenly spoke up, "You should be arresting me."

"For what?" Steen asked. "Did you shoot those two men back there?" referring to Monster Bradshaw and Kent Simons.

"No. For what I did in Nam to those women and kids…"

"That was war, Ritchey. One of the horrors of war, for sure. But I can't arrest you for that. You guys were already charged and acquitted."

"Not me."

"Forget it Ritchey."

"Damn it, Steen," Hodge said, "Do *your job* and arrest the real killer here."

"He's right, Steen," Welker said.

"You don't have to admit to anything more here, Welker," Steen warned him.

"Yes I do, Martin. Just read me my rights, and arrest me, damn it!"

"If that's the way you want it, Scott," Steen said. "Arrest him."

One of the troopers knelt on the ground beside him and cuffed his hands behind his back, while quoting him his rights.

"Can I sit up? I've got to get the rest of this off my chest."

Help him up, troopers. They did, then led him to an oak tree ten feet away, and helped him sit down with the top of his back resting against it.

"How much have you heard, Martin?" Welker asked.

"All of it," Steen said.

Hodge squinted at Shane. Both were thinking, why did Steen let it go this far?

"Go on from where you left off, Scott," Steen said.

"When I got closer to Ellen," Welker continued, "she began screaming hysterically. I had to shut her up before anyone heard and came looking for her. If they found me with her, they would think I was trying to rape her. I couldn't let that happen. As she ran, she fell again and hit her head pretty hard on something; her forehead began bleeding. Just as I got to her, she got up again, still screaming frantically. I tried to talk to her, to calm her down, but I don't think she knew it was me. Nothing worked. Finally out of desperation to shut her up, I grabbed a nearby broken branch that was about three feet long and three inches around, and hit her with it. She fell to the ground on her face. I hit her again, on the head...Then again and again—several times." Welker was bawling now, his body was shaking. "She didn't scream anymore."

Everyone listened in horror, imagining what it must have been like for Ellen. A couple of the men wiped their eyes.

"Steen, can't you take the handcuffs off Hodge now?" Shane

said. "You've listened to this, same as us. Hodge doesn't deserve to be under arrest."

Steen walked over to Hodge and removed the handcuffs, without speaking.

Then Shane said, "Welker, tell us why you took her shirt and the bracelet."

"When I quit hitting her, it was as if I had just watched someone else do it. This teenage boy was standing over this little girl he had just clubbed to death. But then I realized the boy was me. *I killed her.* I killed that sweet, playful little girl. I was horrified. I expected people to show up any second because of the screaming. But no one came. I don't know how they didn't hear it. The wind must have been blowing from the bean field toward me and Ellen.

"I quickly picked her up and carried her farther away from the bean field toward the neighbor's property line, and down by the slough, in the thick blackberry bushes. I spotted a big old maple stump covered in moss and laid her in the crevice under that."

Hodge and Shane looked at each other, shaking their heads.

"What about the shirt and bracelet, Welker?" Shane pressed.

"I started to cover her up with moss and leaves, but then noticed the large letters on her shirt. I had been so panicked earlier that I hadn't noticed them. 'Daddy's Angel.' I cried uncontrollably. I had killed Ellen's daddy's little angel. Then I noticed the bracelet on her left wrist. It said the same thing. I don't know why, but I pulled her back out enough so that I could take that shirt and the bracelet. Maybe I thought if I kept those, somehow an angel would do something. Maybe undo everything I had just done. I put her back under the stump and carefully covered her with moss. Then I crawled out of the blackberries and ran as fast as I could to my truck, with the shirt and bracelet."

"You're lying to us, Welker," Hodge said. "You took the shirt and bracelet for a sexual reason, didn't you? You got excited about what you had just done, and you wanted to be able to experience that excitement again later."

"No! No! No!" Welker shouted. "It wasn't that at all. I've never sexually molested anyone. I'm not a sexual pervert. I'm telling you the truth. I've lived with the horror of what I did for fifty years. I can't take it anymore. I've had horrible nightmares repeatedly since I did it—

"We don't care about your nightmares, Welker," Hodge said. "What about *all the nightmares you caused*? When I was a boy I was afraid to go anywhere alone because of you. I picked in Duncan's bean field. So did Shane, Kent and Bill. We lived with the fear of knowing Ellen Brock's killer had never been caught. How do you think that was for us and every other kid? Or for the parents of every other kid? What you did terrorized a peaceful country community for years. You should rot in hell for what you did."

"Hodge! Ease up, buddy," Shane said. "It's over now. He can't hurt us anymore. It's finally over."

No one spoke for half a minute, each contemplating what had just transpired. Then Steen said, "Let's saddle up."

As Steen and the others reached the two wounded, but stable, men, the Air Life chopper that Steen had radioed for earlier—when he and the troopers had encountered the wounded men—was setting down in the clearing just below Monster Bradshaw and Kent Simons. Sheriff's deputies were also on the scene.

The April 24, 2010, Saturday evening news broadcasts on all local and Oregon state-wide, and many national, radio and television stations reported—

Bean Field Homicide Case Solved Fifty Years Late
Former Dexter Postmaster Arrested

The horrendous murder of nine-year-old Ellen May Brock in a Dexter-area bean field in August 1960 was solved today when Oregon State Police apprehended former Dexter, Oregon postmaster Eugene Scott Welker. Spokesman for the state police,

Myles Bettinger, said Welker confessed late this morning, and gave a detailed account of the murder that—according to Welker—began as just an accident. The Oregon State Police and the Lane County Sheriff's Departments are not releasing anymore details at this time.

(Photos of Ellen Brock and Scott Welker accompanied the broadcasts.)

34

Conclusion

Upon further questioning at the Lane County Jail by sheriff's detectives and OSP Captain Martin Steen—with Hodge Gilbert and Shane Coleman present—Scott Welker denied being the man in the road when Desiree wrecked her car. He also denied having anything to do with Bessie Roger's death. Bessie's body was never exhumed, and her relatives were never tipped off to the possibility of foul play. Her cause of death remained "natural age-related causes." When Desiree's sister Riva told authorities that she was no longer sure if she really did see a man with a gun in the road, Hodge was furious. He and Shane believed she said that because she still held out hope of some day finding Sam's money. She later relapsed into her drug addiction.

Scott Welker admitted that right after he joined the army, he began making monthly payments to Randy Samuel James for him to keep his mouth shut. After paying him monthly for twenty-five years, Welker said he stopped making payments, and told Sam if he ever said anything then, the law would prosecute him as an accomplice, for obstruction of justice, for receiving payoff money for a capital crime, and numerous other felony crimes. Welker estimated he paid Sam about fifty thousand dollars, but never knew what he did with the money.

At the Pleasant Hill Cemetery, May Day 2010—

As the two couples walked through the cemetery, hand in hand, Shiela said, "There it is," pointing to the two-foot-high light lavender, granite gravestone on their left. The four of them stepped up in front of the stone, and Marlene and Shiela each placed a red rose to go with the dozens of other colorful fresh flowers and plants that surrounded the grave.

Shane then wrapped an arm around Marlene's narrow waist, while Hodge did the same with Shiela.

Marlene read out loud—

Ellen May Brock

March 3, 1951- August 17, 1960

Our Dearest Ellen,
Though now you are far away, you are,
And always will be, near and dear to our hearts.
Love Dad, Mom, Brett and Amy

The clouds overhead began to sprinkle, as Shane said, "I had a lot of doubts along the way whether what we were doing was the right thing. But I know now that it was. Not only do Brett and Amy Brock finally have closure, a whole community does."

Scott Welker's case never went to trial. He pleaded guilty to voluntary manslaughter, and on July 9th, 2010, was sentenced to five years in the Oregon State Prison, and three years of probation. The light sentence was mainly because he was only sixteen when the crime occurred and had to be sentenced under guidelines in place at that time. The only evidence that Welker may have been the man in the road when Desiree and Riva wrecked—the plaster cast Hodge had taken from boot tracks near the accident scene—were ruled inadmissible, even though they were a perfect match for Welker's boots. Therefore Welker was never charged in Desiree's death. Welker also was not charged for shooting Monster Bradshaw or Kent Simons, because the judge had earlier ruled that their actions, and those of the other three men that day, constituted an illegal vigilante assault—regardless of the historic result. None of the five vigilantes were charged, however.

Cambell Ritchey was not charged for shooting Bill Starnet's dogs. He went back to living his hermit life at his shack in the woods. The authorities never followed up on rumors of his booby traps. Nor have any neighbor kids risked going onto his place, because he remains a legend among them as *the crazy Vietnam vet* who murdered women and children in 1968, and wouldn't hesitate to do it again.

Monster Bradshaw and Kent Simons recovered from their gunshot wounds, though Monster now has permanent metal plates in his lower right leg and has a slight limp. Bill Starnet bought and began training a pair of three-month old Doberman Pinschers.

Sam's money was never found. No one knows whether he ever spent any of it, or whether it did in fact burn up in the fire that burned down his old barn.

Shane and Marlene sold their place at the edge of Springfield and bought a thirty acre ranch on upper Lost Creek, where they continue to deeply love and support each other as they have for their entire marriage.

Hodge and Shiela Gilbert were remarried on June 10th, 2010, and also bought a home on Lost Creek, a quarter mile from the Colemans. Hodge finished writing his Lost Creek Valley History book. *You* just completed reading it.

*End note- Chapter 12:   To Everything there is a Season— Ecclesiastes 3 (King James Version Bible), Hebrew King Solomon; Pete Seeger; The Limelighters; The Byrds; and numerous other 1960s folk singers and groups. The song, Turn! Turn! Turn!— quoting directly from Ecclesiastes chapter three— sung by The Byrds, became a top hit as the Vietnam War escalated.

*End note-Chapter 16: The fictionalized events in this chapter were created using information gained from several sources, most notably the online Wikipedia record of the actual My Lai Massacre event which occurred on March 16, 1968—a horribly sad fact of the Vietnam War.

An Interview with author Wesley Murphey

Lost Creek Books Consultant Marie Peterson: **A Homeless Man's Burden** is your first novel to be published, but it is actually the fourth one you've written, all in a twenty month period.

Wesley Murphey: That's correct.   The second novel I wrote, **Trouble at Puma Creek**, which Lost Creek Books is publishing next, is my favorite novel of those I've written so far.

Peterson: Judging by the homeless novel, it must be good.

Murphey: I'm not sure whether it is classified a suspense-mystery, a historical suspense, or a thriller. It takes place in the backwoods of Lane County, Oregon in 1980-81. The idea for the novel came from an actual double homicide that occurred at the Puma Creek Campground in the early eighties, though none of the book's details relate to the true crime at all. I've always had a fascination with the forest, and—as a Navy submarine veteran from 1975-79—was also intrigued with the Vietnam War, its soldiers and the war's immediate aftermath, as well as the whole POW/MIA issue. So I combined those interests in writing **Trouble at Puma Creek,** a tale which I believe will stir the hearts of many people. The book does a great job of taking the reader back to that tragic period in America's history, when it seemed most everyone wanted to forget *Vietnam* ever happened, let alone acknowledge that the war may not have ended for many POW/MIA's, or in the minds and daily lives of hundreds of thousands of Vietnam veterans and their families.

Peterson: The book portrays a crazy Vietnam veteran teamed up with his surrogate son, the surviving son of the vet's former baseball coach who was killed in Vietnam. Tell me a little about that.

Murphey: I have to be careful here because I don't want to steal any of the book's thunder. But *I will say* that the crazy vet and the coach's son are involved in two horrendous killings. The lead detective is a Korean War vet who never gives up in his pursuit to bring the killers to justice. Along the way, he discovers that one of the homicide victims, also a Vietnam vet, was involved in a US Government cover up of the POW/MIA issue. I should tell you that after I had completed writing the Trouble at Puma Creek manuscript in the summer of 2009, a retired US Army general who did two combat tours in Vietnam read it and wrote up a wonderful review referring to the book as "an excellent work of crime fiction." But he said I can't use his name publically because in the years following Vietnam he worked for the Defense Intelligence Agency, and he can't support the idea of a government cover up of the POW/MIA issue. I know you were about to ask me for his name, weren't you?

Peterson: Yes, but I won't press it. Tell me where you got the idea for **A Homeless Man's Burden**.

Murphey: The Homeless book idea came to me from the memory I had as a kid of an actual crime that occurred in Lane County during the heyday of pole bean growers. But unlike in my book, the actual crime was never solved.

Peterson: Do you care to elaborate on the actual crime?

Murphey: Not really. I've brought some of the possibilities and many of the emotions to life in the novel, though I completely changed the details and people involved. When I began writing the book in March 2010, I contacted the Lane County area police departments to verify a few details of the crime to ensure that I had the year correct, but that none of the other details I used in my book were factual, at least to the extent I learned about them. I have to admit that I *was* going to get a hold of some of the local newspapers that covered the actual crime in 1960, but I found that I couldn't bring myself to read the stories. They would have hit too close to home.

Peterson: Where did the idea for the trapper and the homeless man come from?

Murphey: My wild imagination. I can't explain it. As a writer I have stuff brewing in my mind all the time. I will admit, however, that certain aspects of the story came from my personal experience, including seeing plenty of homeless people and their shanties while I have been floating on rivers.

Late Breaking Interview conducted two weeks before "A Homeless Man's Burden" goes to press—

Peterson: Today's Eugene Register-Guard has an article saying the actual fifty-year-old bean field homicide case from which you got this novel idea has just been reopened. Had you heard that?

Murphey: I just heard about it this morning from a lady at my church who grew up in the Dexter area in the fifties and knew I was writing a novel related to the bean field crime.

Peterson: Did you have any idea the case might be reopened, and what are your thoughts about that?

Murphey: I had no clue, after all the case was suspended in 1975— that's thirty-five years ago. I'm not sure why it would have been reopened now, but it's amazing that it happened just before my novel was going to press. I'm sure the publicity from the actual case won't hurt what we're doing. But people need to remember that my book is fiction whose idea came from the true crime. Since the details of the crime were never known to me, at least factually, I had to fabricate them just as I fabricated the characters. I'm sure readers will come away from my book with an excellent idea of what it must have been like for the actual people—relatives and those in the community—who lived through the horror of the actual homicide.

Peterson: I'm excited for you and know this book will be a success. And I'm *really* looking forward to reading your future novels.